WHO

ILLEGAL ALIEN

MIKE TUCKER & ROBERT PERRY

BBC BOOKS

Published by BBC Books
an imprint of BBC Worldwide Publishing
BBC Worldwide Ltd, Woodlands, 80 Wood Lane
London W12 0TT

First published 1997
Copyright © Mike Tucker & Robert Perry 1997
The moral right of the authors has been asserted.

Cyberman character reproduced by permission of
Lemon Unna & Durbridge Ltd
© Estates of Kit Pedler & Gerry Davis 1997
All rights reserved and enquiries to The Agency (London) Ltd
24 Pottery Lane, London W11 4LZ fax: 0171 727 9037

Original series broadcast on the BBC
Format © BBC 1963
Doctor Who and TARDIS are trademarks of the BBC

ISBN 0 563 40570 8
Imaging by Black Sheep, copyright © BBC 1997

Printed and bound in Great Britain by Mackays of Chatham
Cover printed by Belmont Press Ltd, Northampton

ACKNOWLEDGEMENTS

Thanks to:
Marc Platt
John Freeman
Gary Russell
Rebecca Levene and Peter Darvill-Evans
Gary Gillatt
Steve Cole
Nuala Buffini
Sophie Aldred and Sylvester McCoy
John Nathan-Turner
The cast and crew of 'the McCoy era'

*Dedicated to the memory of
Howard Tucker,
father and friend*

PART ONE

CHAPTER 1

'London, England, November 1940. Three months in this dumb-assed country and not a sniff of a case. I wish I'd never shipped out of Chicago… except I had to. Too many people in Chicago wanted me out of the way – permanently. A new start in an old country. Figured I could clean up in sleepy old England. I was wrong. The hoods are too slow and the cops are too fast. It's all small-time. All the real crooked talent is away fighting the Nazis or running black-market eggs in from Suffolk.'

Cody McBride pulled back the edge of the blackout curtain, and stared out over the rooftops of East London. Below him the city was dark and empty. He scowled. This was not how a city ought to be. He was used to people, noise, and bright lights. Now all the noise and light came from the bombers overhead, and the gunners trying to shoot them down.

In the distance he could see tracer fire arcing into the night sky, the glow of fires. The city was dying just as surely as its people, and McBride hated it. He craned his neck round to catch a glimpse of St Paul's Cathedral, silhouetted against the glowing night sky. How long before that became no more than another pile of rubble in a London street? He was amazed that it had weathered this blitz as long as it had – it stood out like a beacon. He hoped it survived. Too many landmarks were being erased from the face of London.

He glanced at the stack of newspapers piled under the window. The Lurker. Somehow in the middle of all this chaos some fruitcake had taken it upon himself to start carving people up. A real psycho. The Limehouse Lurker, the press had dubbed him. He'd left a trail of disembowelled, disembodied, and generally messy corpses scattered around East London for the past two months. He was even managing to grab headlines from the Luftwaffe. It was strange, McBride thought: even when death was raining indiscriminately from the skies every night, the Lurker had still managed to spread panic among the population. Give death a human face and somehow it all becomes so much more horrific. The police hadn't come close to catching him: Cody McBride hadn't even tried. That would be a coup – to catch the Limehouse Lurker. McBride laughed to himself. How could anyone solve anything when the Nazis kept bombing the crime scenes?

His attention shifted to the paintwork that read CODY MCBRIDE – PRIVATE DETECTIVE across the top of the glass. The paintwork was already beginning to peel, even though it was barely three weeks old. It seemed that it wasn't only the criminal talent that was away fighting the Nazis.

He let the curtain swing back and contemplated his darkened office. Even by his standards it was sparse. A couple of large filing cabinets stood against one wall, a freestanding safe against another. A couple of trench coats and a hat hung on a stand in the corner, next to an old table with an even older typewriter on it. In front of him was his desk, a large walnut affair, bare save for an ink blotter, a telephone, a bottle of whisky and his shoes. The shoes were full of his feet; the bottle was empty.

He took a long, deep drink of the whisky in his hand, swilled the last mouthful around in the bottom of the glass, and leaned back in his creaky old swivel chair. He really shouldn't be here during an air raid. He should be in the shelters with everybody else. He had watched as the streams of people made their way across the street while the sirens had droned out their warning cry; watched as, one by one, the lights of the city had been extinguished. Staring down at the tide of people, he had shut off his own light, pulled the blackout curtain, and proceeded to get drunk.

At first he had complied with the regulations, sleeping on tube platforms and stairways as the Germans bombed seven bells out of London, but the oppressive atmosphere, the proximity to people who were slowly having all the hope drained out of them, had proved more than McBride could stand. As the weeks had gone by, he had found himself spending more and more air raids in his fourth-floor office with a bottle of whisky. He knew that he was risking his life. He didn't care. This, at least, was life on his terms, a personal game of Russian roulette with Hitler and the Luftwaffe. He had always lived a solitary life. It seemed fitting that, if he was to die, it should be a solitary death.

He pulled a packet of Lucky Strike cigarettes from his pocket and lit one. As he watched the smoke curl towards his office ceiling he rattled the packet. Two left. If he lived through the night he would have to head over to O'Rourke's or Mama's Bar and restock. He inhaled deeply – a taste of home. He thought back to what he had left behind. Not much if truth be told. A good string of enemies and a good string of failed relationships. McBride had never been good with the opposite sex. A lot of women had liked him, but very few had loved him. The relationships that had got started rarely lasted long and never ended well.

He could still see the look on Delores's face as he had boarded the boat for England. She was one of the few who had genuinely cared for him. If he'd asked, she would have married him there and then. She'd been a client of his. He had helped clear her father's name in a nasty little blackmail scandal. He could have left Chicago far behind him and settled down with a good job in her father's company – it had been offered. Instead he had run, though few people would accuse him of taking the easy way out. He had thought that he'd be safe in England, but 'safe' was a relative term. When this onslaught had started, two months ago, McBride couldn't have been in a worse place.

He had come over on the pretence of joining the Volunteer Ambulance Corps, but had made inroads with the local criminal fraternity almost as soon as the boat had docked at Southampton. Within days he had been able to set up his business in East London. The old Jew he rented the rooms from had been less than happy to discover that there would be a private detective in the building, but McBride's money was as good as anyone else's.

The dull crump of an explosion, much closer than before, pulled McBride from his reverie. He swung his feet from his desk and drained the last of the whisky from his glass, crossing to the safe. With a practised hand he spun the dial back and forth until the door opened with a satisfying clunk. Inside stood another, full, bottle of whisky, a soda siphon and four cut-crystal glasses. The glasses were expensive; the whisky wasn't.

McBride put the cheap tumbler that he had been drinking from on the top of the safe, reached inside and pulled out one of the fancy glasses and the bottle. Cracking the seal, he poured himself a very large drink. The glasses had been a birthday present from Delores, and the only thing that he had brought with him from America. He took another deep drag on his cigarette and crossed over to the window, twitching the curtain back and contemplating the deadly firework display being played out in the sky in front of him.

He held the glass of whisky up to one eye, watching the lights of conflict through the cut crystal, turning death and destruction into a miniature kaleidoscope in his hand. In his drunken state, McBride found the lights almost hypnotic, and felt his eyes becoming heavy.

A searing flash brought him back to his senses and he snatched the glass away from his face, spilling whisky down the front of his shirt. Cursing loudly, McBride rubbed at his dazzled eyes, desperately searching for the source of the flash. In the night sky, amid the tracer fire and smoke, a brilliant ball of light plummeted into the tangle of nearby buildings with an impact that shook the windows of the small office.

McBride placed the empty whisky glass on the table, watching as the brilliant glow slowly faded amid the rubble.

'Holy Mother…' Suddenly sober, McBride snatched his trench coat and fedora from the hat stand and dashed from his office, vainly trying to remove some of the whisky from his sodden shirt with a piece torn from the blotter on the desk.

He hurried out into the street, discarding the whisky-soaked blotting paper in the gutter, and desperately tried to regain his bearings. A voice from up the street made him start.

'Put that blasted light out! This is supposed to be a blackout. Do you want them to drop one on you?' In the distance an ARP warden was shouting through the letter box of a terraced house. McBride hurried over to him, pulling his trench coat tight against the chill of the November night.

The ARP warden, a stocky man in his sixties with a handlebar moustache, straightened up as McBride crossed the street. 'You shouldn't be out here. The all clear hasn't been sounded. Why aren't you in a shelter?'

McBride didn't have time to argue. 'Did you see that thing up there?'

'What?'

'In the sky. Something glowing.'

The warden gave McBride a long-suffering look. He sniffed. 'You've been drinking, haven't you?' He pulled a notebook and pencil out of his jacket. 'I'm going to have to take your name.'

McBride shook his head vigorously. 'Listen, Jack. Something has come down. I think it fell a couple of blocks away.'

The warden harrumphed, loudly. 'Don't be ridiculous, man. If a bomb had gone off I'd have heard it. And the name isn't Jack, it's Potter. Colonel T.P. Potter, retired.'

McBride's patience was beginning to wear thin. 'It wasn't a goddamn bomb.'

Potter prodded McBride in the chest. 'I've got quite enough to deal with without pranksters like you causing trouble. Now, what's your name?' A light was suddenly visible in one of the houses, as someone pulled back a curtain to investigate the noises in the street. The warden was off like a dog after a rabbit.

'Put that damn light out. Do you want me to report you?'

Cursing, McBride tried to reorientate himself. The thing had come down to the east of St Paul's. 'Watling Street,' he muttered under his breath. 'Must be near Watling Street.' He headed off through the deserted streets, trying to ignore the rattle of gunfire and the distant noise of explosions, aware that his nightly game of Russian roulette had become a little more dangerous than he had banked on.

9

His progress through the city was slow; there was too much bomb damage that had yet to be cleared away. As he approached the area where he had seen the ball of light come down he had to skirt around several small fires. McBride was unsure whether or not the damage he was walking through was the result of the object's impact.

He stopped, his eye caught by a pulsing glow on the far side of a row of bombed-out terraced houses. Cautiously, he began to pick his way through the rubble. He passed a child's crib with a slate roofing tile embedded in it. He felt sick to his stomach, unsure whether to take it as a memorial to a tragic death, or a shrine to a miraculous escape. Deciding that there was too much blackness in his life, he opted for the latter and continued his unsteady progress through the shattered house.

He reached what would have been the kitchen and peered up over the half-demolished wall. There, in the rubble before him, was a sphere, about eight foot in diameter, glowing softly with an inner light. Several fires burnt around it, and bricks and timbers sporadically clattered down from the building in whose side it had embedded itself.

McBride pushed his hat back on his head and pinched the bridge of his nose, trying to clear his fuzzy head. It certainly wasn't a bomb – at least no bomb that he'd ever seen before. Summoning up his courage, he crossed to the sphere, watching his distorted reflection in its polished surface as he approached. He walked around it once. There didn't seem to be any break in its surface – no seam, no cracks, no indication of its construction.

McBride tentatively reached out to touch the surface. Surprisingly, it wasn't hot at all, and with more confidence he placed both palms on the cool reflective surface.

With a hiss like the opening of a million bottles of Coke the sphere began to split down the middle, dazzling light spilling out, lighting up the rubble like a searchlight. McBride staggered back, throwing up his arms in a futile attempt to shield his eyes from the glare. Through streaming tears he was aware of something indistinct moving inside the sphere, but the light in his brain was getting brighter and brighter until, suddenly and mercifully, everything went black.

McBride woke with the worst hangover of his life. There was a thump in his head that threatened to break his skull, and his mouth felt as though he had a sock in it. He drew in a ragged breath and gagged. The stench of stale whisky clung to him like a cloud.

Tentatively he forced his crusted eyes apart. It was morning. Not long after dawn. The sun was creeping up over the landscape of devastated buildings and, although the light was nowhere near as bright as the previous night, it still took McBride a few minutes before he could see without his eyes streaming.

In front of him the sphere sat in its crater, now two neat hollow hemispheres. He heard rubble shift and the crunch of footsteps on gravel. He tried to sit up and immediately regretted it. With a groan he slumped back on to the pile of brickwork where he had fallen and twisted his head to try to identify the source of the footsteps. A man was picking his way over the rubble towards him. His attention was fixed firmly on the sphere, barely aware of McBride's presence.

McBride frowned. The man was in his late fifties, smartly dressed with an expensive briefcase clutched in his hand. He was also absolutely terrified. McBride shifted slightly and the man turned towards him with a start, noticing him for the first time. The man raised a hand and gestured towards the sphere, his mouth moving but no sounds emerging. McBride tried again to sit up but the blinding pain in his skull proved too much for him.

The pain became marginally worse as the sound of police cars cut through the silence. McBride watched as two uniformed policemen, tin helmets slung at their belts, grasped the businessman by the arms and swiftly escorted him to one side.

A figure in plain clothes – brown overcoat and bowler hat – entered McBride's frame of vision. He groaned and let his eyes shut. Mullen. Of all the strange, glowing, flying-sphere-filled bomb craters in all the world, Mullen had to walk into his.

'Morning, McBride. First on the scene again I see.' Mullen sniffed the air, his nose wrinkling at the overpowering smell of whisky. 'Your aftershave's getting cheaper.'

'Yeah, so are your gags. Give me a hand up here.'

McBride held out his arm and Mullen hauled him to his feet, steadying the American as he swayed uneasily. Mullen was a large man. A thick-set, sardonic Irishman, and a chief inspector in Special Branch. He and McBride had crossed paths on more than one occasion and there was no love lost between them. Mullen didn't like private detectives in general and this one in particular. He didn't care much for Irish-Americans either – Fenians to man. As for Cody McBride, he just wished Mullen would give him a break once in a while.

Two stretcher-bearers clambered over the piles of brickwork and were beckoned over by Mullen. McBride shook himself free of the chief inspector's grip.

'I don't need one of those things. I'm fine. I'm OK.'

He picked his hat up off the floor and dusted it down. On the roadway a couple of policemen were struggling to keep back the ever-growing crowd of public and pressmen. McBride could see the businessman watching him through terrified eyes. No, not him. The sphere.

Mullen had crossed to the sphere and was peering inside. McBride stumbled over to him. The interior of the thing was not round, but contoured and ridged. Of the figure that McBride had seen briefly in the night, there was no sign.

Mullen looked at him sternly. 'Any comment, McBride?'

McBride rubbed his scalp and jammed his hat on to his head, shielding his eyes from the low sun. 'No, but if you find out anything, let me know. I'm going home.'

He turned to go, but the chief inspector caught the sleeve of his coat. 'Oh, no. You're up to your bloodshot eyeballs in this one, McBride. You're coming down to the station.'

The two men stared at each other, preparing for one of their inevitable and long-winded confrontations, when an army staff car burst into view from a side alley. It pulled up on the road and several soldiers sprang out, joining the police and pushing the crowds back, setting up a cordon around the bomb site.

A young, thin man with a young, thin moustache and an immaculate uniform strode through the squaddies, barking orders. Satisfied that the crowd were being kept under control, he crossed to McBride and Mullen. 'Ah, Chief Inspector.'

Mullen caught McBride's eye and muttered under his breath. 'Saints preserve us from Military Intelligence.' He spun round with a smile. 'Good morning, sir.'

The young man nodded, curtly. 'Major Lazonby. Military Intelligence. I'm afraid that this is out of your hands now. Military jurisdiction and all that. I needn't say it's a classified matter, of course.' He peered past Mullen at the open sphere. 'We'll have this thing on a lorry and out of here within the hour.' He glanced at McBride. 'Is this the man who found the bomb?'

'Yes, sir. Cody McBride...' Mullen paused and smiled. 'Private eye.'

McBride shuffled awkwardly. His eyes were red, his hair dishevelled, he was covered in mud and he reeked of whisky. He tried to summon up some dignity. 'It's not a bomb. If it was I'd be dead by now. I was right next to it when –'

A shout from the road cut McBride dead. The commotion building up in the crowd had reached a head and, spurred on by the press, the pitiful cordon of police and soldiers had been broken by people eager to see the mysterious sphere. Mullen and Lazonby were suddenly shouting for their men to restore some kind of order. The press were swarming around taking notes and photographs. Someone with a camera pressed right up in front of McBride and, for the second time in twelve hours, he was blinded by a bright white glare.

* * *

13

By mid-afternoon, the bomb site was empty, save for a lone policeman. The only indication that the sphere had ever been there at all was a smooth indentation in the soil. Soldiers had hoisted the halves on to a low truck and sped off into the depths of London, pursued by the story-hungry press.

McBride had been loaded into a car by Mullen and driven over to the station in Spitalfields. There he had been bundled into an interrogation room and given a cup of foul-tasting coffee. He had now drunk three cups and had lit up one of his remaining cigarettes. He had been there for seven hours.

Mullen looked over the notebook in front of him and leaned back in his chair with a deep sigh. 'Is that all you've got to say for yourself?'

McBride stayed silent, flicking his ash into the empty coffee cup.

Mullen dumped a gun on the table. A 9mm Browning automatic. 'Know anything about this?' McBride just took another drag of his cigarette. 'We could go on all day like this. We will if we have to!' His tone softened. 'Look, I don't care about the gun. Military Intelligence are dying to get their hands on you. They won't be as easygoing as me. All I want is a statement.'

McBride looked at the chief inspector through weary eyes. 'I've said what I've got to say. If you don't believe me then that's your problem.'

Mullen sighed and turned to the young policeman who had been standing at the doorway. 'Dixon, ring my wife and tell her that I'm going to be late home.'

The frightened businessman from the bomb site was still frightened. He had watched as the hapless American private eye had been bundled into the back of a police car and whisked away. He had stayed on as the army had arrived in force and loaded the two halves of the sphere on to their truck, covered it with tarpaulins and driven off with it. Some of the press had tried to get his version of events, but he had brushed them angrily aside, becoming almost violent when one of them had taken his picture.

He had hurried through the slowly gathering bustle of London to a large, secure building lurking in the shadow of Southwark power station. The sign across the top of the building proclaimed it to be PEDDLER ELECTRONIC ENGINEERING – TESTING AND EXPERIMENTATION.

The girl at the reception desk looked up in alarm as the shaken figure of her employer hurried in through the door. 'Dr Peddler…'

He almost threw his coat at her. 'Not now, Rosemary. No callers today. I'll see nobody.' He had vanished into his office and pulled the heavy oak door to behind him.

Once inside his office he began to regain some of his composure. He pulled open the deep drawer in his desk and poured himself a large whisky. He began to sort through a variety of letters and electronics diagrams, putting his lighter to them and watching them burn one by one in the small metal litter bin that stood in the corner of his spacious office. He opened the window to let the smoke clear, looking out over the tangle of buildings and railway lines that formed most of south-east London. At the end of the day there would be nothing left, nothing to connect him with those… things.

He pulled a cigar from his jacket and lit it, watching the tobacco smoke mingle with that of the burning documents. He felt at ease for the first time in months. That ease left him as he looked down into the yard behind the factory. He choked on the cigar smoke. There in the yard was the truck that the army had used to transport the sphere. Before he could come to terms with this development there was a timid tap on his door and Rosemary's head appeared.

'I'm sorry, Dr Peddler, but they insisted…' The door was pushed open and a small, smartly dressed man oozed into the office, smiling unnervingly and rubbing his hands as if in anticipation. His skin was white, and glistened like unbaked dough; his eyes were invisible behind a pair of small, round, black glasses. Behind him two huge figures – well over seven feet tall – stood motionless and silent, swathed in trench coats with high collars, gloves, scarves, and huge fedoras, their features invisible.

'Thank you, my dear, you may go.'

The small man spoke with a high, squeaky voice that made the receptionist feel sick.

She looked at her employer for some assurance. Peddler nodded and she slid thankfully past the two huge figures as they lumbered into the room, shutting the door behind them. She scurried back to the comfort of her reception desk.

Almost immediately she could hear her employer's voice, rapid, garbled, anxious. Every so often the other man's voice would cut across him, slow and high and revoltingly childlike.

She was worried. She had never seen her boss like this. Quietly she left her desk and edged across to the door of his office, stooping until her eye was level with the keyhole.

She leapt back, frantically straightening her skirt as the door swung inward.

'Rosemary, call security to show Mr Wall and his... colleagues... out of here.'

His voice was trembling.

'It's all right, Dr Peddler. I think we have said all we needed to say.' The little man pulled a business card from his pocket and handed it to Peddler. 'Call me if you change your mind. I shouldn't take too long, though.'

He turned and strode past Rosemary. His two silent partners remained motionless.

'Come,' he said, clicking his fingers.

As one they turned and followed.

'Sir...' Rosemary sounded concerned.

Peddler interrupted: 'The extra guard detail. Are they in place?'

'Yes, sir, but –'

'Good... good...'

He turned away from her and trudged back into his office.

Allowing the door to swing shut behind him, he sank to the floor, his head in his hands.

By the time McBride finally escaped the interrogation room it was early evening. By the time he had walked back to his office in the shadow of St Paul's it was pitch black and freezing cold. He had definitely had enough of this city. He'd been knocked out, made a fool of, treated like a criminal – treated like a *Nazi* – and locked up all day in a police interrogation cell.

He pulled his packet of Lucky Strikes from his trench coat, feeling the comfortingly heavy shape of his gun. At least Mullen had had the good grace to let him keep that. He flipped open the packet of cigarettes. One left. He pulled some loose matches out of his pocket and looked for something to strike them on. A police box loomed out of the darkness. McBride snorted and pulled the match contemptuously along its blue-painted side. He lit his cigarette and tossed the packet away.

Leaning back against the box, he stared up at the building where his rooms were. He suddenly straightened. It had been a blackout when he had left last night – now the lights were on. Someone was in his goddamn office!

CHAPTER 2

McBride waited until he was inside the tatty, green front door before pulling his gun from its holster. It wouldn't do to draw the attention of any local busybodies. He began to edge his way up the stairs, slowing his approach as he came to the final flight that led to his office. He tried to creep up as quietly as possible but the old stairs creaked and protested with every step. Slowly and painfully, he creaked his way to the top.

Through the frosted glass of his front door he could see figures moving, hear low voices. Taking a deep breath, McBride took a good grip on the gun with both hands and kicked open the door.

A little man in a dark jacket and a lurid sweater was sitting in the swivel chair behind his desk, pointing out London landmarks to a teenage girl wearing a T-shirt that was far too short and trousers that were far too tight to be decent. As the door crashed open, the man swung in the chair and raised his hat. 'Good evening, Mr McBride. I'm the Doctor and this is my friend Ace.' He noticed the gun and swung his other hand above his head, joining the one holding his hat. 'Oh… All right, we surrender. Actually, we're on your side, you know.'

McBride swung the door shut with his heel. 'How did you get in here?'

The little man smiled. 'It wasn't that difficult. You left both doors unlocked.'

The girl gave a sharp laugh. 'Some private detective.' She peered at the gun in McBride's hands, and her eyes lit up. 'Hey, is that a Browning nine-millimetre?

McBride looked down at the gun, suddenly feeling foolish and self-conscious. 'Uh, yeah.'

'Can I have a look?' The girl – Ace? – held out her hand.

She was pretty, with a mischievous glint in her eye, and McBride had almost handed the gun over before he realised what he was doing. He checked himself abruptly and slid the gun back into its holster.

'Look, who the hell are you? I've had a bad day and I'm really not in the mood. Come back tomorrow.' He shrugged off his trench coat and hung it on the hat stand, next to a badge-covered jacket and a duffel coat that definitely weren't his. He tossed his hat on to the table. Ace picked it up and slouched back over to the window.

The man who had introduced himself as the Doctor leaned across the desk, resting his chin on his hands. He fixed McBride with a piercing stare. 'Mr McBride, the capsule that you discovered…'

McBride threw his hands up and shook his head. 'Oh, no. I've had just about enough of that. The cops think I'm crazy, Mullen thinks I'm a jerk, the army think that maybe I'm a Nazi spy…' He stopped. 'How the hell did you find out about it?'

The Doctor pushed a newspaper over the desk towards McBride. He took it. Plastered over the front cover was a picture of him looking very startled, the sphere in the background. Other pictures showed a furious Lazonby and the frightened businessman. The headline read: NEW GERMAN BOMB FAILS TO EXPLODE.

'Where did you get this? There isn't another edition today.'

'It's tomorrow's paper, dummy.' Ace didn't turn round. She was trying on McBride's hat.

McBride glanced up at the date: 14 November 1940. She was right. This was *tomorrow's* newspaper. He slumped down in the chair that he kept for clients, his head reeling. The Doctor smiled comfortingly at him. 'Cheer up, Mr McBride. You're famous.'

'I look like a jerk.'

The Doctor picked up the paper and studied it closely. 'Who's this man?' He pointed at the picture of the businessman.

McBride shrugged. 'Damned if I know.'

The Doctor frowned. 'I'm sure that I know the face. If I could just remember from where…' He scanned the text quickly. 'Well, the authorities seem convinced that it's some new type of German weapon.'

'And I've spent all day telling them that it isn't a bomb. I don't know... I'd swear that there was something inside it – moving about inside it.'

The Doctor smiled at him. 'Oh, you're quite right. It's not a bomb. I should say it's some kind of transport.'

Ace came over from the window and peered over his shoulder at the picture. 'A ship you mean? Looks a bit weedy.'

'Simple but efficient. A shuttle. A homing pod of some kind. Perhaps an escape vessel.'

McBride found his curiosity being poked with a stick. 'German, you think?'

The Doctor lowered the paper and peered over the top at McBride with those brilliant-grey eyes of his. 'Alien.'

'What...?'

'From another planet.'

McBride looked pained and pulled himself out of the chair. 'Are you crazy? Get out of here.' He crossed to one of the filing cabinets, opened it, and began to leaf through a selection of clean shirts.

The Doctor placed the paper on the desk and leaned back in the chair, staring out of the window. 'And, of course, it's an empty vessel. You see the problem?'

Ace looked puzzled. 'They make the most noise?'

The Doctor waggled his hands at her in irritation. 'No, no, no.' He paused, and McBride turned from the filing cabinet to see the grim smile on his face. 'Whatever was inside it is now running around London.'

Peddler was still in his office when Rosemary was leaving. She poked her head around the door, shocked at the state of her normally immaculate employer. 'Are you all right, Dr Peddler?'

He looked up through tear-filled eyes. 'Hm? Oh, yes, thank you, Rosemary. Lock up, would you? I'm going to be some time.'

He smiled weakly at her as she pulled the office door closed. She hurried through the reception area, locked the front door of the building and scurried away into the East End, not knowing what was going on, and not wanting to know.

For more than an hour Peddler sat at his desk, turning Wall's card over and over in his hand. There was no name on it, just a number. A London number. He reached for the telephone on his desk and dialled.

The phone at the other end was answered quickly: 'Wall.'

'Wall –'

'Have you changed your mind?'

'I…' Peddler took a deep breath and sat in his plush leather swivel chair. He looked across the ordered landscape of his mahogany desk – his empire-in-miniature. Nothing was left now.

'No.' He was suddenly resolved. 'Damn you, Wall. Never. It's obscene! Do what you want with me. You won't find me such an easy target.'

'No?'

There was a click and the line went dead. Peddler replaced the receiver.

A faint noise made him start, and he crossed over to the open window. The yard below him was silent and empty. He pulled the window shut, making sure that the lock was tight. He crossed to the office door and locked that too. Happy that he was secure inside his office, he settled into one of the chairs and poured himself another drink.

Suddenly something smashed through the window, showering the desk with glass. There was a hole the size of a brick was in the pane. Peddler's terror evaporated into anger. Was petty vandalism all that Wall and his heavies could threaten him with?

Slamming his drink down on to the desk, he crossed to the window. There was something on the floor in the shadows. He reached for it, puzzled. His puzzlement turned back to pure terror as he realised what it was.

A desperate scream welled up in his throat as the thing came at him – a scream that was lost in the sounds of the air-raid sirens starting up, as the German bombers crossed the coast once again for their nightly attack on London.

* * *

The Doctor's ears pricked up as the first notes of the sirens reached him. Ace's face lit up, and she bounded across the office to the hat stand. McBride watched as she rummaged in the capacious pockets of her jacket, pulled out a small black box and bounded back to the window. As she slid the front of the box open, McBride saw the glint of a lens, and realised that the device was a small camera. He experienced a moment of panic. Miniature cameras were normally the province of spies. He glanced back over at the Doctor and relaxed. If the Nazis were going to send two spies over to England, they were hardy likely to choose a barely dressed teenage girl and a man in a pullover covered in question marks.

He did up the last buttons of his clean shirt and pulled a tie over his head. 'Come on, you two. You'd better get into the shelters.'

Ace, perched in the window with her camera, turned pleadingly to the Doctor. 'Oh, come on, Professor. I've not seen a single explosion yet.'

The Doctor picked his hat up from the desk and rolled it up his arm on to his head. 'There'll be plenty of time for photo opportunities, Ace.' He turned to McBride. 'Where would the nearest shelter be?'

'Chancery Lane tube is your best bet. It's only a few minutes' walk away.' He crossed to the window. 'I'll show you.'

'Aren't you coming with us?' Ace looked at him quizzically.

McBride shuffled uncomfortably. He had intended getting shot of the two of them and settling into his nightly routine. He was aware of the Doctor's eyes burning into the back of his head. Without knowing why, he crossed to the hat stand and began to struggle into his trench coat.

'Come on, then. I'll walk with you over there.'

He shut off the lights and opened the door for them. Ace grabbed her jacket and pushed the camera back into the pocket, grumbling as she made her way out on to the stairs. As she passed him, McBride tweaked his hat from her head. The Doctor followed, pulling his duffel coat on and, although the room was dark, McBride was sure that he was smiling.

The trio made good time towards Chancery Lane, carried along
by the throng of people heading for safety. ARP wardens kept the
crowds orderly and, although there was an undercurrent of
anxiety, there was no panic.

The Doctor seemed totally at ease. He kept pointing out
landmarks to Ace, jabbing this way and that with the point of his
umbrella. They attracted a few curious looks but most people
were too concerned with the imminent air raid to be bothered by
this eccentric little man.

McBride was still unsure quite why he was out in the street
with them at all. Somehow, the Doctor had persuaded him to give
up his dangerous nightly game without saying a word. That he had
been so easily manipulated annoyed McBride, but he wasn't going
to argue. Perhaps it was about time that he looked after himself a
bit better. There was no way that he would go into the shelters,
though. About that he was adamant.

They approached the entrance to the tube station and McBride
reached into his pocket for his cigarettes. He cursed. He'd smoked
his last one. Suddenly he knew where he would sit out the air
raid. Mama's Bar.

He caught the Doctor's arm. 'This is as far as I go, Doc. I'm off
to Mama's.'

The Doctor stared at him, his head cocked on one side. 'You're
going to visit your mother?'

McBride grinned. 'Something like that.' He pulled the collar of
his trench coat up, and sauntered off towards the river. The
Doctor watched him go, tapping his umbrella handle against his
lips. Ace appeared at his shoulder. 'Is he going to be OK,
Professor?'

'Yes, I think so.' He linked arms with her and turned towards the
tube station. 'Come on, Ace, let's find ourselves a space to spend
the night.'

* * *

24

The night seemed to drag for Ace. The underground station had filled with people. The platform was overflowing, stairwells and even the space between the tracks crammed with Londoners sheltering from the onslaught.

Ace looked over to a young mother, desperately trying to get her baby off to sleep. An older woman, probably the baby's grandmother, was waving a small knitted teddy bear in the air in front of them. Ace smiled. Her own grandmother would have joined the WRNS by now. Sometime this year she would meet Frank William Dudman, of the merchant navy, and they would get married. Ace's smile faded. In three years Frank Dudman would be dead, his ship struck by enemy torpedoes. Kathleen Dudman would have to bring up a baby daughter on her own. Audrey Dudman – Ace's mother.

Ace glanced back over at the young mother. The baby was sleeping now. Ace wondered what would become of that child, where fate would take it. Her gaze wandered around the tube station. There were no teenagers. It was all adults or the very young. Everyone else had been evacuated or called up. She had been used to her evenings in Perivale being filled with people of her own age. Been used to cinemas and amusement arcades, to evenings spent trying to get served in pubs, to clubbing with the old crowd – Shreela, Midge, Ange, Flo, Stevie and Manisha.

Ace scowled. Every time she tried to think about her past, something bad had to come floating to the surface. Manisha; burnt to death in her flat. Killed because she wasn't white. Murdered by… Nazis. Neo-Nazis, for God's sake. There shouldn't be any neo-Nazis. This was supposed to be the war that put paid to fascism. Except it wouldn't. Creeps would still be peddling the same old prejudices in half a century – she'd met them herself. Maybe they would always be there, always have to be fought and guarded against. The Doctor would never stop fighting, she knew – and neither would she.

She craned her neck to see where the Doctor was. He was at the far end of the platform leading a group of octogenarians in a rousing singsong of music-hall favourites. The man who had fought some of the most heinous terrors of the universe was conducting an off-key choir with a stick of rhubarb. Ace didn't dare to think where he'd found that.

Someone pulled out a harmonica and began to play, and Ace groaned as the Doctor hauled his spoons from his pocket and began to provide a clattering accompaniment. Within minutes the entire station had fallen under the spell of the little time traveller and the devastation that was going on overhead was temporarily forgotten. Ace settled back on to the blanket that she had been given. To the sound of bombs overhead and the tune of 'My Old Man', she felt her eyes closing, and within minutes, and against all her expectations, she had fallen asleep.

CHAPTER 3

Ace was woken by the Doctor gently shaking her arm. She pulled herself upright, rubbing the sleep from her eyes. The Doctor thrust a half-eaten stick of rhubarb towards her. 'Breakfast?'

She shook her head at him. 'I think I'll skip it, thanks.'

The Doctor folded the remains of the stick in half with a snap, and stuck it in the pocket of his duffel coat. His eyes were shining with glee.

'I've remembered who that businessman is. He's an electrical entrepreneur by the name of Peddler, head of Peddler Electronics.'

'So what?'

'I'm not sure yet.' He grabbed her hand. 'Come on. Let's go and say good morning to Mr McBride.'

He led her through the mass of sleeping people and out into the early morning light. It was grey and cold. The air was hazy with fog, and the clouds overhead threatened rain. All around, Ace could see firemen and soldiers clearing away the debris of the night before. Fires burnt in the street and a thick pall of smoke hung like a shroud over the distant East End.

Ace stopped and looked around her. This used to be quite a regular haunt of hers, particularly when she had been working at the McDonald's on Tottenham Court Road. She used to browse for hours in the Virgin Megastore, then head over to Darth Vader's flat in Stepney. Darth was a plumber, Flo's boyfriend. God, she still couldn't believe that those two had got married.

'Come on, Ace!' The Doctor was waiting for her down the street. She hurried to catch him up passing several buildings that she recognised, and dozens more that she didn't. Presumably, these were ones that wouldn't survive the bombs. It was all far more elegant than the city she knew. By the time the rebuilding was over, London would be ugly and modern.

The Doctor was on the move again. She had to jog to keep up with him.

'How long does this go on for, Professor?'

'Until the end of July next year. Almost nightly attacks. It's incredible so much of the city survived it. Then there were the V1 and V2 attacks in 1944. After that the city survives pretty much intact until the Dalek invasion. Then, all this –' he gestured expansively – 'is just so much gravel.'

Ace hated it when he began to talk about the Daleks. His voice acquired an edge, a viciousness that didn't suit him. She quickly changed the subject.

'Why are we going back to McBride's?'

'Because our friendly private detective is going to be very useful in getting me to see Dr Peddler and that sphere.'

Ace was puzzled. 'How does getting to see this Peddler bloke help you track down the sphere?'

'I want to know what he was doing at that bomb site. Rich industrialists and company directors don't usually go stumbling around craters in their business suits. I'm curious.'

'Do you know who the sphere belongs to?'

The Doctor stopped and picked up the pieces of a broken doll and a wireless set from the street. 'No, not yet. But I've got some very nasty suspicions.'

McBride was on the phone when the Doctor and Ace arrived at his office. He gestured at them to keep quiet and continued to talk to his mysterious caller in hushed tones. Ace wandered to the window to look out over London again, while the Doctor began to play idly with the dial on the safe.

McBride slammed the phone down and leapt to his feet, pulling on his trench coat. 'That was one of my stoolies. My informers. A case. A decent case at last! Now, if I can just get one jump ahead of the cops.'

The Doctor didn't look up. 'I'm pleased that you've finally got something to pit your considerable talents against, Mr McBride, but we do have some other, more pressing business.' He gave the dial a final twist and the safe door swung open to reveal its meagre contents. McBride made a mental note to get himself a new safe, and to keep his whisky somewhere more secure.

The Doctor stood up, looking smug, and dusted his hands off. 'I've remembered who that man in the newspaper photograph is. A Dr Peddler. It's imperative that we get to see him as soon as possible.'

This time it was McBride's turn to look smug. 'Then tag along, Doc. I'm off to his factory. Peddler's been murdered.'

Chief Inspector Mullen took a long drag on his cigarette, ignoring the pointed look that the forensic officer gave him. This was the last thing that he needed. His run-in with McBride had put him in a foul mood, and given him a headache. He had got home to a dinner of swede and liver (which he hated), and a row with his wife. The row had been in full swing when the sirens had started up, and he'd been forced to spend the night in a tiny Anderson shelter at his mother-in-law's. The night had been passed with her constant snoring and his wife's whispered accusations about how he never spent any time with them.

He'd left the shelter as soon as dawn had broken, not even going home. He'd slipped out through the alleyway behind the house and gone straight to the station. He'd just brewed himself a cup of strong tea when he had received the call about the Peddler death. Looking down at the body now, he knew that there was no way that this could become anything other than a murder inquiry.

The police photographer shouldered his way past him and began to take endless photographs of the body. The flashing made Mullen's head throb and he turned away, finishing his cigarette and looking for somewhere to flick the stub. Aware that the man from forensics was watching him like a hawk, he called to the young policeman at the door, beckoning him over and handing him the remains of the cigarette. 'Get rid of this outside, would you, Dixon.' The policeman was just heading out of the door when McBride appeared, a strange little man and a teenage girl close behind him. Mullen groaned.

'McBride, go away. I've seen enough of you in the last twenty-four hours, and I dare say you have of me, too. Go and find another bomb. One that works this time.'

McBride ignored the gibe, taking in as much of the crime scene as he could. The body was hidden from view, behind the desk. He craned his neck, trying to get a better look. 'So, uh, what happened here?'

'Oh, I'm sorry.' Mullen held up his arms, clicking his fingers to get everyone's attention. 'Right, everybody. Let's go home. Mr McBride's going to be solving this one. The police aren't needed here.'

A snigger ran around the room. McBride and Mullen faced off, ready for a rerun of the previous day. The confrontation was interrupted by the arrival of a large police officer. Oblivious to the atmosphere in the room, he crossed straight over to Mullen and passed him a small notebook.

'Got the secretary's statement, sir.'

Mullen looked at him with a pained expression. 'Constable Quick, the poor woman's in a state of shock. It could have waited, man.'

Constable Quick merely continued giving his report. 'Yes, sir. She's being sedated now, sir. Says that she locked up herself. Dr Peddler was working late. Says he'd been behaving funny. Had an appointment with a couple of villains earlier on. A Mr Wall – little fellow, foreign she thought – and his two 'ssociates. Well, two heavies, really. They were massive, she said, and looked a little bit like…' The policeman tailed off, realising that the entire room was listening to him 'Well, a little bit like American gangsters.'

Mullen looked McBride up and down. 'American gangsters, yes…'

The policeman tried to elaborate. 'Built like brick –'

'Yes, thank you, Constable. I'm sure that your report will be invaluable – later.'

'Yes, sir.' Constable Quick saluted clumsily and stomped out of the room. Mullen rolled his eyes in despair. He was about to continue with his attack on McBride when one of the forensics team hurried over.

'Excuse me, Chief Inspector. This was in Peddler's hand.' He handed over a business card. Mullen took it, handling it by its edges. 'Our shady Mr Wall, to be sure…'

A hand appeared over Mullen's shoulder and plucked the card from his own. Mullen's jaw dropped in astonishment. It was the little man who had come in with McBride. He'd been taking in everything that had gone on, and somehow, by not saying anything, he'd almost made himself invisible. He was turning the card over and over in his hands, oblivious to the fact that he was removing any trace of fingerprints. He held it up to the light, sniffed it, and finally waggled it next to his ear. Aware that he was being watched, he beamed over at Mullen. 'Well, Inspector, what do you think?'

'I think that I should put you on a charge. Obstructing a police officer in the course of his duty. Is this man a friend of yours, McBride?'

McBride shuffled uncomfortably, appalled by the Doctor's complete lack of knowledge of police procedure. 'Uh, sort of.' He winced in embarrassment as Ace took the card from the Doctor and tried to bend it.

'It's plastic. It looks like some kind of credit card, Professor. Did they have credit cards in the war?'

The Doctor snatched it back from her, slapping her hand. 'No, they didn't. Any more than they had "bombs" made from alien alloys.' He began fiddling with the edge of the card. He spoke without looking up. 'You realise what this means, Inspector?'

The entire room was mesmerised by the exchange. Barely a breath was drawn. McBride wondered if he could sneak out of the room while no one was watching. Mullen answered through gritted teeth. 'What?'

'That this killing and your mysterious "bomb" are linked in some way.' He peered up at the chief inspector with twinkling eyes, and smiled. 'I don't suppose you want to tell me where the "bomb" is?'

The smile that Mullen gave him back could have frozen hell over. 'No.'

The Doctor shrugged. 'No... Ah, well. Aha!' With a pinging noise, the 'business card' sprang open like a tiny cigarette case. McBride caught a glimpse of electrical components, far smaller than anything that he had ever seen. He pushed in next to Mullen for a

31

closer look. 'Hey, that's neat. What the hell is that thing?'

Despite himself, Mullen was impressed. He took it from the Doctor and began to study it closely. 'Yes, what the hell is it?'

The Doctor shook his head and pulled a set of jeweller's screwdrivers from his pocket. 'I don't know. I'll have to take a closer look.'

Mullen pulled the card close to his chest. 'Oh, no. The lab boys can sort it out, thank you very much.'

The Doctor gave him a disappointed look, like that of a small boy who's just been told that he can't go and play. He thrust the screwdrivers back into his pocket and crossed to the window, peering through the small hole in the glass.

'Now don't tell me – let me guess. The building was completely locked up, there was no sign of a break-in, and the security man on the front gate saw nothing.'

Mullen stared across at him. 'Well, yes, since you ask.'

The Doctor smiled that brilliant smile again. 'So, how did our killer get in?'

With the forensic officer having to be physically restrained by his colleagues, the Doctor snapped open the catch on the window, slid it up and peered out into the yard. He nodded and pointed at something. 'Aha. There we are, Inspector.'

Mullen reluctantly crossed the room to the Doctor's side. He placed the card on the desk and peered out to see what the Doctor was pointing at. A drain, perhaps six inches in diameter, its cover lying upside down several feet away on the tarmac. He looked at the Doctor in puzzlement. 'What?'

The Doctor pointed again at the drain as if it was patently obvious. 'The drain. It came up through the drain and jumped through the window.'

Mullen gave the Doctor an extremely sceptical look. The two men pulled themselves back in through the window. The Doctor looked at Mullen with utter conviction. 'How did he die?'

'He was stabbed through the heart.'

'Stabbed?'

32

'Sort of… It looks to me more like… something burrowed through his ribcage.'

Ace was there in a trice. 'Ugh! Like an animal, you mean?'

Mullen crossed to where the body was covered with a sheet. Ace tried to cross with the Doctor, but he held her back, shaking his head. She opened her mouth, ready to argue, but the look in the Doctor's eye made her stop. She crossed back over to McBride and watched as Mullen lifted the sheet.

The Doctor's face was unreadable. He bent down and made his grim examination. 'A very small, vicious animal.'

Mullen made a decision. The policeman who had disposed of the cigarette butt had re-entered the room. Mullen pulled him over. 'Dixon, go back outside and take a look at that drain in the back yard.'

The Doctor called McBride over. Ace watched McBride's face go white.

'Jeez. What got to him?'

The Doctor looked down with sadness in his eyes. 'Surprised, shocked, terrified. Poor man.' He let the sheet fall back over Peddler's face and picked up the card again.

There was a call from outside the window. Mullen leaned out. Dixon was shining a torch down into the depths of the drain. 'It's all scratched inside, sir. The scratches look new.'

Mullen looked over at the Doctor with a degree of respect. The Doctor snapped the card shut, slipped it into his duffel-coat pocket and beamed at McBride. 'Come on, Mr McBride. We mustn't stand between the police and justice. The Mountie always gets his man.'

He began to usher McBride and Ace towards the door when Mullen stopped him.

'Hang on. The card please. Wall's card.'

The Doctor thrust his hand into his pocket and pulled out the stick of rhubarb that he had been conducting his impromptu choir with the night before. 'It's in here somewhere. Hold this a minute would you, Inspector.'

He thrust the rhubarb at Mullen and rummaged in his pocket

again, pulling out the card and triggering its opening mechanism. 'There we are.'

He snapped it shut and passed it over to Mullen, taking back the rhubarb.

Mullen studied him with interest. 'If I should want to talk to you, is there any way that I can get in touch with you, Mr…'

'Doctor. I'll be at McBride's office.'

Mullen grimaced. 'Do we have to have him along?'

'Inspector, I am merely Dr Watson. This –' he gestured at McBride – 'is Sherlock Holmes.'

McBride decided that the Doctor had pushed his luck far enough and grabbed him by the hood of his duffel coat. 'Come on, Doc. Ace.'

McBride hurried the two of them out of the office. The Doctor doffed his hat at Mullen, realised that he was still holding a stick of rhubarb, and waved it cheerily at the ashen forensics man as he trotted out of the office. McBride shrugged at Mullen and followed them out. Mullen stood in the middle of the room as the rest of his team let out their pent-up breath. His day definitely couldn't get any worse.

CHAPTER 4

The air in Major Lazonby's office was a thoroughly military one. Everything neat, ordered and, on the whole, green. Lazonby didn't like chaos. There was a place for everything and everything could be forced to conform. That had been the ideal that he lived his entire life by. Even as a small boy he had been impossibly ordered. No nagging needed from parents to keep his room clean, no teachers insisting that his handwriting had to improve. At school or at play he was always immaculately turned out, but, while his elders looked on him as a model pupil and son, children his own age shunned him, finding something sinister in the intense precision of the boy.

And so Lazonby's life had gone on; a solitary one. He played alone, he studied alone. He didn't seem to worry about the fact that he had no friends – he just accepted it. It was almost as if friends would clutter the tidiness. As time went on even his parents began to be excluded from his life.

His college years were just a natural progression of his schooldays. He had grown into a handsome young man and was the subject of much speculation among female students. After endless terms of rejected advances, they finally gave up on him, deciding that he wasn't interested in women, but even the men who tried to coax Lazonby out of his shell were met with firm, and sometimes violent, rebukes. The truth of the matter was that Lazonby just wasn't interested in forming any kind of relationship with the chaotic, disordered people who inhabited his world.

It was a natural progression for him to enter the armed services. His grades at university were superb, and the regimented lifestyle of the army allowed him to flower spectacularly. Without any outside distractions in his life, he swiftly climbed the ladder of rank, and became one of the youngest captains in the British army.

Shortly after the war had started he had been approached by Military Intelligence and promoted to the rank of major. No one was quite sure how far his duties extended, and very few wanted to know. Lazonby was a man to be avoided and feared. This new business with the sphere had given a maniacal edge to his precision, and he was driving his men hard. The truth was, Military Intelligence were worried. Over the past two months there had been a number of explosions in East London of devastating power. Power far in excess of anything the Luftwaffe ought to have been able to drop on them. Even amid the carnage of this protracted bombing blitz these things had stood out. There had been speculation that the Germans had made a breakthrough in the new atomic weapons the Americans were only now starting to whisper about. They needed a result. The sphere had to provide it.

He had had it brought to the military testing facility secreted within the Peddler factory – his centre of operations for nearly a year now. There he had commandeered nearly all of Peddler's men and had set them to work trying to identify every part of its make-up.

He had allowed himself and his team no rest since the sphere had been brought here. He had drawn up a round-the-clock rota. Scientists and technicians, their names picked out in different colours in Lazonby's mechanical handwriting, had protested at the inhuman hours he was expecting of them, but Lazonby had set his rota in motion and heaven help the man who disrupted it.

He himself had not left his office since the sphere had arrived here. Despite forty-eight hours without sleep, he still looked immaculate: his moustache neatly trimmed; his hair combed with military precision; every crease on his jacket perfectly straight.

The technician standing in front of him was a shambles. His hair was unruly, the white lab coat he wore was covered in streaks of grease and burn marks. He slurped his tea noisily out of a cracked mug as Lazonby scanned the man's report. Lazonby didn't like dealing with these civilians. The report was sloppy – the paper was dirty and the spelling and grammar appalling.

Lazonby placed the report into his 'pending' tray and glanced at the name tag on the man's coat. B. Harkness. 'So what success have you had?'

Harkness took another slurp of his tea, wiping his mouth with the back of his hand and wiping that in turn on the grimy front of his coat. 'Nothing. We've tried everything. We can't pierce it, we can't melt it, it doesn't conduct. We can't even begin to analyse it.'

Lazonby stared straight into Harkness's face. The technician had mismatched eyes. One brown, one blue. More disorder. Everywhere that Lazonby looked there was disorder. 'Are you telling me that the Germans have developed an impenetrable metal?'

The technician shrugged. 'I'm not sure what I'm telling you, Major Lazonby.'

'It simply doesn't add up. Jerry isn't stupid. Why should he develop a bomb casing that won't shatter? And why should he dump it on our doorstep?'

The phone on Lazonby's desk rang. He answered it and, as he listened to the voice on the other end, he felt his face flush with rage. 'Dr Peddler? Why wasn't I told sooner?' His grip on the receiver turned the knuckles on his hand white. 'I want this place sealed off completely. Now! Do you understand?'

He replaced the receiver with barely controlled anger, took a deep breath and then picked it up again. He spoke in slow, measured tones, but the thinly veiled threat in his voice made Harkness shudder.

'I want to see Chief Inspector Mullen. I want to see him *here*, and I want to see him *now*.'

McBride unlocked the door of his office and let Ace and the Doctor in. He would have to take more care about security if crazy strangers were going to walk in every time he left his door unlocked. He didn't quite know what he'd got himself into but he was starting to enjoy it. The Doctor was weird, but he believed the story about the sphere and he'd managed to shut Mullen up. That was good enough for McBride. The kid was cute, too. Odd taste in clothes, and sometimes she lost him with her slang, but she was bright and sassy.

She was dancing around the Doctor. 'Aren't you glad that we came now, Professor?'

He waved his umbrella at her. 'Well, I still don't like the motive behind it. You're a barbarian, Ace.'

'But it's history. The pensioners in Perivale were always droning on about the Blitz.'

The Doctor nodded wearily. 'So you had to come and see it.'

McBride shook his head in disbelief. Perhaps 'weird' wasn't the right word...

The Doctor tossed his duffel coat in a heap in the corner and sat at McBride's desk. He pulled the set of jeweller's screwdrivers out of his pocket and, to McBride's astonishment, placed Wall's calling card on the centre of the desk.

'Hey, I thought you gave that thing to Mullen.'

The Doctor had already sprung the card open and was poking and prodding in its interior, trying to keep Ace out of his light. 'No. I gave him an Arcturan gambling chip. They look very similar.'

McBride was both amused and impressed. 'Sonofagun...'

The phone on McBride's desk rang and he reached for it. But Ace got to it first and dropped into her best American drawl. 'Mr Bogart's out of the office at the moment...' She stopped. 'Oh, right...' She passed the receiver over to the Doctor. 'Mullen.'

The Doctor gripped the receiver beneath his shoulder and chin and continued his investigation of the inside of the card. 'Hello, Inspector... The card. What card would that be? A Christmas card? Birthday, perhaps? Oh... that card. No, I thought that you had it. No? Well, now, let me think. Ah! I gave it to that nice young policeman. What was his name? Swallow? Swift?... Quick!' His eye's opened wide in surprise. 'Really, Inspector, I'm sure that isn't language fitting for a police officer.'

He let the receiver fall back on to the phone. 'McBride, would you do something for me?'

'Sure.'

'I take it that you've made certain contacts with the seedier strata of London society.'

McBride looked confused 'What?'

'You know a lot of criminal types.'

'Well, yeah.'

'People who would know what was going on. Know about any

new faces – anyone trying to… "muscle in", I believe you'd say, on their business.'

'Sure.'

The Doctor looked pleased. 'Good. I want you to find out something about Mr Wall and his associates. Also, see if anybody knows where the army are hiding a huge silver sphere.' He pushed Ace out of his light again. 'Take Ace with you.'

'Professor, it's raining.'

'Well, take my umbrella, then. Off you both go.'

He shooed them towards the door. Ace grabbed the Doctor's red-handled umbrella and bounded down the stairs. McBride jammed his hat on to his head and was about to pull the door shut when the Doctor stopped him

'One more thing…'

McBride turned back. The Doctor was silhouetted against the window. 'Peddler's business. Find out if it was all above board. Were they up to anything at all… dubious? You needn't count working for the British government – I'll try Inspector Mullen on that one, though I doubt he'll tell me. See what you can do.'

McBride turned to go but the Doctor's voice stopped him in his tracks again. 'Oh, one more thing.' The Doctor was still nothing but a silhouette against the morning sky, but McBride was aware that his eyes had turned to slivers of ice. 'Take care of her, Mr McBride.'

He shut the door and hurried down the stairs to join Ace. The Doctor may act like a clown, but McBride had finally realised that it was all a front, a shield concealing something more dangerous and more alien than he could possibly imagine. All the Germans' bombs and bullets would be as nothing to the wrath of that little man if anything happened to this girl, and McBride didn't want to see that wrath.

He pulled the collar of his coat up against the chill November day. The first spots of greasy rain were beginning to fall, washing the soot from the buildings and forming black pools on the road. He crossed over to where Ace was waiting for him. She was trying to put up the umbrella, but the wind was swirling and she was having trouble hanging on to it. McBride took it from her, pulled off his hat and thrust it into her hands. She put it on and grinned cheekily at him. He struggled with the umbrella for a moment before it flipped open, and the two of them headed off into the mist.

The Doctor watched them vanish into the fog. He stood for a few moments, watching the raindrops form patterns on the window pane, then turned and contemplated the card on the desk. He took a deep breath and picked up the screwdrivers again.

'And now for you...'

Elsewhere in the drizzly darkness of the East End, something huge and dying lurked in the doorway of a ruined warehouse. Shrouded in tarpaulins, its frame shook, its body consumed with an infection that got worse with every passing day. It didn't know where it was, or what it was. It didn't know anything before waking months ago. All it knew was that this entire place was hostile to it, and that it had to survive.

It had paused in doorways and basements through this and every other night, as the bombs had fallen, bricks and shrapnel tearing into what remained of its body. Now it crawled out of its hideaway, pulling the tarpaulin tight, desperately trying to hold itself together, a huge shambling figure stumbling through the smoke.

The tremors got worse. It needed to feed again. Its desire for survival was all-important, overwhelming, crushing all other needs. It had to find another victim. It didn't know what the small bipeds were that inhabited this place, but the fluid they contained helped to subdue the fire that raged within it

It had already killed many times since it had been here. Sometimes it was lucky and the bombs did the work for it. It had plucked bodies from the ruins, drained them and let the fires consume the husks. The victims were needed more frequently now as its condition worsened. It kept moving, trying to remain out of sight, keeping to the dark places, but the tremors had got worse and the pain had made it bold. It lumbered through the foggy daylight, aware that the source of its craving was near: it could smell the raw, crude reek of its addiction.

In the ruins of a house it could hear the sound of movement, bricks and rubble being moved. It speeded up, its tarpaulin flapping around it like huge, ragged wings.

Old Josh had had better days. The mornings after the air raids had usually afforded him better pickings. He was out most of the time before dawn to avoid the police and the firemen. He scavenged through the bomb sites to gather enough food for the day. He never took from houses where there were bodies – he could never have lived with himself stealing from the dead – but if the houses were empty, their owners safely in the shelters, then he felt happier. If the houses were bombed out then the occupiers had more to worry about than a few missing tins of soup or loaves of bread. He never took valuables, only food, and then only enough for one or two meals. It seemed pointless trying to store anything because you never knew if your store would still be standing the following day. His current bolt-hole had proved more successful than most. He had found a way into the crypt of a church in Spitalfields. An empty sarcophagus had provided the most comfortable bed he had had in months.

Today had been a particularly bad day for him. One house had had a well-stocked larder, but the bombs had done too good a job. He had been through several houses in the street but none had had anything that was of any use to him. The kitchen of this house looked promising. A few small fires still burned but the rain was starting to put them out. He was fairly sure that there were some tins under the rubble – it was just taking him a little longer to get at them than he would have liked.

Josh stopped as he heard something move out in the street. He was usually well out of sight by now. It was too light, but the fog afforded some protection, and the firemen were busy in the more elegant areas of town. He listened for a moment. There it was again, a shuffling, flapping noise. He peered through the smoke. There was something moving in the gloom. He abandoned his tins and made his way to the shattered back door. The flapping got louder and Josh began to get scared. He stumbled over the piles of bricks, trying to get to the gate in the back wall. He heard a crash from behind him and spun to see a huge figure in the doorway of the house.

Smoke curled around the tarpaulin wings, turning the figure into a huge angel of death. Josh felt his heart pounding fit to burst. 'Oh, Gawd, you're the Lurker, ain't you? The Limehouse Lurker.' He scrabbled desperately at the gate as the giant shambled towards him, rain dripping from its outstretched hands. 'I ain't worth killing, guv, honest I ain't…'

Josh's pleas were cut short as the two huge hands clubbed him to the ground. The tarpaulin wings curled around the two of them, muffling the screams of the old tramp as the Lurker tore him apart. The screams were mercifully short, and the Lurker stood, smearing as much blood as it could over its body, feeling the fires inside it subside.

It stopped, suddenly, its twitching head on one side, listening. Ever since it had been in this place it had been aware that it was being followed. Something small and dogged and lethal that always hovered just out of range. Something that was not of this earth. It was near again. Gaining.

Scooping chunks of flesh against its chest, the Lurker pulled its cloak around itself again and shambled off into the ruins, looking for somewhere to hide.

In the back garden of the house, the sightless eyes of old Josh filled with rainwater, running like tears into the bloodsoaked earth.

signal detected>
activate>
locate signal source> signal source moving>
compensate>
analysis of terrain> uneven> many artificial structures> condition unstable>
compensate>
scan for hostile life forms> none>
lock on to signal source>
follow>

42

CHAPTER 5

Ace and McBride threaded their way through a city that was slowly coming alive around them. Ace was like a sponge, absorbing sights, smells, sounds – drinking in everything. Of all the experiences that she had been through with the Doctor it was this, wandering through her near past, that made her spine tingle. So often visits to Earth ended in remote areas of the country – desolate moorland or quarries. London was always so vibrant and exciting, no matter what the decade. She had resisted the offer of visiting the future. She had an overwhelming dread of meeting somebody she knew, seeing them old and wizened, and she unaware of everything that would have passed for them. She realised that she was living outside of time, and that the longer she stayed with the Doctor, the harder it was going to be to reintegrate herself into a 'normal' life.

She shook her head. She was getting morbid. For the moment she should enjoy the experience of wandering through a time years before her birth. She giggled at the absurdity of the situation, pulled her camera from her pocket and began taking snapshots of what was going on around her. Tube stations were slowly disgorging their tenants on to the streets in a steady stream and people were beginning to emerge from Anderson shelters, blinking like moles in the morning light.

Families returned to their homes, not knowing what they might find. Shop owners made their way to their businesses, praying that they had been spared the bombs and the looters. Ace watched a woman break down in floods of tears, burying her face in her husband's chest as they regarded the bombed-out shell of their small shop – windows broken, clothes and mannequins scattered across the road. Abruptly the woman pulled herself straight, dried her eyes and began to clear away some of the wreckage, standing dummies up and piling rubbish into sacks, determined that they would open as usual.

Ace felt a pang of guilt. No wonder her grandmother had kept talking about the Blitz. She was proud of it. Proud of how she had coped with it.

Ace resolved that if they should ever meet again she would listen to the stories with a little more interest, not dismiss them as the boring afternoon ramblings of a nostalgic old woman.

She suddenly felt an urge to stay and help, but McBride dragged her away, keen to get over the river and out of the rain as soon as possible. He was cold and miserable. His hair was plastered to his forehead. Ace huddled up to him under the umbrella. 'What's up with you?'

'You mean apart from being cold, wet, and very probably out of my depth?'

'Yeah,' Ace grinned, 'apart from that.'

McBride fixed her with a serious look. 'Where are you from?'

'Me? I'm from Perivale.' Ace's expression was one of pure innocence.

McBride grunted. 'The Doc sure ain't from Perivale.'

Ace remained silent. Explaining quite where the Doctor came from was tricky at the best of times. She found it best to say nothing.

The two of them walked in silence for a while. To McBride's surprise Ace linked arms with him, grateful for some extra warmth. She hadn't really dressed for the occasion. She had the offer of using the TARDIS wardrobe, but she always felt more at home in the clothes that she had brought with her from Iceworld. It gave her a degree of independence and, despite the fact that the Doctor was the only adult she had ever been totally comfortable with, she still needed that slight independence, an emotional crutch that said no matter what happened, she still had control over her own destiny.

It was McBride who broke the silence.

'The Doctor... he isn't a violent man, is he?'

Ace looked puzzled. 'The Professor? No.' She stopped. 'Not unless you've got sink plungers instead of hands, that is. Why?'

'Oh, nothing. Just don't go running off and getting yourself into trouble. Deal?'

'Deal.'

A flurry of wind blew autumn leaves in eddies around them, and Ace had to help McBride hold on to the umbrella. The two of them battled on towards Blackfriars Bridge. The bridge was blocked by the burnt-out shell of a Routemaster bus. A dozen men were straining to push it to the side of the road. To McBride's irritation, Ace ran over and added her weight to the others, eager to help. The men gave her a curious look but she was stronger than she looked and her help was gladly accepted.

Ace grabbed a London Transport badge as a trophy and she and McBride headed off over the bridge. Beneath them, the Thames, dark brown and turbulent, made its way inexorably towards the sea. Ace liked the river. It had seen plagues, fires, and wars before, and this would not be the last. Despite all that humans could do, it would still be here, a constant companion to London and its people.

By the time they arrived at Mama's Bar the two of them were soaked through, and the Doctor's umbrella had seen better days. Mama's was unimpressive from the outside, a shabby wooden frontage under a railway arch. A badly faded sign that might once have been cheerful and brash swung in the wind.

Ace and McBride hurried under the railway bridge, grateful for the shelter. Ace shook the water from the umbrella and McBride pushed the door open.

Ace's senses were assaulted by warmth, light, and smoke – a total contrast to the street outside. Mama's was a huge room. There was no attempt made to hide its railway arch origins. A few people looked up as Ace and McBride entered, but soon turned back to their own business. Ace dumped the sodden umbrella into a stand near the door and followed McBride towards the bar. Tables were scattered everywhere – different styles, heights, and colours. One wall had been separated off into booths with crude wooden screens and figures lurked within them, wreathed in cigarette smoke. The roof looked as though it had been patched more than once. A metal bucket stood on the bar, water dripping into it from overhead with a steady tattoo of tinny pings, and tiny rivulets of water trickled from all sides across a concrete floor which sloped towards a metal drain in the middle of the room.

A huge, old-fashioned jukebox stood in one corner. Ace stopped and mentally pulled herself up. Old-fashioned to her, maybe, but at the moment it was, no doubt, the height of modern music technology. Music was playing – nothing that Ace recognised, something about the 'Santa Fe Trail'.

The long, low bar filled the back of the room. It desperately tried to affect a stylish American feel and fell a long way short of the mark. Baseball memorabilia were scattered over the back wall amid posters, pennants, and too few bottles of spirits. A grubby and torn American flag was draped over the counter. McBride was in conversation with the barman, a huge black American in a white vest, furiously polishing beer glasses. He looked up as Ace approached. McBride pulled out a stool for her.

'Ace, this is Mama. Mama, Ace is a friend.'

Mama flashed her a smile that made his vest look grey, put down his glasses and leaned across the bar. 'Any friend of Cody's is liable to be bad news, but you're a good deal prettier than most, so what can your Mama get you?'

McBride butted in. 'A beer for me, a cream soda for the kid.'

Ace grimaced, 'I hate cream soda. I'll have a beer too.'

'Make that a Coke, Mama, and a couple of doughboys. Is Sharkey in yet?'

Mama jerked a thumb towards one of the booths. In the gloom, hunched over a beer, was a small ratty-looking man whose clothes were several years too old and several sizes too big. Sharkey had been McBride's stool pigeon since the private eye had arrived in London. Most of the time he just concerned himself with small-time crime – black-market stockings and cigarettes, an outlet for merchandise looted from bombed-out shops – but McBride had quickly learned that Sharkey had a good pair of ears and a nose for other people's business. If there was something big going down, then Sharkey was liable to know who, where, and when, and in McBride's business that was very useful.

Pale and nervous, Sharkey nodded a greeting at McBride, immediately checking all corners of the bar to see if anyone was watching. McBride did a quick check of the room himself to see if Sharkey's paranoia was justified. The bar was just beginning to fill up with the early-lunch crowd – a few of the Ambulance Corps, a couple of the locals – no one of any significance. He crossed to the booth, calling back at Ace.

'Bring the drinks, will ya, kid.'

Ace stuck her tongue out at him. She hated being called kid. Mama pulled a pint of cold beer and set it down in front of her. As he turned to get her bottle of Coke from the huge clunky fridge behind the bar she gulped down a few mouthfuls.

Sharkey and McBride were deep in conversation when Ace slumped into the chair next to the private eye. She thought that the little informant was going to go through the roof. McBride calmed him. 'Don't worry, Sharkey, she's with me. She already knows about Peddler.'

The ratty little man calmed slightly, taking a long, deep drink of his beer, his hands trembling.

'What is it that you need to know, Mr McBride.'

'There's a couple of hoods – big guys – going around with a little guy named Wall. Know anything about them?'

Sharkey shook his head thoughtfully. To Ace's disgust a light shower of dandruff settled on to his collar. McBride was right when he said that he had lowlife contacts.

McBride wasn't surprised. He hadn't been expecting instant results. 'What about that silver ball? The one that fell on me?'

Sharkey grinned, revealing crooked yellow teeth. 'Yeah, I saw that. In the paper.'

McBride looked embarrassed. 'Yeah, well, the army took it away. I gotta find out where it went. I also need to know the lowdown on

Peddler's operation. What they did, anything crooked.'

Sharkey pulled on a battered trilby and finished off his beer. 'Let me make a phone call.' He scurried over to the door and out into the rain, looking more and more like a sewer rat. Ace didn't disguise her distaste. 'Doesn't he ever take a bath?'

McBride shrugged. 'I guess not. Best goddamn lead in the city, though.'

Mama shambled over from the bar with a plate and thumped it down on the table between them 'There you go.'

He grabbed Sharkey's empty glass and began a circuit of the room, wiping ashtrays and clearing glasses until he had half a dozen grasped in each enormous paw.

McBride pulled a napkin from under the plate. 'You ever had doughboys before?'

Ace shook her head, dropping unconsciously into an almost American accent. 'Uh-uh.'

'Well, tuck in. We're here until Sharkey gets back and this is going to be the closest we get to having any lunch today.'

Back in McBride's office the Doctor put his screwdrivers down on the desk, stood up and stretched. He'd been working without a break for hours and his back ached. It had been a while since he'd done something this complicated. Being chased up and down faceless alien corridors by huge slavering monsters had its disadvantages but at least it kept you fit.

He had known for a while that the card was some form of signalling device – he'd seen enough of them in his life to know that. The problem was that he didn't know what it was signalling to. He had his suspicions, but the only way to test them was to reactivate the card and see what happened.

It was an unfamiliar sensation for the Doctor not to know what was going on, and he didn't like it. He thought back to the expression on Peddler's face. Whatever it was that attacked him – and its modus operandi was naggingly familiar – it had no right to be on this planet at this time. Humans had enough trouble at the moment with monsters of their own.

The TARDIS had taken them here purely at Ace's behest, to let her experience the Blitz first-hand. Would the devastation, the loss of life, temper her enthusiasm for explosives? She'd been on at him for days to let her use the TARDIS labs to manufacture an improved Nitro Nine, and he didn't dare think what she might come up with if she ever got loose in the chemical store.

Dropping back into the swivel chair, the Doctor picked up the mysterious card. Holding it by its edges, he brought it up to his forehead, closed his eyes and concentrated. There was an almost imperceptible click from the card as the calling beacon activated. The Doctor placed it back on the desk and smiled grimly.

'Right… now we wait.'

He rummaged in his pockets and pulled out a packet of sweet cigarettes. He peered at the small print on the bottom of the battered cardboard pack: 'Use before end of September 1977'. 'Marvellous!' he beamed, happily. 'Thirty-seven years before their sell-by date!' He stuck one in his mouth, then put on his hat at a rakish angle and leaned back in the chair, swinging his feet up on to the desk. 'Letsh shee what comesh crawling out of the woodwoik, blue eyesh.'

The chair began to slide backward and the Doctor dropped slowly towards the floor until he touched the ground, his feet still on the desk. He pulled the sweet cigarette from between his lips. 'This obviously isn't as easy as it looks.'

Ace had finished her doughboy and was half-way through McBride's when Sharkey slithered back to their table. If possible he was jumpier than ever. His wet hair stuck slickly to the top of his head and he looked constantly back at the door. He spoke quickly and quietly to McBride.

'I'm taking you to see someone. Deals in scientific stuff, anything crooked. Clever though. Calls himself the Professor.'

Ace spluttered, nearly choking on her food.

'What's up with her?'

McBride was pounding her on the back. 'I don't know.'

Ace took a long swig of her Coke. 'I'm OK. Don't mind me.' McBride turned back to Sharkey, but Ace's mind was racing. She'd been calling the Doctor by the nickname 'Professor' ever since she'd been travelling with him. Was it possible that this, or some later regeneration, had set himself up in wartime London as some kind of seedy underworld adviser?

The thought faded as she listened to Sharkey. The Professor was an old man by the name of George Limb. The Doctor had used many aliases over the years, but this didn't have his style at all. Had this man been called John Smith, then she might have been worried. The Doctor seemed to think that John Smith was nicely inconspicuous but Ace cringed every time he used it – she would have to talk to him about finding another name.

She pulled her chair in closer to catch what Sharkey was saying.

'He used to be some kind of adviser to the government, until they dropped him. I don't know all the details. Now he tries to make a living like the rest of us. If you want scientific know-how, scientific gear, he can get it. That heist over in Acton last year? Word on the street was that the Professor planned every step of that. I don't know who his contacts are, but they're powerful. If anyone is going to know where your blessed sphere is, then it's him.'

McBride gulped down the last of his beer. 'OK, let's do it.'

Sharkey looked suspiciously at Ace. 'You takin' her?'

Ace bristled. 'Yes, he is taking her, ratbag. And don't start giving me any of that "it's-too-dangerous-for-girls" crap. Tell him, McBride.'

McBride's heart sank. He had been hoping that he could leave Ace under the watchful gaze of Mama while he and Sharkey tracked down the sphere, but it was obvious that if he didn't take her with them then she would just sneak off and follow them anyway. At least he could keep an eye on her if she came along.

'Of course she's coming, Sharkey. Just think of her as my junior partner.'

Ace tipped McBride's hat back on her head at a rakish angle, swung her feet up on to the table and tipped her chair back with practised ease. 'Wicked!'

The Doctor was pacing restlessly around McBride's office. He hadn't expected to get any instant results, but rather thought that his reactivation of the homing beacon would result in *some* reaction from whoever had provided it.

He had sat at McBride's desk for a long time, clearing his mind for the battle to come. Eventually, he had got bored and started poking around the office for things to do. There was a time when he would have just sat and waited. Some of his older regenerations would have settled themselves down with a plate of cheese and a bottle of wine, or a good book, patiently waiting for the enemy to show their hand. He, on the other hand, had taken McBride's typewriter to pieces and reassembled all the letters in a different order, rummaged through the filing cabinet until he had found every pair of socks and filed them according to colour, and made a small sculpture out of empty whisky bottles. He was currently repairing a hole in the sole of one of McBride's shoes.

He crossed to the window for the hundredth time and stared out into the drizzle. It was getting dark now; shops were shutting up; people were making their way home, nervously waiting for the sound of sirens. The Doctor frowned. Ace and McBride must have found something out, or they would have been back by now. He didn't like sending them off on their own but, if he was right, then they were far safer than he was.

Ace had never been to Belsize Park. Posh area. She didn't know anyone who lived there. The houses lined the sides of wide avenues in elegant, terraced rows; broad steps cascaded from large front doors, through black wrought-iron railings to the street. Storey upon storey, tall windows atop taller windows gazed down upon the shabby detective and the bomber-jacket-clad tomboy.

It was giving Ace the creeps.

The streets seemed eerily still. Her footsteps seemed to echo unnaturally off the pavement. The sound of people, of traffic, of London life, seemed distant. Where was everybody? No cars. Did many people have cars in 1940? Ace couldn't remember. There was no one at all in the streets. No dogs, no cats... no birds were singing. Ace stopped and tugged at McBride's sleeve.

'Should be up here somewhere, on the left... What?' He sounded irritable.

'Have you noticed anything?'

'No. Now, come on.'

'Some detective. Listen.'

'Can't hear anything. Now come on.'

'Wait.' Ace leaned over the railings and peered through the huge front window of first one house, then another. Another. It seemed incredible. Every room she looked into was properly arranged – curtains, furniture, here and there a piece of ornamental porcelain posed behind glass – but completely empty of people. There was no one in any of these houses.

'It's like the *Marie Celeste*.'

'That was a ship, kid. This is a street. You should check out your history.'

A plant – a huge fern – luxuriated in one window. It was the only sign of life Ace could see. It was still alive. The people must have only recently left.

'Cody, why would a whole area of London suddenly be deserted? There's no air raid.'

'Dunno, kid. Could mean a lot of bomb damage. Structural stuff. Gas main gone, maybe. Had to move everybody out. Or it could mean an unexploded bomb. Why d'you ask?'

An unexploded bomb. A recently dropped unexploded bomb. Very dangerous. Very, very unstable.

'Cody...' Unconsciously Ace let her voice fall to a hoarse whisper. 'I think there's an unexploded bomb around here.'

The detective stopped dead in his tracks. 'Holy Mother.'

'Keep calm. There's nothing we can do but hope for the best. And keep our voices down.'

'Maybe we should ask in one of these houses.'

Ace let out a sigh. 'Do you ever actually manage to solve any of your cases?'

'Look!' McBride was gesturing down a side road – slightly narrower, the houses still huge but a bit shabbier. Midway down the street an old man stood on a front step – the door open behind him, scattering bread to the non-existent birds.

'That must be him.' McBride set off at a run. 'Hi there!' he shouted at the top of his voice.

'I'm afraid you must have thought me dreadfully foolish out there.'

The old man had ushered them in, taking the soaking umbrella from Ace and placing it in an elephant's-foot umbrella stand by the door.

He must have been in his mid-seventies, thin and slightly stooped, frail-looking, with the characteristic transparency of age. The old man smiled a warm, sad, watery smile. He blinked his warm, sad, watery eyes. There was something strange and slow about the way he blinked.

In some ways he reminded Ace of the Doctor.

'A silly old man's notion. I thought perhaps if I put out bread the birds might return. The bombs fell three days ago. The street you just walked up is a façade, on one side at least. The back of the entire row has been blown to pieces. Beyond those immaculate front rooms is a mélange of chintz and rubble, I'm afraid. It looks so perfect, but it's an empty shell. Very unstable; very unsafe. So they moved all the people out. Along with the birds.'

McBride sighed noisily, but Limb carried on as if not noticing.

'But, you know, the birds knew before. The day before the night the bombs fell, they didn't come. All day, they didn't come, nor any day since. It's as if they know something else. It's as if they know of some further violence to be visited upon our little hamlet. I've put bread out every day, but to no avail. It's strange how they seem to know…'

'Why weren't you evacuated?' asked Ace.

'Oh, they tried. I refused to go. Been here too long, you know. Too old. Too old…' For a moment the old man seemed far away, in a place of infinite, long-ago beauty. He shook himself slightly. 'I'm sorry – I'm neglecting my guests. Tea?'

They were sitting in a small back parlour of the rambling house. A fire roared in the little grate; a teapot steamed on a painted tray on an embroidered tablecloth on a carved and fluted occasional table.

'Nah,' McBride spat, after a few moments' deliberation. 'I don't buy it. These are rich houses. They'd have been looted, for sure. The gangs would have a field day round here.'

'Yes,' the old man agreed, 'we do by some stroke of good fortune seem to have been spared the attentions of the looters. Perhaps they, too, believe there is an unexploded bomb here.' He smiled. 'Like the birds.'

He poured hot, weak tea into delicate porcelain cups.

'I must admit,' he continued, 'I rather like the peace and quiet now that everybody's gone. But I do miss the birds.'

His high, soft, lilting voice, his gentle eyes and faded tweed jacket, patched at the elbows, reminded Ace of kindly, dotty old vicars and headmasters in 1970s English sitcoms, images she mused on as the old man continued his ramblings.

'It baffles me, how they do it. How en masse they seem to sense danger. Have you ever watched a shoal of fish acting like a single organism, usually in response to a threat? I really believe that it isn't a question of how quickly each reacts to the signals transmitted by its neighbours. I think there's something more… fundamental going on. I wonder what that might teach us about the fabric of the universe…'

'Hey…' McBride's gruff interjection made Ace start with a sudden flash of anger. 'Are you the guy we're looking for or not?'

'Oh, I'm sorry. I didn't introduce myself. My name is Limb.

George Limb. And yes, some of my… less salubrious acquaintances do call me the Professor. Although quite what field they think I might – as it were – profess in, I couldn't tell you.'

'You sell information to crooks, yeah?' McBride dashed his tea down in one loud mouthful. Ace winced. McBride took out his Lucky Strikes.

'I… must confess I am less scrupulous about the company I keep nowadays than I ought to be. It all began as rather an accident. I trained as a scientist – a physicist – but made my career as a civil servant, working close to government. As a favour to a friend in politics – naturally, I cannot divulge his identity – I allowed certain documents to be made available to the press. This caused a certain chain of political events which both my august friend and myself considered germane to the long-term good of the country. As I am sure you know, the government quite properly relies upon absolute discretion from its civil service. Security, one might say, needs to be watertight. I – as it were – sprang a leak in the system. A leak… yes, I rather like that…'

He sipped slowly at his tea. To his left McBride struck a match and took his first gasp.

'Parliament was not happy. The resulting furore began to look as if it might lead the baying hounds of the back benches to my friend's door. And so, like a loyal civil servant, I stepped in and, as it were, took the fall.'

Again the old man's eyes seemed unfocused, gazing past Ace to the back wall of the room, and its one door.

'I resigned, but for a while that did not seem to be enough. There was talk of prosecution. I was not a rich man – any more than I am now – and could simply not have afforded to fight such a case. That was when my newly acquired notoriety came to my rescue, and –'

'Look, Professor,' said McBride impatiently, his words emerging on a tide of cigarette smoke. 'I don't want to seem a pain in the ass, but… well, we don't have a lot of time.'

If the old man was offended by McBride's interruption he didn't show it. He smiled and carried on. 'A certain wealthy criminal seeking specialist advice sought me out. He offered me a generous fee, and as the information he required was relatively harmless in nature, and in any event – I happened to know – shortly to become declassified, I gave it to him. Unfortunately, once one has begun to tread such paths one can rarely leave them. My reputation spread among the London underworld and… well, one hardly likes to refuse such people. By and large I find them tolerable.'

'Why didn't your friend help you out?' asked Ace. 'Seems a bit of a scummy thing to do, dropping you in it and then leaving you there.'

'Oh, no, young lady,' Limb replied. 'He had a great political destiny to fulfil. I was a mere functionary, and dispensable. Still, enough about me. May I ask how you came to know about my little… consultancy?'

'Sharkey,' said McBride, between lungfuls of American tobacco smoke. 'You got an ashtray in here?'

The rain had settled into drizzle by the time Ace and McBride left George Limb's house. Ace had found his company spellbinding; McBride's excruciating.

'Why did you have to do that?' she complained to the detective as they walked back through the high Regency ghost town.

'We got what we came for, didn't we?'

That was true. George Limb had kept the pair – or Ace, at least – entertained for more than an hour, talking freely and gently, describing the changes to the life of the city forced by the war, talking about life before the war, before the previous war, far back into the reign of Queen Victoria. If history at school had been like this Ace might actually have passed her O-level. He had fed them tea and sandwiches, commented wryly on Ace's singular mode of dress and speech, and politely tried to ignore Cody McBride.

Finally, McBride had cut in once again – and just as rudely as the first time.

'Look, Mr Limb, I hate to break up the history lesson but we need some information. You might have read about the thing that came down a couple of nights ago. Big silver ball.'

'Oh, yes,' Limb had replied with a smile. 'I thought I had seen your face somewhere before. Celebrity... such a fleeting mistress nowadays. And becoming more so. Have you noticed how more and more people seem to become famous for briefer and briefer periods of time? Who knows where it might all end?'

'The sphere, Professor,' McBride had snapped. 'We need to find it. Military Intelligence took it away. We need to know where they took it.'

'And what, might I ask, do you intend to do with this knowledge? I'm sorry, but I always make it a rule to ask. You surely don't intend to steal it?'

Ace had shot McBride a guilty glance. Obviously, the thought had occurred to him, too.

'I see...' Limb had spared them the awkwardness of answering. 'Well, I might as well tell you... the Peddler factory on Lavington Street.'

Ace groaned. 'But we've just –'

McBride shushed her. 'What goes on at the Peddler factory, Mr Limb?'

George Limb looked at McBride carefully. 'The government carries out certain... activities there. But I really should counsel against attempting to gain entry.'

'Security tight, I guess...'

'Well... actually, no. The last time I was privy to this sort of information I have to say that security at the Peddler factory was a shambles. Of course, that was some time ago. My political friend – the one I told you about – once threatened to drive a number eleven bus full of passengers into the factory, just to make the point. He didn't, of course. A shame, really. I wouldn't have put it past him...'

'Peddler. OK, thanks.' McBride was on his feet. 'Well, it's been great chewing the fat with you. We must do it again some time.'

And with that the detective had swung through the door and out into the hallway. Limb had followed him, stopping only to straighten a picture hanging next to the door. Ace had paused to look at it as she too exited the room. There was Limb – younger, but unmistakably Limb – playing chess with… Talk about friends in high places. Playing chess with Winston Churchill.

CHAPTER 6

The foyer of the Peddler building was quiet and empty, in total contrast to the bustle and noise of the morning. At Rosemary's reception desk, a lone army corporal sat, idly flicking through a novel, his mind elsewhere.

A slight noise made him look up. He grunted. Just someone on the first floor. No doubt Lazonby had asked for yet another report from those poor bastards in the lab. A smile crossed his face. The fireworks between Lazonby and Chief Inspector Mullen had been worth seeing. There was a point where he thought the two of them would come to blows. The policeman should have known better than to try to cross swords with the Major, particularly while the war was on. Several phone calls had been made to Whitehall, and Mullen had been told to continue his investigation without interfering with Lazonby's operation. Lazonby, in turn, had been told that if the chief inspector needed access to the crime scene then he was not to be obstructed. Both men had parted company in foul moods and the factory had been placed under military guard.

The young corporal looked at his watch. He was due to be relieved at six o'clock. He didn't envy whoever pulled night duty. The factory was well built, but he doubted that it would survive a direct hit from a German bomb. He turned back to his novel, hoping that the story would eventually engage his enthusiasm and help the hours pass a little faster.

Another noise made him look up again. A scraping from one of the internal doors. He put down his novel and picked up his rifle. He crept across the foyer, unsure whether he was being foolish or not. A further metallic scrape convinced him that he wasn't and he snapped off the safety catch. 'Who's there?'

He reached out cautiously for the door handle. He stopped. Billowing, choking white vapour poured from under the door. Before he could cry out he was enveloped in the evil smelling cloud and crashed to the floor.

It was a grumbling and petulant Ace who had followed McBride back across London to the Peddler factory. As far as she was concerned they were going around in circles. McBride had told her to stop griping, that this was what detective work was all about: following leads, making connections until a pattern began to emerge. He did have to admit, though, that the Peddler factory was the last place he had expected the sphere to turn up.

First, he had said, they had to 'case the joint'. Then they had to wait. Wait for the workforce to go home, wait for things to quieten down. Simple.

Now that they were standing outside the rear gate of the factory, however, McBride had to admit that something seemed wrong. Breaking and entering was a serious enough offence at the best of times, but breaking and entering a factory doing secret war work for the government was liable to get them shot. At least it would get them shot if there was anyone about to shoot them. The factory was dark: there was nothing unusual about that – there was a blackout in force – but McBride expected to see some sort of security. His unease wasn't helped when he pushed at the rear gate and it swung open. Not only unguarded, but unlocked.

'I don't like this, kid. Not one goddamn bit.'

He was about to suggest that they call their break-in off and go to get the Doctor when Ace slipped nimbly through the gate. Cursing, McBride followed her.

They found themselves in a cobbled yard. Crates and boxes were stacked in every corner and a couple of trucks stood in the shadows of the loading bay. Ace was about to make her way over to the shutter doors when McBride grabbed her by her collar. 'Let's take things a bit slower, shall we?'

She shook herself free. 'There's nobody here, McBride. Maybe they're all in the shelters.'

He shook his head. 'The sirens haven't sounded yet.'

'Well, perhaps they've gone early to avoid the rush – you know, book now to avoid disappointment.'

McBride scowled at her. 'Don't get smart, kid. Come on, we'll go in through here.' He crossed to a side door, pulling it open and peering into the darkened corridor. He pulled his Browning from inside his coat. Ace was about to make some quip, but the look on McBride's face made her stop. She realised that she was becoming blasé. She and the Doctor had broken into so many alien strongholds that getting into an old factory on Earth had seemed like child's play. That sort of attitude was liable to get her killed. She made a mental note to take things more seriously in future, and followed McBride into the gloom.

The factory interior was drab and regulation. It reminded Ace of school. The walls were covered with posters – CARELESS TALK COSTS LIVES and WALLS HAVE EARS. One in particular made Ace grimace – KEEP MUM, SHE'S NOT SO DUMB.

McBride tugged at Ace's sleeve.

'They've made it easy for us, kid.' The corridor to their left was peppered with dire warnings about dangerous substances and what might befall unauthorised personnel. 'I guess that must be the way to the lab.'

They followed the 'Keep Out' signs and passed a wide staircase. They stopped at the sound of movement from one of the upper floors – footsteps and the chink of mugs.

'Probably squaddies,' Ace whispered.

McBride nodded. 'Or police.'

'Where do you suppose security have got to?'

'Beats me. All I know is that there's no way we should have been able to get this far without someone spotting us.'

The Doctor had finished the repair to McBride's shoes and had spent the last hour bringing his spoons to a high polish with a tin of Brasso that had been lurking in a desk drawer. He held them up, looking at his reflection in the curved metal surface. He was about to launch into an impromptu performance when a faint metal-on-stone clang made him stop.

He placed the spoons on the table and crossed gingerly to the door. There. Another noise. A metallic chittering. The Doctor tensed; it was time. He moved over to the far wall of the office, tucked himself next to the open safe, and waited.

McBride and Ace continued their passage into the depths of the building until the American stopped and beckoned her over to an office. He eased the door open and the two of them slipped inside. The room was small and cramped – a manager's office looking out over the main laboratory. There in the centre of the room, surrounded by a plethora of benches and equipment, was the sphere, still in two neat halves.

'Jackpot!' breathed McBride.

He tried the door to the lab. Locked. He wrapped a handkerchief around the butt of his gun and tapped the glass until it cracked. After carefully picking the glass out of the frame, he reached through and unlatched the door. The two of them crossed to the sphere and Ace clambered into one half, running her hands over the contoured surface. 'It's bigger than I thought it would be.'

McBride scratched his head. 'Yeah. It's bigger than I remember it. We'll never move it.'

'You were hoping to take it with you?'

'I… Yeah.'

'Well, you should have thought of that before we got here, shouldn't you?' Ace hopped out of the sphere and pulled her camera from her jacket pocket. 'I'll get a couple of snaps. The Doctor can get the film developed in the TARDIS.'

'OK, OK. Just do it quickly and let's get out of here.'

Ace began to take flash stills of the sphere, the blue-white glare lighting up the darkened laboratory. Something caught McBride's eye. Something huddled under one of the workbenches. He crossed over to it, his eyes trying to compensate for darkness interspersed with blinding flashes.

The flashgun went off again and a chill went down McBride's

spine. The shape was the slumped body of a lab technician, tea from a smashed mug spreading across the floor. McBride knelt down and dipped his finger into the tea. It was still warm.

He turned to tell Ace that they had to get out of here when the main doors to the lab slammed open. Filling the doorway were two enormous figures clad in trench coats and fedoras - the classic American gangster. They lumbered into the room.

The scratching outside McBride's office had continued for a while, but now it had gone suspiciously quiet. The Doctor was about to go and have a look when the glass panel in the door shattered as something small and silver hurtled through it.

The Doctor stared as the small, metallic ball uncurled on the floor.

'Ah, yes,' said the Doctor, nodding with grim satisfaction.

Metallic cilia writhed and skittered on the carpet as the thing scanned the room. Gloss-black eyes fixed on the Doctor and, with a high-pitched, tinny scream, it launched itself at him.

Ace backed away as one of the figures bore down, towering over her. McBride launched himself across the workbench, pulling Ace out of the way. He levelled his gun, but the gangster swiped it out of his hands, sending it clattering into the shadows on the far side of the lab. McBride dodged as the huge arm swung back at his head, stepping in closer to his assailant. He'd been quite a good boxer back in the States, and was sure that his agility was more than a match for this lumbering thug.

He swung his best right hook, a perfect punch that should have sent the guy sprawling. It was as though he had punched a mailbox. Pain exploded inside his head and he collapsed to the floor, clutching his hand in agony.

McBride's collapse saved his life as the huge arm swung back again, sending glass and equipment flying from a shelf. Ace watched in horror as the giant figure tore off its hat and scarf, and the collar of its trench coat settled back on to massive shoulders.

Twin handles, glinting in the cold light, slid from either side of the monstrous head. It turned its face towards Ace.

It was a face she knew.

It was the face of a Cyberman.

PART TWO

CHAPTER 7

'For the moment President Roosevelt was keeping America out of the war. For the moment. Still, I always knew America was quite capable of dealing with Germans. I had been in New York when Joe Louis met the challenger to his world heavyweight title, Max Schmeling. After two minutes of the first round Schmeling was on the canvas and the Brown Bomber was champion of the world again. Two years later and I was stuck in a top-secret limey research factory, with a teenage girl from God knows where, hoping to make the Bomber proud of me by taking down another German thug with my best shot. Problem was that the meat-head had turned out to be a tin-head, and I damn near broke my wrist.'

Ace watched as the Cyberman towered over the oblivious McBride. After the initial shock of seeing the creature, she realised now that it was different from the Cybermen that she had encountered before, cruder somehow, its features less defined. But it looked just as powerful. The face was totally blank, a cruel parody of a human face, but the eyes had two indentations below them, like teardrops. It reminded Ace of a clown's mask, and she hated clowns. Beneath the trench coat, its huge frame was covered in a fine tracery of filaments and cables, coiling their way to the mass of controls that clung to its chest. Lights flickered on complex regulatory devices and there was a mechanical wheezing, like the breathing of some great leviathan. The other Cyberman was still swathed in its gangster disguise. It seemed unaware of Ace and McBride, more concerned with making a series of adjustments to a control panel inside the sphere.

McBride let out a groan of pain and the Cyberman that was looming over him turned its blank stare to the crumpled figure at its feet. It raised a huge silver arm. Ace looked round for a weapon, painfully aware that there was nothing here that would be effective against the remorseless silver giants. A length of gas barrel lurked in the mess of materials on a workbench. Ace gripped it with both hands and screamed over at the poised Cyberman.

'Oi! Jug-ears! Pick on someone your own size!' She pivoted on the balls of her feet, sweeping the gas barrel off the bench in an arc that brought glass and equipment showering over the workshop. The impromptu weapon connected with the Cyberman's head with a deafening clang and an impact that tore it from Ace's hands, jarring every bone in her body. The Cyberman staggered, momentarily taken off guard. Those precious seconds were all that Ace needed.

She dived in under the monster's flailing arms and hauled McBride to one side. The private eye was pale and obviously in considerable pain.

'McBride, are you OK? Cody!'

He glanced up at her, then his eyes widened in horror as he got his first proper glimpse of the thug he'd hit. 'Holy Mother!'

'Come on, McBride, we've got to get out of here.' Ace glanced back at the giant figures. To her satisfaction and delight her attack had managed to put a dent in the handle that protruded from the side of the Cyberman's head. That satisfaction was short-lived as each Cyberman pulled a stubby silver tube from inside its coat. Cyberguns. When they had proved no danger the Cybermen might have ignored them, but now that she had attacked one... Ace closed her eyes and braced herself for the shots, but they never came.

Silently, and in unison, as if responding to some unheard message, the two silver figures turned away from her and crossed back over to the sphere. One of them pressed a control and there was a hissing, like a million steam baths, as the two halves of the sphere neatly resealed themselves. With childlike ease, the Cybermen picked up the sphere and carried it out through the shattered double doors. McBride turned to Ace.

'What the hell were they?'

* * *

The Doctor threw himself to one side as the silver creature hurled itself across the office. It bounced off the wall and clattered to the floor, chittering angrily. The Doctor skipped nimbly into the centre of the room, snatching up the homing device from McBride's desk. He'd been expecting this, or at least, something very like this. Cybermats. Small cyborg killing machines. And if there were Cybermats in London then their cybernetic masters couldn't be very far behind.

He peered into the gloom. He couldn't see any sign of the little assassin. A noise from under the window made him start. He was being hunted. The Cybermat was lurking near the skirting board, waiting for an opportunity to pounce. The Doctor tried to move towards the light switch near the door; there was a blur of silver to his left. He dodged to one side as the Cybermat came screaming at him from under the desk. He felt the rush of air as it sailed past his head and bounced off McBride's filing cabinets with a resounding clang.

The Doctor regained his vantage point in the centre of the office, his eyes darting around all the gloomy corners, trying to determine where his attacker was lurking. He had encountered the tiny killers on several occasions, and each time they had been equipped with a different form of weapon. Some emitted piercing sonic waves, others injected a lethal strain of poison – all forms of attack that he had been able to deal with. This one seemed to be in possession of nothing more than a sharp set of big pointy teeth. The Doctor frowned. No subtlety at all. His solution would have to be equally unsubtle.

There was a sudden glint of metal from the corner of the room. The Doctor slowed his breathing to a whisper. 'Now then. Are you movement-sensitive, heat-sensitive –' he waggled the business card – 'or are you just after this?'

There was an explosion of movement from the other side of the office. The Doctor dropped to his knees, flicking the card across the room. The Cybermat flew after it – straight into McBride's open safe.

The Doctor hurled himself against the heavy safe door, slamming it shut and spinning the dial. Inside he could hear the sound of splintering lead crystal as the thrashing Cybermat destroyed McBride's expensive glasses. The Doctor slumped to the floor and mopped his forehead with a large paisley handkerchief.

'Oh dear. Mr McBride isn't going to be very happy about this.'

The Cybermen carried the sphere into the yard and loaded it on to the back of a canvas-topped truck. Wall watched as the two giants straightened and crossed over to him. He pointed at the Cyberman still in its disguise. 'Now, you can kill them.' The gangster figure turned and lumbered back into the factory. Wall tittered like a small child.

The Cyberman re-entered the gloomy laboratory. There was no sign of the two humanoids. It pulled the stubby tube of its Cyberweapon from the housing under its chest panel. Internal processors switched its visual circuits to infrared and it began to sweep back and forth across the room.

Ultrasensitive audio receptors could hear sounds of movement from the far side of the laboratory and the Cyberman began to move towards them, pushing benches and equipment out of the way. There was another noise from the gloom of the lab. The Cyberman triggered the stud on its gun and bolt after bolt of energy surged across the room.

Ace clamped her hands over her ears as her hiding place was torn apart. Wooden splinters showered around her as the energy beams shattered the bench.

The noise stopped. The Cyberman continued its remorseless advance. Ace waited until the Cyberman was almost level with her, and then leapt into the open. She pressed the flash of her camera right up against the Cyberman's face plate and pressed the trigger.

The flash lit up the laboratory, momentarily overloading the Cyberman's infrared sensors. It staggered backward.

'Now, McBride! Now!'

Ace was hurled to one side as the Cyberman lashed blindly out at her. Internal computers transferred optical circuits to battle conditions and the Cyberman tried to re-establish a target. There was suddenly a dazzling plume of light as the flame of an oxyacetylene torch arced through the darkness.

McBride lunged at the Cyberman, sweeping the flame down and slicing through the stubby Cybergun. It exploded in a shower of sparks. Dodging the lethal, chopping arms, McBride swept the flame back up the length of the towering figure, and the lab was lit up in an orange glare as its trench coat caught light and the towering monster was turned into a pillar of flame.

'Way to go, McBride!' Ace was ecstatic.

'Don't get your hopes up, kid.' McBride nodded over at the Cyberman. Although the clothes were burning, the creature itself was completely unscathed. It tore off the burning garments, scattering them over the lab. Ace and McBride dived for cover as the Cyberman lifted one of the heavy workbenches and hurled it towards them.

In the reception area of the Peddler building the young army corporal staggered to his feet, leaning on his rifle for support. He shook his aching head, trying to lose some of the grogginess. What the hell had happened? He brushed at his uniform. He was covered in a thin layer of white powder, like talc. Some of the dust caught at the back of his throat and he coughed violently. He remembered the white mist pouring from under the door. Gas! He'd been gassed. They were under attack! As if to reinforce the fact, there was suddenly the sound of breaking furniture from the lab. He punched the fire alarm with the butt of his rifle.

Wall was sitting in the cab of the truck, rocking back and forth, murmuring happily to himself when the sound of the alarm tore through the evening air. He shot upright in his seat, his head twitching in panic. 'Something's gone wrong.' He turned to the

Cyberman crammed into the passenger seat alongside him. 'Get that alarm off!' The Cyberman squeezed itself out of the cab and lumbered towards the building, rain streaming off its silver casing.

In the reception area the young corporal heard the crunch of heavy boots on gravel. He struggled with the latch of the front door, eager to hand responsibility to some senior authority figure. But the door was torn from his hands as... something hurled it open. The soldier backed away from the advancing silver monstrosity, raising his rifle with shaking hands. 'I'll shoot! I mean it.'

The thing reached for its gun and the young soldier unleashed a barrage of shots at point blank range. The silver giant reeled, sparks flying from its chest panel, as bullets ricocheted around the reception area. It righted itself and tore the rifle out of the young soldier's hands, twisting it into a tangled knot of metal.

The corporal turned and ran, but there was a harsh rattle and a burst of energy from some sort of gun – and he crashed to the floor, acrid smoke curling from the cuffs and collar of his uniform.

The Cyberman stepped over his charred and twisted body and tore the alarm bell from the wall.

In the laboratory, McBride and Ace were playing a bizarre game of tag with the now charred and steaming Cyberman. Whenever it got within reach, McBride lashed out at it with the harsh flame of the oxyacetylene torch, bringing up deep, oozing welts in the silver skin of their attacker. The problem was that, as a weapon, the torch wasn't exactly manoeuvrable. Ace was wheeling the gas cylinders about like a woman possessed, but they were rapidly running out of space, and the Cyberman showed no sign of tiring. Their only hope was to try to sever some vital system. Their hopes had been raised when they had heard the alarm bell, but swiftly dashed as the alarms stopped abruptly.

The Cyberman lunged again and McBride brought the torch up, wielding it like a sword, and slashing the flame across the huge silver arm. A thin silver hose burst open, spraying the air with a fine foam. Tiny silver mites, no bigger than pinheads, swarmed over the creature's arm, sealing the damage. McBride felt sick.

Suddenly the door at the other end of the lab crashed open. Ace spun. Another Cyberman, the one with the bent handle that she had damaged, stood in the doorway. It levelled the silver tube in its hand.

'Down, McBride!'

The two of them dived for cover as energy bolts blasted across the laboratory. McBride dragged Ace under one of the workbenches as the gas cylinders exploded, sending shrapnel slicing across the room. The two Cybermen advanced.

McBride hugged Ace to him as the bench was lifted from over them.

'This is it, kid.'

The charred Cyberman reached down... and was thrown to one side, as a hail of bullets slammed into it. The other Cyberman raised its gun and fired. Ace could hear screams over the rattle of the energy weapon before there was another deafening round of gunfire.

The lab was lit up as bullets streamed into the two aliens. Sparks flew from the silver armour under the repeated impact of heavy machine-gun fire. Stray bullets whistled around the room. Ace and McBride crawled through chaos. McBride could hear orders being barked out in a clipped English accent. Lazonby! There was a lull in the noise, and then the lab lit up again as the terrifying rattle of a Cybergun broke the silence.

Lazonby had been in his office inspecting his rota chart when the alarm bells had sounded. He had always expected that the Peddler factory would be the subject of an enemy attack. He had snatched his service revolver from his desk, and had been satisfied to see that his troops were already in the corridor, rifles poised, waiting for his orders. He could hear the distant sounds of fighting, and the rattle of something unfamiliar. He gestured to his men and they fell in behind him.

At the foot of the stairs, in the bullet-riddled reception area, they had found the remains of the corporal who had been left on sentry duty. One of Lazonby's men turned the body over, a broken husk that had once been a soldier. Lazonby's grip tightened around the butt of his revolver. 'They must be in the laboratory. Come on, men.'

They had entered the wreckage of the laboratory to see McBride and that young girl cowering from... Lazonby stood in awe. Even in the gloom of the lab these creatures were impressive. Huge figures of glittering metal. The blank metal face turned towards him. Impassive. Unblemished. Perfection.

Machine-gun fire, harsh and brutal, shattered the moment, then the man next to him erupted in a ball of heat and smoke, and Lazonby the Officer took over. He levelled his gun and fired four rounds into the head of one of the armoured figures. 'Wait for a clear shot! They're wearing some kind of armour – aim for the joints!'

He noticed Ace and McBride crawling through the wreckage. 'Somebody get those civilians out of here.'

In the drizzle outside in the yard, Wall cowered at the sound of gunfire. He hopped from the cab of the truck and scurried over to the loading bay. There was another burst of gunfire and the crackle of energy weapons. This wasn't how the operation was meant to be at all. He chewed at his nails. The Cybermen were invulnerable to most forms of attack, but if the soldiers managed to get reinforcements... He peered into the gloom through his little black glasses and hissed under his breath. 'Withdraw. Do you hear me? Retreat. We will regroup.'

He scurried around to the cab of the truck and clambered in, fumbling with the keys and bringing the diesel engine into roaring, shuddering life.

Inside, the Cybermen straightened, hearing Wall's instructions. They turned in unison and strode out of the shattered laboratory. Bullets bounced off their huge shoulders as one of the bolder troopers tried to halt their retreat. A slicing chop broke the neck of the soldier and he slumped to the floor in a crumpled heap. The Cybermen vanished through the external lab doors.

In the office overlooking the workshop floor, Ace's ears pricked up at the sound of a truck engine. 'They're getting away!'

McBride winced as he nursed his throbbing his hand. 'Thank God for that.'

Ace turned, her face set with grim determination. 'But I know what they are. I'm going after them, McBride.'

Before the American could object, Ace had dodged past the soldier on the door and was sprinting across the lab. She could hear the cultured English tones of the officer, and the American twang of McBride shouting after her.

'Stop that girl!'

'Ace! Goddamn it, come back here.'

She bounded over one of the shattered workbenches, feeling glass crunch under her Doc Martens. She darted out into out into the cool evening air, ready to duck back into the lab at the first sign of Cybermen. The truck was just rounding the gate and heading out on to the road. She sprinted after it. She could hear people close behind her. McBride called out again. 'Ace! What the hell d'you think you're doing?'

The truck was picking up speed, now. Ace began to run faster. She didn't have a plan, she hadn't even begun to think about what might happen if she was caught. She just had to find out where the Cybermen were going. The back edge of the truck was almost within her reach, now, the spray from the tyres splattering her face. Her heart pounded in her chest. A trailing rope dangled from the flapping canvas covering the back of the truck – she caught it and hauled herself up on to the back of the speeding vehicle.

McBride caught a glimpse of her smiling face as the truck vanished in a cloud of spray. He threw his hat down on to the wet tarmac in dismay and disgust. 'Goddamn it!' He'd lost the sphere, the – what had she called them? – Cybermen, and now Ace. How the hell was he going to explain this to the Doctor? He turned to head back into the factory, to find himself confronted by a grim-faced Lazonby.

'She's gone.'

'Yes, so I see. Very convenient. We'd better make sure that *you* don't make any sudden disappearances then, hadn't we?'

Lazonby raised his gun.

CHAPTER 8

Cybermats were unpredictable little biomechanoids; this the Doctor knew. You could never tell quite how their brains – tiny, dedicated computers interlaced with thin skeins of primitive, animal nervous system – would react to a given set of circumstances. It all depended on the way their masters had programmed them. This one was revealing a spirit the Doctor had never before encountered in the lethal little machines. Having successfully homed in on the tiny transmitter, it had seemed dormant for a while. Listening from outside the safe, the Doctor had oh-so gingerly eased the latch back. Slowly… nothing. Silence within. Gently he had eased the door open a crack – and a mini-hell had broken loose. The thing had hurled itself at the shaft of light that had pierced its darkness. The Doctor had slammed the safe immediately, but now the Cybermat was throwing itself continuously at the walls and door of its prison. The safe would hold – of that the Doctor was sure – but now there was the question of what to do with the little monster. He couldn't leave it in there for ever; neither had he the means to destroy it. He sat back in McBride's chair, staring at the heavy, grey, metal box, playing idly with his hat, pondering the problem.

A sudden sound jerked the Doctor to his feet. Those creaking stairs. Somebody was coming up. The Doctor gauged the sound of the footfalls. Too light to be a Cyberman.

'Hello…' An Irish brogue. The Doctor smiled.

'Come up, Inspector.'

'*Chief* Inspector.' Mullen's tread on the creaky stairs grew brisker and louder. 'Doctor… I was hoping to find you here. About that card –'

'Ssshhh…' Gently the Doctor hushed the policeman as he entered the office. 'Listen.'

The policeman paused, eyes suddenly scanning the room, head slightly cocked. The dull, repeating thud from inside the safe continued.

'What do you think that is, Inspector?' asked the Doctor in a low, conspiratorial voice.

'It's *Chief* Inspector, Doctor, and I haven't got time to –'

'Time.' The Doctor was suddenly brisk. 'No, you're right. Do you have a gun on you, Inspector?'

'Well, I –'

'Off the record, of course.'

Somewhat self-consciously the policeman drew an army-issue Webley from inside his overcoat. 'You haven't seen this, Doctor.'

'Quite, quite. Now, I want you to train it on the door of the safe, and when I open the door I want you to pump every bullet you've got into the thing inside it. Do you understand?'

'I'm not sure I do, Doctor.'

The Doctor flapped his hand impatiently. 'It's simple enough, man. I'll explain everything afterwards. The important thing is that you don't hesitate for even a second. The thing in there is lethal. Now, do you understand?'

Mullen took a deep breath. 'I understand.'

'All right. Ready…' The Doctor gripped the handle of the safe. 'Now!'

In one motion the Time Lord jerked on the handle and levered the door open. The Cybermat, amid its thrashing and jerking, was facing away from the door. Momentarily disorientated, it spun around and gathered itself to leap. Gun held out in front of him, Mullen seemed transfixed by the writhing metal worm which even now had the policeman in its fatal sights.

It occurred to the Doctor that he had no idea if Mullen was a decent shot.

'Mullen!' yelled the Time Lord as the beast sprang forward with a low electronic warble. Mullen fired. The Cybermat was thrown back into the safe. Mullen fired again, again, again. All six chambers discharged their bullets into the thing, which jerked and buckled under the impact, metal shards ripping from its casing, hydraulic fluids hissing out as it died.

Mullen stood, breathless, gun still levelled at the safe.

'Well done, Inspector. You can relax now – it's dead.' Casually the Doctor picked up the now-limp Cybermat and tossed it on to the desk. He sank back into McBride's chair.

'Doctor,' Mullen croaked, 'what in the name of Jesus is that thing?'

'Shall I tell you, Inspector? It's our killer.'

'What are you saying man? That's what killed Peddler?'

'That, or another one identical to it. You see, the card left by our friend Mr Wall was a transmitter.' The Doctor crossed to the safe, plucked out the card, and handed it to Mullen. 'It sent out a signal to this thing, which could then home in on the card. Having made contact with the card, the thing was presumably programmed to kill any humans in the vicinity. Very, very nasty.'

The Doctor was prodding inside the shattered casing of the Cybermat. Mullen caught a glimpse of bloodied flesh among the gleaming metal. The remains of… goodness knew what! A cat? A bird? Pieces of human flesh?

'But what is it, Doctor? Where did it come from?'

'It's a piece of alien technology, Inspector. It's in the wrong place and altogether the wrong time. The chaos could be incalculable.'

'And you say there are more of these things about?'

'Inspector, these are just the tip of the iceberg. What we really have to worry about is the race of beings who made this thing.' He picked up the Cybermat and stuffed it into the pocket of his duffel coat.

Mullen ran a hand across his forehead. He was sweating. Sometimes he wished he'd remained an ordinary copper. Never joined Special Branch.

'This is all a bit beyond me, Doctor,' he said.

The Doctor smiled to himself. How many times in his travels had he heard those very words?

'It makes what I was going to ask you about seem… trivial.'

'What's that then, Inspector? I'm all ears.'

'Well… it's just this Lurker business. We're not really getting anywhere, and –'

'Lurker business?'

'You know, Doctor. The one they're calling the Limehouse Lurker. He's been at it two months, now. Killed at least six. Maybe more. It's difficult to tell with all these bombs falling. It's the Ripper all over again, and we're just as in the dark about this one…'

'Ah, yes. I think I saw something about it in McBride's newspaper.'

Mullen shuddered. 'He literally rips his victims apart in some kind of frenzy.'

'Two months, you say… Well that rules the Cybermen out. We know they only arrived the night before last. Besides, if there's one thing they're not, it's frenzied.'

Slapping the desk with both hands, the Doctor sprang to his feet once again. 'No, I'm afraid you're on your own with this one, Inspector. I've got far too much to worry about.'

For a moment his eyes strayed to the blacked-out window; his thoughts to the besieged city beyond. 'I do hope Ace is all right…'

His reverie was interrupted by the ring of McBride's telephone. Time Lord and policeman looked at each other. 'Well, it won't be for me…' said the Doctor.

'Mullen,' the chief inspector barked, snatching the phone from its cradle. 'Yes… What…? Who…?'

The voice on the other end of the phone sounded high and agitated to the Doctor.

'Anybody else? I see. I'll be right there.' Mullen slammed the phone back down. 'There's been an incident at the Peddler factory. A break-in of some kind. It seems our friend Cody McBride was involved.'

The Doctor looked sharply at Mullen. 'But I left Ace in his care! Come on!'

Mullen placed a hand on the Doctor's shoulder. 'There was no mention of her, Doctor. Lazonby's got the place nailed down tighter than a Scotsman's wallet.'

'Lazonby…' The Doctor was puzzled. 'Why would Military Intelligence be there?'

Mullen exhaled, short and heavy. 'If anybody asks, I didn't tell you this, Doctor. The wireless sets and gramophones are just a cover. Peddler has been doing highly classified research and development work for the military. McBride's in a lot of trouble, Doctor. He's under armed guard on suspicion of treason, and I'm afraid if you turned up you'd cop it too. Lazonby would have you arrested on the spot – perhaps even shot. I wouldn't put it past him. He even regards my presence at the factory as an interference.'

'Right now, Inspector, my only concern is for Ace.' The Doctor's face was creased with concentration. 'McBride isn't stupid. I think he's almost chivalrous, in a way. Surely he wouldn't drag her into that… Then again, this is Ace we're talking about. All right, Inspector, you go to the factory. Find out what you can.' His fists were clenched; his eyes once again seemed to stare through the folds of the blackout curtain. 'Oh, Ace…' He yanked open a drawer in McBride's desk. 'Now, Mr McBride, where would you have taken her?'

It was useless. Why didn't the man keep proper files? His drawers were full of creased correspondence, much of it bearing the postmark of the United States, much of it unread, the envelopes still sealed. His filing cabinet was full of clothes. Empty or half-empty bottles of whisky seemed to doze in every cranny of the dingy office. His big black address book was devoid of names or addresses, full of scribbled, disembodied telephone numbers and bulging with newspaper cuttings. Many were about the Lurker. Some, older, faded now, recorded past triumphs and disasters for the sleuth, snippets from the *Chicago Tribune*, here a stolen painting artfully recovered, there a police caution for a drunken breach of the peace involving a municipal fountain. There was a photo of a younger McBride with a pretty, dark-haired woman.

Nothing to indicate where he might have taken Ace.

What was it that McBride had said to him the previous night? He was going to see his mother. It didn't make sense. McBride's mother had died in a Chicago nursing home some five years before. The Doctor had seen the newspaper cutting, buried with the rest. He should have gone with Mullen. Under arrest or not, he had to get to see McBride.

As he prepared to leave, the Doctor's eyes scanned the office a final time. They stopped on the noticeboard. There had seemed to be nothing of importance pinned there. A bus timetable, a menu from a local pie-and-mash shop, a beer mat. A beer mat. Stained, faded; the writing barely legible. The Doctor leaned forward, squinting. *Mama's American Bar. Glasshill Street. Your Home From Home.*

That was it. It had to be. The Doctor looked at the clock on the wall. It was nearly six o'clock in the evening. In a few hours the bombing would start and the daring and decadent rich, convinced of their invincibility, would be sipping champagne under chandeliers in Claridge's, listening to the mellifluous tones of a jazz quartet. And, he hoped, the dishonest poor would be propping up Mama's Bar, perhaps listening to Glen Miller on the jukebox.

Having snatched his duffel coat from the hat stand near the door, the Doctor descended the stairs and went out into the dark evening.

A low, friendly murmur of voices greeted the Doctor as he approached the ramshackle building beneath the arches on Glasshill Street which was Mama's Bar. Scarcely a chink of light showed itself through the door or windows. Probably more to do with flouting licensing regulations than adhering to blackout regulations – the Doctor couldn't imagine this place chucking out at eleven twenty.

He eased open the door and slipped inside. Instantly the buzz of conversation, the chink of glasses, even the music from the jukebox died as the Dorsey Orchestra hit the last big note of 'The Peanut Vendor'. All eyes were fixed on the little stranger. He walked over to the bar. The enormous black barman in the stained and sweaty vest made no move to serve him.

The Doctor looked at the array of caps, pennants, and photographs of baseball players that covered the wall behind the bar. 'Tyrus Cobb...' he said, to no one in particular. 'Hack Wilson... And of course the Babe...'

If anything, the silence thickened. Slowly, the barman walked over to the stranger. 'What you know 'bout baseball, mister?' he challenged.

This guy sure didn't look like no baseball fan. He had to be taking the rise.

Mama towered a good foot over the little stranger. If it came to it he wouldn't need the baseball bat he kept under the bar to deal with this one. He must have had a hundred pounds on him.

'Oh,' said the little man casually, 'I was there in 1926 when Babe Ruth hit three home runs in a single game.'

'You was there?' said Mama, his voice high with incredulity. '*I* was there.'

'I think, though, that the best I ever saw was Joshua Gibson. Pure poetry in motion.'

Mama felt his face crease in puzzlement.

'How you seen him?' he demanded. 'He plays Negro League.'

'Oh, I've seen the Pittsburgh Crawfords many times,' said the stranger, a nostalgic smile playing across his lips. 'Though not for many years... I suppose you could say I'm a bit of a fan.'

At last Mama's face relaxed into a rueful smile. 'Well, I'll be. The Pittsburgh Crawfords, eh? OK, friend, what you drinkin'? On me.'

The Doctor allowed himself to be poured a cold beer. It was rare that he drank – the potent brew sent a shudder up his spine.

'Are you... Mama?' the Doctor asked.

'I might be,' the big man replied, still smiling.

'Perhaps you can help me,' said the Doctor. 'I'm a friend of Cody McBride's. I'm looking for him.'

'Cody ain't been in all night. He came in here maybe three o'clock this afternoon, with a girl. A kid.'

'And then…'

'They was talking to Sharkey. Usually that means Cody's got a job on. They stayed maybe half an hour, then left. Sharkey – he had a couple more beers, then took his ass home to sleep it off, I reckon.'

'Sharkey…' The Doctor didn't like the sound of the name. 'And where can I find him?'

'Oh, stay awhile. He'll be here. An' who do I say is wantin' to talk to him?'

'Oh, the Doctor. Just… the Doctor.'

The Time Lord stationed himself at a remote table to wait and watch. It had been a long time since he had had the leisure to sit and observe the human world going about its everyday business. He scarcely had it now, or the inclination: he was too worried about Ace. Nevertheless, waiting and watching were all he could do. He watched a small man in a voluminous, dark, pin-striped suit, a thin cigar jutting out from beneath a thin moustache, holding court in a nearby alcove as women with bleached, stacked hair and pencil-skirts ebbed and flowed from his presence, shimmying and giggling, and men whispered to him in low voices, hanging and darting on his every nod.

He watched a group of English soldiers, so very young in their ill-fitting khakis, nervously enter the bar, grinning AWOL grins, and order American beer.

He watched two men, big and bearded, arm-wrestle each other to a standstill at a nearby table, shaking and straining, blind to everything but their struggle, until the table collapsed beneath them. Without a word, without a smile, they picked themselves up, re-erected the table and began to wrestle anew. He shook his head sadly. It would be many millennia before humankind finally learned the simple lesson of the futility of blind conflict. They wouldn't learn it from this war, nor the next. No, for generations they would go on trying to master one another, tables being re-erected and collapsing endlessly beneath them.

It was two hours before a shifty-looking man slipped through the door of Mama's, ever wary, eyes darting between the shadowy corners of the huge room. The Doctor watched the little man sidle up to the bar, watched Mama talking to him, nodding in the Doctor's direction, watched the little man turn furtively, momentarily catching the Time Lord's gaze, then look away. Must be Sharkey, the Doctor concluded. More words were exchanged with Mama before the little man made his way cautiously to the Doctor's table.

'Mama says you're looking for McBride,' he muttered, staring into the table top.

'Yes,' the Doctor replied. 'Or, more specifically, I'm looking for a young woman whom I left in Mr McBride's care. I understand you might know something of their whereabouts.'

'Like you say,' said Sharkey in his never-more-than a whisper voice, 'I might know something…'

'I take it you're angling for some sort of financial incentive,' said the Doctor, coldly.

'Well…' The informant glanced momentarily up at the Doctor. He started. Those eyes. They seemed to hold him, to penetrate him, to know him.

'Mr Sharkey, I'm not here to play games,' said the Doctor, suddenly harsh, 'I suggest that you tell me everything you know forthwith.'

'I…' Sharkey hesitated.

'Forthwith, I said.'

'McBride and the girl came in here earlier – they was asking about that new bomb they found down Watling Street, the one the soldiers took away. They wanted to know where it might have been taken, like. I sent them off to see a man I know, calls himself the Professor. Knows all about that sort of thing, bombs and science and what have you. Used to work for the government.

Lives up Belsize Park way – fifteen Primrose Gardens.'

Sharkey stopped, breathless, shaken. He had never been so forthcoming in his life. One thing he wasn't was a babbler. You couldn't be in his profession. Information was his currency; it was his bread-and-butter. Information was power. When had he first heard that? Sharkey was not a powerful player in the information game. What little nuggets he could gather he sold, usually to McBride, for a few poxy quid here and there. Always small-time stuff; never worth more than a few quid.

And now this. Almost afraid to meet those eyes again, Sharkey lifted his head and looked across the table at the little man who had opened him up like a tin of soup.

But the little man was gone.

CHAPTER 9

High Regency period, probably Nash, some slight evidence of neglect and disrepair. Nothing like the grime and corrosion of the end of this century. Deserted. Evacuated.

Possibly an unexploded bomb: typical of Ace. Her talent for walking into danger sometimes seemed to rival his own. A hasty telephone call to Mullen had revealed that she too had been seen at the Peddler factory. McBride had been arrested; she had vanished. The Doctor's hopes of finding her were not high. Still...

He walked briskly up to George Limb's front door and rapped on it, hard. He waited impatiently as soft footsteps behind the door shuffled slowly towards him. Only when the door creaked open a few inches did his face break into its most charming smile. He doffed his hat and stretched out his hand in greeting.

'Good evening. Am I to take it that you're the gentleman known as the Professor?'

'Well... yes... George Limb is my name. How may I help you?'

'Excellent. I'm sometimes called the Professor too. By an insolent young girl who should know better. Her name's Ace, and I'm looking for her. Can you help me?'

Limb smiled his warm, weak smile. 'Ah, yes. Ace. Perhaps I can help you. Would you like to come inside?'

The Doctor followed Limb down the long, high hall, stopping to pull his red-handled umbrella from the elephant's-foot stand. He was led inside an airy room into which light flooded from two huge, street-facing windows.

'So should I refer to you as Professor?' the old man asked.

'Doctor will do,' the Time Lord replied.

'Very well then, Doctor. Yes, I received a visit yesterday from the young lady in question, accompanied by a rather brusque American gentleman named Cody McBride. They came here seeking... information. Do you play chess?'

Dominating the room was a large oak dining table, bare except for a simple wooden chessboard, the pieces large, classic Staunton shapes.

'As a matter of fact I do,' replied the Doctor. 'I'm rather good. Had I the luxury of time…'

'Time… Ah, yes. That is indeed a luxury…' That faraway smile once again suffused the old man's face. 'But you must forgive me – I presume you would like to know exactly what I told your young friend and her companion.'

'If you please,' replied the Doctor, gazing at the chessboard.

'I'm rather embarrassed,' replied Limb. 'I'm afraid the information I gave them was technically in contravention of the Official Secrets Act. I revealed the location of a highly secret government research complex.'

'Don't feel too bad,' the Doctor replied. 'I sent them looking for that information. Stupidly, I failed to anticipate that they would take it upon themselves to act upon it.' Limb blinked his strange, slow blink. 'They broke into that highly secret government research complex.'

'Oh dear,' said Limb. 'Oh dear, oh dear. I did try to stress to them that such a course of action would be extremely foolish.'

The Doctor was still staring at the chessboard. 'Mr Limb, might I ask how you knew about the Peddler factory?'

'Before my… retirement, I was a civil servant.'

'Would you happen to know what sort of research they were conducting there?'

'All I know is that they were conducting experiments into the battle-effectiveness of the British foot soldier. It was all pretty fantastic. The intention was to give the individual soldier the speed and strength of many men. The strength of the Lurker, no less.'

'Lurker…' The Doctor was still staring at the wooden warriors ranked before him.

'The Limehouse Lurker. The East End Fiend, Doctor.'

'You seem to have a most remarkable situation here.' The Doctor tapped the black king lightly. 'The most complete stalemate I have ever seen. Who was your opponent?'

'Oh, I was playing against myself, Doctor.'

Limb reached down and moved his white queen directly into the path of a black bishop.

'Sacrificing the queen…'

'As Mr Conan Doyle's famous consulting detective says, once you have eliminated the impossible, what remains, however improbable, must be the right answer.'

Eyes still on the board, the Doctor nodded slowly.

He stopped.

Suddenly his eyes shot up.

'Mr Limb, tell me about the Lurker. You said he was strong.'

'Oh, yes. If you read the reports…'

He shuffled across to a bureau against the far wall, opened it, and hauled out a pile of newspapers.

'I've been following the case with some interest. In spite of the fact that the press is calling him the new Jack the Ripper, there is something unique about this case.'

'Please, go on.'

'Well, first there is the nature of the deaths. These unfortunate people were not attacked with any kind of edged weapon, nor bludgeoned with a blunt instrument. According to the police and coroner's reports, the early victims were literally torn apart down the middle. I suppose that this might be possible given appropriate machinery and of course time, but the Lurker seems to work fast. No one has come even close to catching him. The last few cases have been even worse: the victims were crushed to death. Quickly, too, judging by the area of the… blast.'

'Blast?'

'Doctor, they were squashed like tomatoes. They literally exploded from the pressure.'

Limb dropped the pile of newspapers with a thud on to the table.

'Do you have these police and coroner's reports?'

'I'm afraid not, Doctor. They are available in the Public Records Office. If you were to make an appointment…'

'No time, no time. What else can you tell me?'

'Well, the press are calling the attacks frenzied, but I'm not so sure. The first killings, at least, seem to show some method. In the first case there was a major intrusion into the body, made, as the coroner rather flippantly said, as if by a fist. The aorta was snapped just above the heart. The end was poking out of the chest. Later, as I said, he literally ripped his victims apart from the chest. Finally, there came the... tomato approach, if you will forgive the phrase. This might seem to betray a gradual loss of control, an increase in frenzy, or on the other hand it might betray an ever more ruthlessly efficient –'

'Efficient way of extracting blood from the body.' Once again the Doctor's eyes were on the chessboard. 'It's damaged, of course. If its casing has been damaged, then the sterile fluid interface between its biological and mechanical parts will be under assault from the atmosphere. Earth viruses. Bacteria. It will need to find some substitute fluid. Earth, 1940. The nearest thing available is... blood.'

'Well, I'm not sure I caught half of that, but –'

'Blood plasma, man! Where will I find the most concentrated supplies of blood plasma?'

'In London. The hospitals, I suppose. Those with blood collection centres. The government has been making constant appeals to the public to give blood. The bombing is taking its toll, you know. I think, from memory, I can give you a few addresses.'

'Please.'

Limb shuffled slowly back over to the bureau, extracted a piece of paper, and began writing. The Doctor studied the chessboard.

'Sacrificing the queen. Suicidally brilliant. I predict mate in sixteen moves. I really would love to play a game with you, Mr Limb, but, as I said –'

'You don't have the luxury of time,' said George Limb, handing the Doctor the piece of paper. 'I know, Doctor. I know.'

A rogue Cyberman.

It was about to rain. Events seemed to be wrong-footing the Doctor. He had underestimated the complexity of the situation. He was no nearer to finding Ace. And there had been no bus for half an hour. Funny how the war seemed not to have affected the London bus system at all.

A rogue Cyberman. Why was there never a bus when you needed one?

George Limb squinted in the rapidly diminishing light. It looked like rain.

'Well, well...' he chuckled to himself. His eyes darted brightly between newspaper reports and an old map of London. He dipped his elegant pen into a silver inkwell and scratched another cross on the map. 'Well, well...'

CHAPTER 10

It was completely dark. Ace had no way of telling whether it was day or night. She had no idea how long she had hidden here, surrounded by towering walls of brick, dripping pipes and the constant, deep sound of water rushing beneath the ground.

Peering out of the canvas back of the speeding lorry, the last thing Ace had seen was the two huge wooden doors which had slammed behind her, cutting off the road, the city, the light. As the van had juddered to a halt she had slipped from the back and into the plentiful shadows, where she had crouched as she watched the creepy little man – it had to be Wall, judging by the description – and his Cyber-henchmen disappear into the darkness.

From what she had been able to make out she was in a tall, narrow nave, criss-crossed high overhead with metal gantries – wrought-iron grilles emerging from and disappearing into the void. Sunk into the side walls were deep openings, corridors more like tunnels, leading to the deep hum and throb of huge machines. Ace had slipped silently past each of these entrances, crouching, watching, then springing like a cat, picking her way cautiously back to the gates. Stealing a look back into the darkness, she had begun feeling her way along the gates, looking for a way to open them.

Nothing. They were well and truly locked. If only she had some Nitro Nine on her. The Doctor was always forbidding her to carry the lethal explosive: this time he had been adamant. If such an advanced weapon should fall into the hands of a nation at war... blah, blah, blah. He had lectured her for half an hour on the danger of advanced technologies falling into the hands of cultures not yet ready for them. When he had finally shut up and got on with landing the TARDIS she had secretly thrown her Walkman into her rucksack, just to spite him. Her Walkman, but no Nitro Nine. She had thought to use the truck to escape, simply by driving it through the locked doors. She immediately discounted that idea: the doors were too solid, the lorry facing the wrong way. She would have to try the stunt in reverse gear. No chance. The only option seemed to be to wait until the doors were opened again. She had slipped back into the shadows; huddled herself against the wall, out of sight under a raft of pipes, rough with lime-scale stalactites, and waited.

And waited. Hours had passed. She was exhausted. She had had to grind her knuckles into the rough sides of the pipes in order to try to stay awake. Finally, in spite of herself, mastered by sheer fatigue, huddled in the dark, she had drifted off into the deeper darkness of sleep.

She awoke cursing. How long had she been asleep? Had the huge doors opened while she was dozing? Had she missed an opportunity to escape?

Nothing seemed to be any different. Apart from the low rhythm of the machines, apart from the constant subterranean flow of water, the place was silent. There was no sign of Wall or the tinheads.

So what to do? Think like the Doctor. Logically, there seemed to be only two courses of action. Either stay at ground level and try to find an exit down one of the side corridors or go up on to the gantries and try to find a window she could climb out of. There must be windows…

As far as she knew, Wall and the Cyber-goons were still on ground level; she decided to go up. She skirted the wall until she came to the nearest of the steeply ascending metal staircases. Silently, she began to climb.

If anything, it was even darker up here.

She stopped. A noise, overhead. Footfalls? She edged slowly forward along the narrow gantry.

There it was again. Too light to be a Cyberman. Too furtive to be Wall. Somehow the footsteps sounded scared.

More boldly now, Ace mounted another staircase. Still the sounds seemed to be above her. How tall was this place? Above, as below, she could see only darkness. She ascended a third staircase. The walkway that stretched ahead of her was narrower than the lower two; on each side of it was merely a single handrail. She must be a good sixty feet up. She was suddenly aware of a faint breath of wind. A good sign – there must be some access to the outside.

She stopped. Overhead, a dragging sound, metal on metal. The sound of someone grunting and straining. And then, a furious blast of cold air, a glimpse of something huge and grey cannoning down from above. Ace dived to one side, skidding across the metal floor. The thing – a huge, obviously full oil drum – crashed on to the walkway, which rocked and buckled beneath the impact. The drum continued to fall, exploding on the stone floor far beneath. Ace felt the metal grille tilt beneath her. She was falling. Hands flailed at the air. With the tips of her fingers she caught one of the poles that supported the handrail. Her fingers burned with pain as she clawed a better handhold for herself. Above her she heard the sound of running footsteps. Breathing – fast, panting, jagged and visceral. A face loomed out of the darkness above her – pale, gaunt, grey with stubble, eyes darting nervously. He stared down, a look of bitter disappointment on his face.

'Pleh… Please… Help me…' Ace gasped. 'I can't hold on much longer.'

His mouth curled into a snarl. He moved a foot lightly on top of one of Ace's clinging hands.

'Why should I? You've ruined my plans. Did they send you up here to get me?'

'Please…' Her hands were slipping now. 'No one sent me…' Slipping. 'I'm just trying to find a way…' The bar wrested itself free. Her hands closed on air. '…out…'

She fell.

A split second later she was dangling again, held hard in the man's grip. Straining, he hauled her back on to the narrow balcony.

Steadying herself on hands and knees, she felt the ironwork again beneath her, then slowly clambered to her feet, dusting herself down indignantly.

'What did you want to do that for?' she barked.

'Ssssh…' The man looked around him in fear. 'Keep it down, will you? They'll hear.'

'I don't care!' snapped Ace.'I'm getting out of here.'

There was no doubt – the wind was coming from somewhere behind the creep, from the level above. Angrily she pushed past him.

'No…'

She ascended the next stairway quickly, ignoring his protests.

'No way out up there… No escape from the Cybermen…'

The wind was actually quite strong now. Ace climbed a final, short set of steps, and found herself reassuringly on stone again. The corridor was narrow, low and dark. She edged along it, heart soaring. She felt the crunch of twigs under her feet. Bird droppings. She never thought she'd be so glad to step in bird crap. After several yards the corridor opened up into a wide stone attic-space. Overhead in the stone eaves a benighted pigeon cooed. At the end of the sudden expanse of moonlight were two huge semicircular openings – windows on to the sky, vast and glassless. She ran up to them and threw herself against the bars that covered them. She shook the bars, then banged on them. Her heart sank. They weren't going to budge – only the pigeons could come and go this way. Ace slumped on to a pile of leaves and litter beneath the window. She felt like crying.

'No escape that way, I told you. When did they bring you here?'

She spun around. Him again. She could see him better now; he must be about fifty, tallish, his clothes, filthy, torn, a battered donkey jacket covering what was once perhaps a white shirt. Pathetically, what must recently have passed for a tie – a limp, strangled, knotted strip of cloth – hung about his neck.

'They didn't, as such. I followed them in. Now I want to get out. Did you drop that drum on me?'

'Yes. Sorry.'

'Sorry! I was nearly killed!'

'Three days I've been locked in here with those monsters. It's driving me mad. I've been hiding up here, mostly. My plan was to lure the two big ones up here then drop the drum on them. I thought you were one of them. Like I said, sorry.'

'Mmm.' Ace had to admit, on paper it wasn't a bad plan.

'Trouble is, they'll be up here like a shot now, the noise the drum made.' He let out a troubled sigh. 'Why did they bring you here, anyway?'

'They didn't,' Ace replied. 'I told you, I followed them.'

'Mad. You don't know what you're up against.'

'I do,' said Ace, hollow-voiced. 'Cybermen. Horrible. I've come across them before.'

'Me, I'm just the caretaker here. This place is supposed to be closed down. Decommissioned. There was only me left here. They just turned up one night – the Cybermen and the one they call Wall. Locked the place up tight with me inside. They know I'm here, but they don't seem too bothered.'

'They'll be bothered now. You tried to chuck a dirty great oil drum on their heads.' The man nodded, slowly, fatally. 'What is this place, anyway?'

'It's a sewage pumping station.'

Of course. O-level history again. London's Victorian sewerage system. They'd done it in painful detail. They might even have studied this place. If only she'd paid more attention she might have some idea how to get out.

'Like I said, it's out of commission. Too much bomb damage to the sewers round here. They're Victorian, you know.'

'Yes, I know,' said Ace, flatly. The last thing she wanted was a chat about London's sanitation problems. Joseph – what was his name? – Bazalgette and all that rubbish.

'They'll be sending a team out in a week or two to assess the damage. See what can be done. Although, between you and me, the main conduits have had it. I think they'll have to just demolish the lot and start again.'

'Sending a team?' Maybe London's sanitation problems weren't so irrelevant after all. 'Where?'

'Here, for starters. They'll –'

'So the Cybermen will be discovered, and –'

'And it will be too late for us.' The caretaker spat. 'We'll have starved to death by then. If the Cybermen don't get us first. I haven't eaten in three days.'

Ace fished deep into one of the pockets of her jacket. 'Here. It's not much, and it's a bit old, but…'

The man was holding the thing up to the light, eyeing it warily.

'What do I do with it?' he asked.

'Eat it, of course. Haven't you ever seen a Creme Egg before?'

As the caretaker wolfed down the sweet, Ace stared out of the huge, barred windows.

'What are they doing here?'

'Mmmff…' He swallowed the last of the gooey chocolate. 'That's another thing I don't understand: they've started the pumping machinery.'

'Why?'

'God knows. There are too many breaks in the system for it to do much good. And I can't imagine public health being one of the Cybermen's big concerns. I've been down a couple of times, looking for food mostly. Heard them talking. Didn't understand most of it…'

'What?' asked Ace, impatiently.

'Well, I know things aren't going well for them. They're on the run, and desperate that no one should know where they are.'

'On the run?' Ace was incredulous. 'Who would the Cybermen need to run from?'

'Search me…' the caretaker replied. 'All I know is they're hiding here. They keep going on about some … escape pod, I think. They came here in it.'

'Wall as well?'

The caretaker nodded. 'Wall and the two giants. And now they've lost the pod.'

Ace shook her head. 'They've got it back. I was there.' She thought for a moment. 'Maybe it's a good thing. Maybe they just want to get out of here. I mean – it's not exactly a great place to escape to at the moment, is it? London, I mean. Where did they come from anyway?'

'I don't know,' the caretaker replied, 'but I don't think they're planning to go anywhere in a hurry. You see, there's something else they're looking for. They keep on talking about some… command unit… Yes, command unit.'

'Command unit?' Ace wished she'd pumped the Doctor for more information on the Cybermen. There had never seemed to be time – there was always so much to assimilate in the Doctor's mad world.

'And I'll tell you something else –' the caretaker's voice dropped – 'they can't find it anywhere.'

Ace paced impatiently about the vast brick loft. Darkness wouldn't last for ever. They had to make their move soon. Finally, her companion had relented and they had begun their silent descent.

On the ground floor, off down one of the darkened stone passageways, she could hear the grating voices of the two Cybermen, and Wall's chilling, childlike wheedle. It sounded as if they were arguing. Ace strained to hear what they were saying, but the throb of machinery was loud here, and drowned the words.

'See what I mean?' the caretaker said. 'The pumping machinery's going full pelt.'

Ace nodded. Her plan was a risky one. The Doctor would have been proud of her. She had – she hoped – arrived by pure logic at the solution to their dilemma. There was no means of exit on the ground floor – that much was clear. She had gone up and found none. Logically, there was only one thing to do: go down.

At first her companion had dismissed the idea out of hand. No one, he had assured her, could get out through the sewers. Even at the best of times they were dangerous – pitch-dark, winding labyrinths of human ordure, pestilent with poisonous gases, and now, thanks to the bombing, structurally in ruins and, it would seem, flooded.

'How long have the pumps been going?' she whispered.

'Ever since they arrived,' came the whispered reply.

'So with any luck they'll have got rid of the flooding.'

'It's not that simple!' He was scared. His voice was beginning to rise. 'It depends on a lot of things. The extent of the bombing, the level of rain – the storm drains empty into the sewers, you know.'

She placed a gentle finger over his mouth.

'I can't do it on my own,' she whispered. 'It's our only chance.'

'I know,' he whispered back. 'I agreed, didn't I? This way.'

He led her away from the awful voices and down another dark, stone corridor. Pipes cut in and out of concrete, hissing and humming. Other corridors intersected; they turned first left, then right, right, then left, until Ace was hopelessly lost.

'This is nothing compared to underground,' her companion assured her.

'Sssh!' she replied. It seemed to her that their voices and footfalls echoed horribly down here.

The caretaker placed a hand on her shoulder. 'Wait a minute,' he said. Set into the wall to their right was a cupboard, its wooden doors painted a familiar corporation green. He opened the doors. Half a dozen torches, some rope, a fireman's axe. The caretaker took out two of the torches and handed one to Ace. 'We'll need these,' he said.

The passageway was completely dark, except for their torch beams dancing on the walls. They came to an entrance. Beyond was only blackness and the constant rush of water, deep underground. The caretaker let his torch play on the inky dark. Dimly, Ace could make out an array of manholes dotted over the floor; raised columns of brick, and on top of each a cover of heavy, disc-shaped metal, hinged, each capped by a horizontal metal anchor-wheel.

'Come on.' Gingerly, she stepped into the room and made for the nearest of the drains. Her hands gripped the wheel and she applied all her strength to it. It didn't budge. Her companion joined her; together they strained and heaved.

'It's no good,' he finally gasped, his voice barely audible over the crashing and sloshing of water below them. 'Rusted shut. These places have been badly neglected since the war started. Let's try another.'

'Wait!' Ace froze. So, she hadn't just imagined it. Something had definitely brushed against her foot. Slowly she lowered the beam of her torch.

The floor was alive – a squirming mass of metallic silver grubs, all identical, all about the size of rats. Ace had never seen such things before, but they reeked to her of Cybertechnology.

She struggled to master her rising panic, to assess the situation coolly. The things seemed docile – drugged, almost. She guessed – hoped – that they required some specific task before becoming active.

'D'you have Rentokill in the 1940s?' she asked.

'What?'

'Never mind. Just don't look at the floor.'

There were sixteen manholes in the room. They picked their way from cover to cover, treading with agonising, faltering precision among the horrid bed of Cyber-things. Every manhole cover was rusted solid.

'The axe,' Ace said, suddenly.

'What?'

'The axe that was in the cupboard. Where we got the torches. We can put it between the spokes of the wheel and use it as a lever. Wait here.'

'I'll go,' the caretaker said, insistently. 'You'd only get lost.'

She nodded. He was right; all the passages had looked the same to her.

'I won't be long. Ten minutes at the outside.' His voice appeared to come from nowhere, his body already swallowed by shadows.

It was the longest ten minutes Ace had ever spent, she was sure. The scuttling and chittering of the buglike creatures was getting louder. She swept the floor with her torchbeam. There was no doubt about it: they were moving more than they had been; some were even reacting vaguely to her light. They were waking up.

Footsteps! Thundering down the corridor. Ace braced herself, ready to run. It was the caretaker, axe in hand, panting, flailing with his arms, trying to get the words out.

'They're coming,' he gasped.

He kicked his way across the floor, driving a path through the Cybercreatures.

'Quickly…' He jammed the axe between the heavy arms of the wheel and threw all his weight against it. Ace did the same. Slowly, then more easily, the wheel began to turn. He tossed the axe to one side. 'Help me lift it.'

The lid rose easily on its hinge, and fell away from the hole with a crash.

'You go first,' the caretaker barked to Ace.

She looked down. Metal rungs were set into close brickwork, vanishing into darkness after only a few feet; the smell of sewage and stagnant rainwater; the rhythmic sloshing of the pumps. She hauled her feet over the edge, dropped nimbly into the hole and began descending the rungs, fast.

'Come on!' she shouted up the shaft. The caretaker was older than she was, and bigger. He was climbing into the hole too slowly. From above she heard the unmistakable flash of a Cybergun. The feet above her head twitched and jerked from the rungs; the twelve-stone weight of her companion bounced down the shaft, rebounding off the walls, catching on the rungs, knocking Ace from her precarious perch and carrying her down into the darkness below.

They landed on damp, clammy stone. Mercifully the fall couldn't have been more than five feet. Ace groped about on the slime until she felt the handle of her torch. It still worked. Thank God. She shone it in the face of her friend. His eyes were wide and dead, staring in different directions. His mouth was open, his neck broken, his body lying like a bonfire-night Guy.

Ace ran her hands over the emaciated, grizzled head. She placed it in her lap and for just a second closed her eyes, feeling the tears well. Then, she laid his head on the ground and limped away into the tunnel, the feeble light of her torch dancing ahead, determinedly not looking back.

She hadn't even known his name.

CHAPTER 11

Every moment the smell of its craving grew stronger. Now the sensation was almost unbearable. It had been following the scent for weeks, and it was so close now. Here – outside this place – the crimson stench hung thick in the air, drowning out everything, making its vision swim, its limbs tremble uncontrollably. Even the high, insistent singing in its head had been replaced by a cavernous silence.

It was dying, it knew. It was drawing on its last reserves of strength.

It stood against a brick wall, perhaps twenty feet high, featureless, windowless. Beyond lay what it sought. It pounded on the wall with its fists. And it could not break through. Its ragged tarpaulin billowed round it in a sudden gust of wind.

It turned.

The wind carried something on its breath. In the distance it could see one of the creatures approaching.

Oh, and this one reeked of it!

'Doctor...'

'Mmm...? Turn right here, Inspector.'

'Doctor, will you stop being so mysterious. You're making the law look foolish.'

'Mmm...?'

'I'm the one who's supposed to be conducting this investigation, Doctor. Both investigations, in fact. Dr Peddler and the Lurker. Now you tell me they're both connected, but don't tell me how. On your say-so I've got half my force chasing round all the hospitals in this part of London asking a load of damn-fool questions to damn-fool doctors without any of us knowing what in the name of God is going on.'

'Mmm...?'

'That's it.' Chief Inspector Mullen slammed his foot on the brake pedal of the police car. 'Not another inch do I go until you put me in the picture, Doctor.'

The Doctor sighed, then smiled.

'All right, Inspector. You win. But I warn you, what I tell you is going to sound bizarre in the extreme. You won't believe me for a moment. And you'll never be taken seriously again in His Majesty's Police Force if you breathe a word of this.'

Mullen nodded, braced for the unbelievable. Glancing in his rear-view mirror he started the car in motion again.

'I believe that the Limehouse Lurker is part of the alien race which made the thing which killed Dr Peddler. They're called Cybermen, and they're very, very nasty. I believe that this particular Cyberman is malfunctioning.'

'You told me that much. That's why it needs blood. That's why it's killing people.'

'Yes. What I don't understand is what it's doing here in the first place. The Cybermen shouldn't have evolved into this form yet. These appear to be sophisticated Cybermen, from a time period far ahead of this one, judging by the Cybermat.'

The Time Lord patted his coat pocket. He stopped. He thrust his hand into first one pocket, then another, then another.

'Oh dear,' he muttered. 'Very careless. I could have sworn I brought the Cybermat with me. I must have left it at McBride's office. One has to be so careful with anachronisms, Inspector.'

'Doctor...'

'Ah, turn left here. And park. This is our last port of call.'

Mullen swung the car into a narrow cul-de-sac and pulled up in front of a sprawling, red-brick and white-stone building, with high, arched windows and steeply pointed roofs. Solid and practical as industry yet rising in elegant angles and planes to become pure thought – a Victorian elementary school.

'A lot of buildings have had to be commandeered, Doctor. Most of the schools are closed anyway, so many kids have been evacuated.' He killed the ignition. 'It looks as if our boys have already arrived, Doctor.'

The two sleuths exited the car. A police constable at the gate saluted Mullen.

'Constable Quick…' Mullen suddenly sounded apprehensive.

'Evening, sir. Nothing to report. Doctor in charge says there's been nothing out of the ordinary, but I 'appen to know the cat's off his food, sir. Which is most unusual, sir, and always means trouble. I got that from one of the cleaners…'

'Now I recognise you, Constable,' said the Doctor, doffing his hat. 'We met yesterday morning at the Peddler factory. You'd just interviewed the secretary.'

The policeman remained immobile, looking doubtfully between Mullen and his chatty friend. The chief inspector pinched the sleeve of the Doctor's jacket and, daintily but firmly, steered him inside.

'I think we'd better look at this one ourselves, don't you, Doctor…? Ah!'

A woman of about fifty bustled through a door into the brick-and-glass corridor in which they stood. She wore a starched white coat about her body and a starched expression on her face. She stopped for a moment when she saw them, and then bustled on.

'You're more policemen, I suppose. Well, you at least,' she said to Mullen, shooting a sidelong glance at the Doctor. 'I've already given the constable a piece of my mind, sir. Please don't make me waste my breath doing the same to you.'

She opened another door and bustled through it. With a sigh Mullen strode after her. Heavy wooden lab desks sat in rows, bolted to the floor. She strode to the front of the former classroom, picked up a notebook and started scribbling furiously.

'Look, madam…'

'Doctor. Dr Ruth Walsh, blood transfusion service, on a gruelling schedule, Mr…'

'Chief Inspector.' Mullen's voice was flinty. 'Chief Inspector Patrick Mullen, Special Branch, in the middle of an important investigation. I must ask you some questions, Dr Walsh. I'm afraid I am not at liberty to reveal the nature of our current inquiries, but your cooperation –'

'Oh, I know all about your current inquiries, Chief Inspector Mullen. The constable has already told me.' She seemed white with rage. 'Have you any idea how short of blood we are at the moment? Have you any idea how difficult it is to get people to come forward at the best of times to give blood? If people think that the Limehouse Lurker might just decide to drop in for tea with a craving for blood…'

Mullen groaned. Nobody was supposed to know that. He hadn't even told the squads of policemen he had sent fanning out across east London what they were looking for. Just any disturbances – anything out of the ordinary. If a moron like Quick had put two and two together then his little secret must be all over the city by now. Panic… Riot… Resignation…

At the back of the classroom the Doctor sprawled across one of the benches and began fiddling with the gas taps.

'Chief Inspector,' Dr Walsh continued, 'you must forgive me…' It sounded more like an order than a request.

'I understand,' said Mullen, defeated. 'The last woman Quick interviewed had to be sedated.'

'I'll tell you what I told him, Chief Inspector. There has been nothing out of the ordinary around here at all. No disturbances. All of our blood has been collected on schedule. Nothing has gone missing.' Standing in front of the blackboard she sounded for all the world like a teacher trying with all patience to communicate a simple idea to a stupid child.

'Should anything out of the ordinary happen,' she lectured on, 'we shall of course communicate the fact to the police at once. Now I don't think I really need add anything to –'

'Aha!'

The shout from the back of the classroom was the Doctor's. He had opened a number of large glass jeroboams, each containing differently coloured powders or crystals. He had made a little dry-mixture in a pile on the desk and was picking up handfuls and sprinkling them into the path of a gas tap. From the gas tap a flame shot across the desk. And as the Doctor's compound hit the flame it danced from yellow to red to green to silver, and then back again.

'Dr Walsh,' the Time Lord called, never lifting his eyes from the shimmering flame, 'where does your blood go after it's collected?'

'Oh…' She was staring into the Doctor's flame, and for a moment didn't answer. The light danced in her eyes. Her hard mouth softened to a gentle smile.

'It, ah…' She shook herself from her dream. But the smile remained. 'It's taken to a central collection point, and from there it's distributed around the city.'

'And this central collection point is… where?'

'Couldn't tell you. That information isn't passed down to me, I'm afraid.'

'Mullen…?' The chief inspector didn't answer. 'Mullen!' The Doctor flapped his arms irritably in the direction of the almost-sleeping policeman.

'Uh… I could find out, Doctor. We'd have to go back to the station.'

'Very well, come on.'

With a snap of the gas tap the Doctor killed the flame and jumped from the desk. His audience snapped to attention with a start. He raised his hat to Dr Walsh.

'Good day to you, Dr Walsh. It's been a pleasure meeting you.'

'Oh, the pleasure was all mine,' the haematologist replied. 'Quite, quite beautiful…'

She drifted out of the room and back down the corridor.

'I said come on,' said the Doctor tetchily, tugging the chief inspector by the sleeve of his overcoat.

'Doctor, I've got to tell you, I feel a little… light-headed.'

'I'm the one who's been light-headed,' said the Doctor dourly.

'Or cloth-eared, or flat-footed, or something. I've been slow, Inspector.' He raised his hands to the sky. 'Oh, Ace... Forgive me. I've been so slow. I should have thought that there would be a central collection point. That's where he'll make for.'

The Doctor pushed open the glass front door of the school. He regarded Constable Quick, standing to attention, his back to them, immobile on the other side. It didn't look as if he had moved a muscle since they went in.

Mullen followed the Doctor through the door, then swung to his right, sauntered up to his subordinate and clapped him chummily on the shoulder.

'You're a good man, Quick,' he said. 'I know that. Dedicated. Dogged. You'll make a good copper, Quick.'

'Yes, sir,' Quick replied flatly.

'Take a breather, why don't you? Go inside. Take the weight off your feet for a bit.'

'Inspector Mullen...' The Doctor's voice was as warm and milky as his old mother's had been. 'Wakey, wakey...'

Mullen shook himself. Where was he? Spinning round, he got his bearings just in time to see Constable Quick through the glass door, inside the school, settling himself into a comfortable chair and stretching his arms and feet.

'What the...'

He took a dumbfounded step back towards the school.

'Quick!' he bellowed. 'What the Devil do you think you're doing?'

Ace, had the Doctor but known it, was almost within earshot of her friend as he begged her forgiveness. He had raised his voice to the sky: she was beneath his feet, sloshing through an underground river of rainwater. Her progress had been slow – she seemed to have been down there for hours. She had left her the caretaker – she had had to – and pressed on with their plan.

Barely six yards along the tunnel Ace had come face to face with her first major obstacle. The German bombs had done their work:

the tunnel was almost entirely blocked with rubble – bricks, concrete, and London clay. She had shone her torch up into the dark gash where the roof had been. It didn't look safe. Gingerly, she had begun hefting the uneven chunks of earth and masonry from the pile, her ears straining for any sound from behind which might indicate that she had been followed into the pit. Nearly an hour later she had managed to clear a space deep enough to reach what she desperately hoped was the end of the cave-in and wide enough – just – to crawl through on her stomach. Wriggling like a worm, she had squeezed herself between unsteady tons of rock and concrete.

After what seemed like an age she had emerged into what she hoped was just water. The tunnel was ankle-deep in it. Just ahead of her it split into two. Ace had shone her torch down each of the tunnels. The one on the right ended almost immediately in more rubble, down which a constant sheet of water sluiced.

Water. It looked clean. It must be rainwater, which – she hoped – meant she was close to an exit to the surface. Eagerly she had begun tearing at the debris, throwing it behind her. The ceiling was higher here. Another good sign. She had ascended the pile of rubble. Her hand had closed on something metallic, buried under the scree. She had tugged, and it had come free – a metallic rod, four or five feet in length, and curiously grooved and notched. She tested its strength against her own. It was strong – good. Wedging it under the largest of the clay-and-concrete boulders which blocked her way, she had heaved downward with all her weight. The rod had held firm – the huge block had stirred. Again she had heaved. Slowly, like a stone giant waking from sleep, the rock had pivoted over, half twisted, and thundered down the rubble slope.

Ace froze. A thin, constant trickle of dust was suddenly showering her from somewhere above. The trickle became a stream. Swearing to herself, she had skidded back down the slope, small clods of earth and pieces of broken brick tumbling around her legs. The metal pole had clanged down after her, catching her in the back of the legs and sending her sprawling.

Barely stopping to think, she had picked herself up and hurled herself down the other corridor as a huge, irregular slab of concrete encrusted around a twisted mass of torn pipes and cables crashed to the floor of the tunnel.

Miraculously, her torch, slung by its carrying strap around her wrist, still worked. Ankle-deep in water, she had struck out down this last available path. At first the journey had seemed straightforward. Ace hadn't eaten since the previous day. The sleep she had managed in the pumping station had been sporadic and uneasy. Aware that she was drawing on her last reserves of energy, she had felt desperately grateful that the tunnel seemed intact, and that it ran straight and at a comfortable head height. She had stumbled onward, ignoring the spray of the mini-cascades of water which constantly sluiced out of much smaller tunnels and pipes, emptying into this larger tunnel at shoulder height. She was almost grateful for their sound, grateful as the remorseless pounding of the vast underground pumps gradually receded into the background torrent.

Feeling more confident now, she had set her mind to planning what she would do when she reached the surface. Go to McBride's office, she supposed. Hope that the Doctor was still there.

Unknown to either of them, the Doctor was fifteen feet above her, waking Chief Inspector Mullen from his dream.

At the pumping station, alone in the room of the drains, Wall looked impassively into the hole that had swallowed the girl. No light glinted off his black-lensed glasses. He stepped back from the hole and let their gaze take in the entire vast space. The floor seethed before him.

There was no hurry. Let her run. The Cybermats had her scent.

They were much more active now. He took a small electronic pad from his pocket and began punching in numbers. His little pets began to wriggle and chitter frantically about his feet. One by one he picked them up by their tails and watched them wriggle in his hand for a moment. The feeling made him chuckle. One by one he dropped them, head first, into the hole.

Ace stopped suddenly. Something was wrong. The water, which had previously been lapping around her ankles, was now nearly up to her knees. The passage was subtly sloping downward. Carrying her deeper.

Closing her eyes, she had muttered a prayer. Pray to God the tunnel levels out. Pray to God the water doesn't rise to ceiling height. There was no doubt: the downward slope of the passage was becoming steeper. Soon she was wading thigh-deep in water. Soon afterward it was above her waist.

Something brushed against her hand, and then swam away. Those Cyber-things! She put a hand against the wall to steady herself. Calm down, she told herself. Calm down. It's only a rat.

She was feeling the tug of the underground current now, trying to overbalance her, trying to tease her feet away from the clammy, slippery floor of the tunnel, dragging her forward and downward.

She peered into the beam of her torch. It was as she feared. Barely two yards ahead the tunnel roof disappeared under water. She would have to go back. Try to find some other way out. Barely holding at bay her terror at the prospect of being stuck down here, of dying underground, dying in a sewer, she would not even admit to herself the possibility of such a fate. She *would* find a way out. She *had* to.

She turned on her heel, resigned to the long journey back. She frowned. There was a wind, a rush of air, a sudden current tugging at her legs – and then a wall of water was bearing down on her.

The brick world turned upside down. Her feet were swept from under her. Water engulfed her head, flooded her nose and eyes. She couldn't breathe. She was caught in the current, flailing, banging against the brick walls and ceiling, thundering downhill. No air. No light. Her mouth filled with water…

Ace skidded to a halt, dragging great gulps of air into her lungs.

For minutes she lay still, curled up, foetal, eyes tight shut. The first thing she saw when she opened them was water, plunging endlessly into the abyss. She was lying on an enormous metal grille – a drain cover, deep underground, a gateway to a deeper, lonelier nether world. Her torch was still alight, although its beam was faint and flickering now. She shone it across the floor and up the walls.

The massive disc of the grille sat at the bottom of a wide, shallow concrete bowl into which the deluges of twenty or more inlets constantly poured, before spilling away through the metal bars on which Ace lay curled. Stone buttresses criss-crossed high above her head, eaves and angles intersected around the classically shaped mouths of the inpouring tunnels. It was like some kind of cathedral. A cathedral underground.

Ace let her head slump to the floor. If she had to die down here, this seemed a good spot. No one gets a mausoleum like this any more on the surface.

She breathed deeply and slowly.

Something was flapping against her cheek. She opened her eyes. Some kind of wrapper, caught in the bars of the drain. Buzz Bar… She picked up the chocolate wrapper and stared at it in the dim torchlight. She lurched to her feet. The wrapper was practically intact.

The air was fresher. The air was normal!

There must be a surface drain really close.

Frantically, she ran from wall to wall, shining the dying torch into the overhead gloom. At last she found it. An alcove – a man-sized groove running straight up the wall as far as she could see, and inset with metal rungs.

'Yes!'

Her shout echoed and bounced between the walls as she pulled herself, rung by rung, up the ladder of salvation. At the top was a cover, similar to the one by which she had entered this strange world. Please, let it open…

The cover tilted up and fell back to the street with a clang. Ace's head and shoulders, bruised and filthy, emerged slowly to the long shadows of darkened buildings, silvery in the moonlight.

CHAPTER 12

Sharkey sipped at his whisky and fingered the thing in the pocket of his overcoat. He didn't normally drink whisky – least of all Mama's overpriced bourbon – but tonight he was both celebrating and in need of as much Dutch courage as he could get. He was exhilarated – and terrified.

Sharkey had never been a likeable figure, and had therefore never been much liked. He had grown up sly and solitary, always on the outside of things, always the spectator. Watching, observing, had become his main pastime. As a youth he had been fascinated by the goings-on behind the brightly lit windows of other people's homes. It was easy in a city as densely packed as London. Watching, listening, remembering. Information had become his trade. The poverty of his upbringing had more or less inevitably led to a life on the fringes of the criminal world. He had begun by carrying tales between the different crooks operating around the capital, selling them out, one to another, for a few quid here and there. Never giving enough to do any real damage or to bring their wrath down on his head, of course. Then had come the cops, and the private investigators.

He had never been a powerful player. He had made a small but adequate living, and that had been enough. Then everything had changed. Nowadays he never gave any information to anyone at all without explicit authority from above. No informer in London did – they valued their lives too much. As one body they continued to watch, to note, but now they were the eyes and ears of a single great organising mind. All that they learned was channelled up the secret network; all that passed the other way was by express authorisation only. There was no money in it for Sharkey – or for anyone. There was only the fear of what would happen if he dared to disobey.

Tonight he was daring to disobey.

Tonight, for the first time in years, he was his own man. For the first time in his life he had something that was really worth selling. Information was power – that was what Sharkey believed, and that was what He believed.

Him.

Sharkey blanched at the thought. Why did He keep returning to his mind? They said He knew everything that went on in this city, however inconsequential. And tonight, for the first time in his life, Sharkey was far from inconsequential.

Tonight he was unique. Tonight he was a power player.

If He found out He'd tear Sharkey limb from –

Sharkey downed the whisky and slunk up to the bar for another. He was playing the most dangerous game of his life. Again he fingered the thing in his pocket – the thing he had picked from the pocket of the funny little man. He didn't know what it was – it looked like some kind of huge grub, part metal, part flesh. Disgusting. It was broken, of course, or dead, or whatever word was most appropriate for the thing. Shot to pieces by the look of things. But it was still central, Sharkey was sure, to whatever it was McBride and his friends were after, whatever it was the military were after, and whatever it was the higher powers that he served were after. For the first time in his life Sharkey knew something really worth knowing. This was his big chance. He had made the crucial telephone call. Now all he had to do was wait.

'Sharkey?'

The Doctor had looked puzzled as he plucked the telephone from Chief Inspector Mullen's fingers.

'Lowlife,' Mullen had said flatly. 'One of McBride's narks.'

'Oh, yes. I met him at that bar Cody McBride likes to frequent. Hello…'

He had slipped easily into the chair behind Mullen's desk. The chief inspector's office was tiny compared with McBride's, and not much more orderly. Empty cups stood in for the empty whisky bottles favoured by the American.

'Make yourself at home, Doctor,' Mullen had said under his

breath, raising his eyes to the ceiling.

'Doctor?' said Sharkey's voice.

'Yes.'

'Today, in the bar, you got something out of me, and I got something out of you.'

'Go on.' The Doctor's voice was a low, alert purr.

'And I reckon that what I got you're gonna want back. You wouldn't want it... falling into the wrong hands.'

'I take it you're referring to the Cybermat that was in the pocket of my coat. Small metal rodent.'

'Yeah, that's it...'

'Mr Sharkey, I should warn you, as long as you carry that thing with you, you are in mortal danger. Dead it might be, but safe it is not.'

'Listen, Doctor. I want money for this. I reckon five thousand's about right. I'll be waiting where we met before. You get the money together, but give it to someone else to bring here. I don't want you pulling that stunt with me again. Get someone else – tell them where to come.'

'You're not listening to me, man,' the Doctor had shouted. 'Get rid of that thing! Throw it in the river! You're in terrible danger!'

But the line was dead.

The Doctor got up and began pacing about the tiny office, weaving an impossibly intricate trail of wet footprints.

'Doctor –'

'Sharkey's got the Cybermat,' the Time Lord interrupted. 'The one we destroyed at McBride's office.'

'And I suppose he wants money for it.'

'The Cybermat is irrelevant. Anybody who possesses it is doomed. I believe the Cybermen are trying hard to conceal their presence here. They will locate and destroy that Cybermat utterly and completely – and anybody who's around to see them do it. Come on!'

The Doctor marched from Mullen's office. The chief inspector hurried after him.

'Where are we going, Doctor?'

'To that bar. To prevent a massacre. Inspector, I want the address of that central blood collection point. I also want a list of all the companies in Britain and as many as you are aware of overseas who're engaged in the same sort of work as Peddler.'

'Duty sergeant!' Mullen yelled.

Alarm bell ringing, the companions roared out into the night for a second time in Mullen's big black car. The rain drove ahead of them.

'I think some time back you were in the middle of giving me an explanation Doctor,' the chief inspector said laconically.

'Very well, very well...' The Doctor sounded testy. 'Our Mr Wall and his large metal associates arrived, I believe, in the capsule. They are in hiding here, and are trying to conceal their presence – hence their attempt to steal back the sphere... hence, I believe, the murder of Dr Peddler.'

'Peddler...'

'Peddler's secretary told us that he had received a visit from Mr Wall the day before. She also said she heard raised voices, and that Dr Peddler summoned security before they left. Obviously, Wall wanted something that Peddler could supply. He tried in some way to engage the services of Peddler, and Peddler obviously refused. He now knew too much, and so the Cybermen had him killed.'

'Sounds all right to me, Doctor.'

'No.' The Doctor brought his hand down heavily against the dashboard. 'I don't like it. Why would Wall need to have Peddler killed? Surely, Peddler can't have learned much in a single meeting. Why was Peddler so terrified? And why did they fall almost immediately into fighting? No, Mr Wall and Dr Peddler are old acquaintances.'

Outside the air-raid sirens were beginning to sound.

'How much do you know about Dr Peddler's past, Inspector?'

'Nothing, really.'

'And could you find anything?'

Mullen scratched his chin.

'Military Intelligence would have a file. We could always ask Major Lazonby.' The drone of the Luftwaffe was already overhead. In the distance bombs began to fall. 'And – dare I ask? – what about the Lurker?'

'That's another thing I don't understand. The Lurker, as you call him, is a badly malfunctioning Cyberman. It has been here for months – we know from the dates of the killings. But why would a Cyberman be hiding in London?'

'So the other Cybermen and Wall could be... What? Some kind of rescue party?'

'Precisely, Inspector. They will be searching for the Limehouse Lurker every bit as hard as we are.'

'We just have to find him first.'

'Yes,' the Doctor replied. 'Or, rather, no. First, we have to get to Mama's Bar. Can't we go any faster?'

scanning>

scanning>

scanning>

possible hostile life forms entering close scan zone>

activate>

analyse> bipedal> humanoid>

two distinct organisms> young, mature> one male> one female>

sentient> speech patterns in evidence>

analyse and translate>

i shouldn't go near it if i was you>

what d'you reckon it is then>

dunno. could be a bit off a german plane a bomber>

nah. it don't look like no bit off no german plane>

aw look at its little legs innit cute>

anyway, come on. that's not why we're here>

gerroff. it looks like a table to me. a little round table>

it ain't no table it's more like a globe what's been cut in half>
bloody funny whatever it is>
look it's probably some fancy record player. these was posh
houses>
why weren't it blown up then like everything else>
i dunno. cummere>
gerroff i said>
i thought we come 'ere to – you know>
i know but i'm not sure>
there's no one about they're all in the shelters. come on>
i can't not with that thing 'ere. i feel like it's lookin' at us>
don't be daft it's only some kind of gadget>
look at them lights on the top and the buttons>
right if you don't like it i'm gonna get it shifted>
i shouldn't touch it if i was you>
hostile entering zone of absolute exclusion>
arm>
prepare to detonate>

The explosion knocked Ace to the floor. How close had that one been? It felt like a mini-earthquake.

She had been pulled, wet and shivering, from the drain by people in a queue waiting at a mobile soup kitchen. Tramps and the bombed-out homeless, side by side in a line. They had given her soup and tea and found a passing policeman who had agreed to take her home. He had summoned a car, which had dropped her at McBride's office. Yes, she assured them, this was where she lived. Even now Ace could never quite get over her mistrust of the rozzers.

She had entered the office to find it empty. Her mind raced. Mama's Bar. Maybe she might find McBride there. She picked herself off the floor and, pausing only to fetch up her rucksack, she thundered back down the stairs and on to the street.

Instinctively, Sharkey leaned back into the shadows. Too much whisky had dulled his terror. He was starting to feel bold, confident… Let Him go to hell. He wasn't that all-powerful. Sharkey was moving up in the world. Dealing with a new class of client.

So the little man had been bluffing after all. Course he had. And he'd sent the girl. Sharkey watched from the shadows as Ace stumbled into the bar.

Outside the first siren was sounding. A momentary hush descended on the bar. Ace heard a low, insistent hissing. Out of the corner of her eye she could see someone trying – and failing – to signal to her without being seen by the rest of the bar. Sharkey. He might know. She crossed to his shadowy table and sat down. 'Now's the Time' by Charlie Parker kicked in on the jukebox.

'You came, then,' he said.

'Sharkey,' she began, not realising that he'd seemed to be expecting her, 'I need to find Cody. I need to find my friend the Doctor.'

'Have you got the money?'

'What?'

Each paused, looking at the other as if they were mad. It was Ace who broke the silence.

'Do you know where Cody is?' she asked insistently.

'You… haven't come to buy this, have you?' His hand reached into his jacket pocket. He could feel the lethal little creature and the power it promised slipping from his grasp. He could feel the fear returning.

Ace got to her feet.

'Thanks anyway,' she said. 'I've had an idea. I'll go and see George Limb.'

She looked down at Sharkey. Suddenly he felt the blood leave his face.

The dead thing in his pocket had twitched.

Mama looked down in annoyance at the drain cover in the middle of the sloping floor. It always rattled in heavy rain, but this was –

'What in the name of –'

The drain cover exploded upward, hitting the stone roof above. From the drain poured … bugs. Little metal bugs. By the dozen. By the score.

Sharkey was yelling. 'Cybermats!' He leapt to his feet and screamed. The one in his pocket was biting into his thigh. A ring of razor-sharp metal incisors had harpooned through the lining of his jacket, through his clothes and embedded itself in his flesh. He tore at it in terror. It came away, still holding a lozenge of skin, blood, and muscle tissue.

Cybermats? Ace leapt onto the table. So *that's* what they were.

Sharkey collapsed on to the floor in pain. Staring, terrified, at the silver army erupting from the ground, he crawled back, further and further under the tables. It was Him. The little man had been right. Madness, ever to dream of defying Him. He knew every thought that was had in this city. Sharkey's head hit the wall. He had crawled on his back into a corner.

'Sharkey!' Ace yelled. She strained to see him beneath the tables. He was dead down there, she knew.

On the ground, equidistant between the whimpering, prostrate man and the advancing host, the broken, clinging-to-life Cybermat – wasn't that what he'd called it? – squirmed and writhed. It seemed to be trying to crawl towards its arriving swarm. They closed on it. They tore at it with their metal mandibles until nothing remained of their brother.

Then it began. Like a feeding frenzy. Scuttling and leaping, they swarmed across the bar. Sharkey screamed as a carpet of Cybermats flowed over him, tearing him to pieces. Ace leapt from table to table, trying to reach the cover of the heavy wooden bar. She could see in a blur customers falling, screaming as the Cybermats attacked. Charlie Parker on the jukebox died with them.

Behind the bar Mama swore under his breath and reached down for his baseball bat. A Cybermat sighted him at two yards and gathered itself to leap. As it launched itself across the bar he swung, sending the little killer flying across the room and into the far wall.

Mama spat into his hand and crouched ready for the next attack.

'Let's play ball,' he muttered.

Another flew at him. He swung. Another home run. A third. And then he heard a chittering to his left. A Cybermat was sitting on the bar next to him, gathering itself.

'Get out the way!' Ace leapt a good five feet from the last table on to the bar. Her feet skidded on the tatty flag spread across it; the flag rucked, and Ace shot down the length of the bar on her back. The Cybermat swung round in time to see her feet cannon into its face. With an electronic squawk it shot off the edge of the bar to the floor.

Ace collapsed behind the bulkhead of the bar, her fingers clinging to the edge of the flag.

'That's it, missy,' grinned Mama. 'You jus' take shelter behind the good ol' Stars 'n' Stripes.'

She hauled herself to her feet as a Cybermat hit the floor behind the bar. Before it could leap, Ace flailed at the rain-filled bucket on the bar. Barely gripping it, she swung it down, mouth first, on top of the Cybermat. She scanned the bar momentarily before hurling herself at the nearest beer keg and toppling it over on to the rattling bucket.

'I need a gun or something.'

'Under here.' Mama nodded down at the bar. 'I jus' got it for show, 'cause I'm a lousy shot. It's loaded, though.'

Ace grunted. A shotgun. She had never used a shotgun before. It would do. She swung the twin barrels out into the centre of the room, where the largest cluster of Cybermats was still concentrated, put the stock of the gun against her shoulder, and pulled back on both triggers. The pool of Cybermats scattered. All seemed momentarily confused.

Mama let out a whoop. Quickly Ace scanned the bar. Perhaps a dozen people were dead. Others had succeeded in running into the night. Many still crawled about the floor of the bar, clutching at gaping wounds. The Cybermats seemed to be losing interest in them. All were now beginning to close in on the bar, on Ace and Mama.

Oh, God, thought Ace.

'They're after me!'

'Say what?'

She broke the gun open. 'Have you got any more cartridges?'

'Same place.' He scooped a handful from under the bar.

Ace thrust a heavy cartridge into each chamber and snapped the gun shut. She thrust it at Mama.

'What? Aw, no… I hate these things,' he moaned.

'It's easy. Just point at the biggest group and pull. You saw what happened when I did it. They all froze up for a moment. It's like… the shock messes up their lines of communication, or something…'

She smiled to herself for a moment. The Doctor would have been proud of her.

'You fire. I'll jump the bar and leg it. They'll follow me, I think.'

'But –'

'Now! They're about to attack!'

Praying under his breath, Mama raised the gun, closed his eyes, and fired.

Ace bounded across the bar and leapt for the door. She had to put some serious space between her and them before they got their wires uncrossed. That would be about now. Her feet pelting against the road, she glanced behind her. Yes, the first of the swarm was scuttling out through the door.

She gritted her teeth, eyes wide, and tried to run faster. A glance back. They were gaining on her. She was exhausted. She had been attacked, chased, and nearly drowned for as long as she could remember. She was slowing down.

She swung left on to a major road, and her heart surged. London Transport to the rescue. A solid, red, double-decker London bus sat, engine purring, at the roadside. She felt obscurely happy. The future she knew and, in her tortured way, loved would survive. She would make sure of it.

Inside the bus she could see the silhouettes of passengers. She could feel the first of the Cybermats nipping at her heels. The bus began to pull away. She jumped, sailed through the open back of the vehicle and skidded to rest at the foot of the stairs.

Leaning back out of the bus she could see the Cybermats already coming to a halt, then turning and disappearing revoltingly into gutter-washed drains.

She turned. The passengers were all silent, staring at her. Mostly men, a few women. They were all in uniform.

'Wh-what's going on?' Ace asked nervously.

'ATS,' said one of the men sternly, rising to his feet. 'This isn't the number seventeen to Walthamstow, you know. We're on ack-ack duty. Did you really expect to catch a bus during an air raid?'

'Please,' said Ace, 'where are you going?'

'Well...' The man shuffled uneasily. 'Belsize Park, since you ask. We're going up on to Hampstead Heath.'

Ace smiled. Perfect. Peaceful Belsize Park. George Limb. Her final hope.

'But you can't stay on here,' the man continued. 'We shall have to stop.'

There was only one thing for it.

Surrendering to the inevitable, Ace collapsed into a heap on the floor of the moving bus.

CHAPTER 13

The passenger door was already open as the powerful, black police Rover screeched to a halt across the road from Mama's Bar; the Doctor was already half out of the car. They had endured a nightmare journey, the path of the bombs forcing them further and further north, away from Mama's. Mullen had tried over the radio to rustle up some other, closer units, with limited success. London was taking another pounding; there were casualties everywhere.

They, too, had felt the force of the explosion that had floored Ace. Mullen had struggled to keep control of the wheel.

'What in God's name was that?' he had sworn.

'Nothing to do with the Luftwaffe, I'll tell you that much, Inspector,' the Doctor had replied quietly.

The car had sped on through the night. Their attempts to navigate through the chaos were constantly thwarted; collapsed buildings, raging fires and floods from the fractured drains and sewers sent them weaving across chaotic, convulsing east London.

'It's like bloody snakes and ladders, this,' Mullen had said, performing another three-point turn in the road.

'Chess…' The Doctor had sounded half asleep. 'The pieces are in disarray, scattered across the board. The game plan is lost. The player who can find it first will be the winner. Order will come to the game on his terms.'

As they had approached the bar, roaring past McBride's seedy office, he had suddenly become alert. Out of the car now, he sprinted the last few yards to the bar, then stopped dead. The place was silent. The door swung open in the wind. Whatever had happened here was over.

Getting out of the driver's seat Mullen looked at his watch. Nearly two bloody hours it had taken.

The Doctor beckoned to Mullen. Slowly the two men sidled

along the windowless wall of the brick-and-tin shack built into the railway arch.

'The place should be much more lively than this,' whispered Mullen. 'Something's definitely… Christ!'

He leapt backward as the silence was split by a pair of rapid gunshots from inside the bar.

'Quickly!' Crouching low, holding his hat on his head, the Time Lord sprinted for the door, and cautiously peered round it.

'Oh dear, oh dear,' he tutted. 'Dreadful, dreadful.'

The Doctor and Mullen listened to Mama explain as they stared round the place in silence. The last of the ambulance crews had gone, taking away the dead and the wounded. The police had just left, promising to return when this insane night was over. They had helped dispose of the victims of the slaughter into the hands of the medics and the morticians, and taken a brief statement from Mama. It had had to be brief – the whole thing had lasted less than five minutes. Less than five minutes from when those things – those Cybermat things – had burst up through the drain to when they flowed en masse out of the door after the fleeing girl. Less than five minutes to do all this, to trash his bar, to leave maybe twenty people dead. The floor was awash with blood, furniture was overturned and broken, the jukebox was smashed.

Mama had surveyed the carnage with disbelief. He had slumped against the bar.

'Time,' he had said, for the first time in his professional life, 'gentlemen, please.'

A rattling at his feet had disturbed him. One of those metal rats was still here.

Under the bucket.

Carefully loading up the shotgun, rolling the beer barrel to one side, he had kicked out at the bucket with his foot. The thing had spun, and glared up at him.

Please, don't let me miss, he'd prayed, silently.

He had pulled the two triggers in rapid succession. Caught the thing right in its tin back. Point-blank range. The mechanical spine had shattered. The innards had been all but pulverised. Cyber-dogmeat.

Ace's passage across London that night had been much smoother than the Doctor's. The bus had danced and dodged, driven ahead of the bombs as it raced north to distribute its cargo of volunteer gunners. How much of the journey Ace had spent unconscious, as opposed to pretending to be unconscious, she wasn't sure. She had caused a stir when she fell, the passengers fluttering around her like black-winged moths. The women had been particularly flappy, refusing to hear any talk of putting her off the bus in the middle of all this. At their direction some of the men had lifted her on to one of the long bench-seats. Someone had pulled a blanket out of his bag, and this was now tucked around her.

Her sleep was short, but deep and black. The ATS woman had difficulty in shaking her awake. Slowly, engine roaring, the bus was drawing up a steep hill. It stopped. They had arrived. Disorientated for a moment, Ace stumbled out of the back of the bus. Her fellow passengers all seemed to be disappearing into a huge, wide pit in front of her. She walked forward until she was looking into the man-made excavation. At the centre of it sat the biggest piece of anti-aircraft artillery Ace had ever seen. Her friends were suddenly a team, orders barked out and responded to instantly, swarming like ants over the gun, arming, loading, angling skyward. She covered her ears against the deafening crump of ack-ack fire.

The sky was bright with fire, the ground lit up with it. Ace appeared to be standing on a huge hill. Behind her, trees and heathland sprawled away into orange darkness. Below her all London lay on fire. Small on the horizon she could see St Paul's, silhouetted darkly red against the light of even more distant fires. Fires on the Thames! A river of fire! Beyond the horizon, in her mind's eye, she could see the bridges, wreathed and canopied in flame.

Booming and flashing, way off to her left; the docks were copping it tonight...

Her eyes drank in the familiar city. Her city. The city that had dumped on her and those she cared about for as long as she could remember. She thought of the posh kids, the pigs, the bloody skins. Her city, but dying. Being cleansed. The thought of chattering government ministers, the law, the schools. What could they say to this? Did they think this could be contained? Authority had broken down there. Anarchy was at the reins.

And she loved it.

She wished her friends could be there to see it. Midge, Shreela, Manisha.

Manisha.

Burnt out by Nazis.

A man was shouting at her shoulder.

'You can't stay here.'

'No,' she said quietly. 'Which way is Belsize Park?'

'Straight down,' the man yelled.

She turned so that the lovely, lethal fire-ballet was at her back and trotted away down the path and into trees.

She had little difficulty finding George Limb's house. The heath path became a road, wandering south through Hampstead Village, until – she was sure – the darkened streets were looking more familiar to her.

She swung into one of the elegant, unlit Regency avenues. She was close now. Two streets down – a turning off to the left – there, half-way down the street. One house with a dim light burning in the front windows. So frail against the canopy of darkness, but warm, inviting.

She banged on the front door for several minutes before it gently opened.

'My word,' the old man exclaimed. 'What are you doing out on a night like this? Come in, come in.'

'I saw your light,' Ace said.

'I know.' He ushered her into the small back parlour. In the grate a fire cracked and spat. 'It's against regulations, but it's such a small light. We should all keep a light burning in our windows, for the lost traveller.' He sat her down. 'My dear, you look exhausted. Let me get you something to eat.'

She was too exhausted to argue. She allowed herself to doze while the old man pampered her, bringing her blankets, rolling a leather pouffe under her feet, serving her hot, weak tea and the warmed-up leftovers of his evening meal.

'Curry,' Ace remarked, surprised.

'Oh, yes,' George Limb had enthused. 'I love the cuisine of the Indian subcontinent. I only wish more of my countrymen had discovered its many delights. They will, I am sure. Given time…'

He had that faraway look in his eyes again.

'But, my dear, you must tell me…' He was suddenly lively again. 'You must tell me what brings you here. What adventures you have had tonight…'

Between breathless hot mouthfuls Ace let the last few days spill out of her. She was still starving. The soup she had eaten on the street had barely scratched at her hunger. She told of her breaking into the Peddler factory with McBride, about the Cybermen and her stowing away in their lorry, about the pumping station and the caretaker, about her escape through the sewers, about the attack on Mama's Bar.

'I'm afraid Sharkey's dead,' she said. 'He was a friend of yours, wasn't he?'

George Limb was silent for a moment. He blinked his sad, slow blink.

'Poor Sharkey,' he said. 'He never could look after himself properly.' He reached for the teapot. 'This calls for another cup of tea. These… Cybermen sound most formidable.'

'Yes…' Ace hesitated. Had she said too much? How could she, in London in 1940, possibly know about alien races and other planets? Anomalies. The Doctor was always warning her. It was dangerous to give information about the future, however vague, to even the most well-intentioned of people. Even a hint could change history.

She decided to concentrate on the matter in hand.

'George, we've got to do something! I've got to find the Doctor.'

'The only thing that you must do is rest.'

She slumped back in the chair. He was like something out of an old, black-and-white British B-movie.

'I'm afraid my telephone line here still isn't restored after the bomb. They won't do it just for me. But there is a public call box out on the main road. I shall go and telephone Mr McBride's office. If the Doctor isn't there I shall try Chief Inspector Mullen's police station. I shall be about twenty minutes. You try to sleep.'

And so she tried. She listened to George Limb clambering arthritically into an overcoat and scarf and shuffling out of the front door. It closed with a reassuring thud. She closed her eyes and tried to sleep.

She couldn't. Her ears were ringing, her senses were jumping. Behind her eyes she could see squirming pools of tiny Cybermats.

And the house was starting to give her the creeps. Ace had never been good in strange old houses. Somehow when George Limb was present the house had seemed aglow with warmth and faded gentility. In his absence it was beginning to seem merely old and creepy. The fire cast long, dancing, witch-finger shadows on to the walls and ceiling. She was starting to imagine she could hear noises. Footsteps, on other floors. How long had he been gone? What was that Cody had said about looters on the streets?

She reached into her rucksack and extracted her Walkman. Some music should soothe her troubled breast. Napalm Death – pirated off Darth – not ideal, but it would have to do. She had nothing else. Anything to drown out the whispers of this damned house.

Three frantic songs later the tape ended. Ace flipped it over in the little device. She stopped, finger paused on the play button. She hadn't imagined it. She could definitely hear muffled movement in the house.

Slinging her miniature headphones around her neck she cautiously opened the door and went out into the narrow, dimly lit passageway beyond. She edged out into the broad, spacious, shadowy hallway. The huge staircase beckoned to her. Gently she tested the front door. It wouldn't open – it was locked.

There it was again. A muffled thumping, followed by a heavy dragging sound.

Upstairs.

She thought of the back door. There must be one, she supposed, somewhere. Suppose that was locked, too. She thought of upstairs.

She couldn't help herself. Slowly she started to climb the ornate, elegant Regency staircase. The sound, clearer now, was still overhead. Another storey. The stairs were narrower here. At the top the landing split in two directions. There was a door to the left. That was where the noises were coming from.

She pressed her ear against the door. The heavy thuds, the dragging, had both stopped. What she could hear now was a slow, falteringly rhythmic wheeze. It sounded like somebody trying to breathe. Somebody old or dying.

She tried the door. Locked.

There was a key protruding from the lock in the door. It turned easily.

Slowly she peered into the pitch-black room. In the darkness she couldn't guess how far away the source of the sounds might be.

'Hello…' said Ace, timidly. 'Don't be frightened.'

Silently, she stepped into the room. It stank. It stank of rancid meat.

Behind her the door clicked shut. Panicking suddenly, she scrabbled at the wall for the light switch.

The rasping, harder now. The dragging, thumping sound again.

Coming closer.

Her fingers connected with the switch. The light came on, dazzling Ace for a moment.

And, with a gurgling, choking snarl, the Limehouse Lurker lunged.

PART THREE

CHAPTER 14

'A cell. For the second time in two days I was in a cell. Locked up again, only this time it was the military asking all the awkward questions, not the police, and they hadn't been so understanding about the Browning. I'd tried to impress upon them that I was a private detective involved in a heavy case, but was told that my licence was worth zilch, and that as far as the military were concerned I was up to my fedora in trouble. Breaking and entering, wilful destruction of property, probable espionage. I was in trouble, big time. And my hand still hurt like hell. Wherever they were, I was damn sure that the Doctor and Ace were having more fun than I was.'

'We're too late. Every move of the game, we're too late.'

The Doctor was once more pacing the already worn carpet of McBride's office.

Breathless from ascending the four flights of stairs, Mullen closed the door behind him and slumped into the private eye's chair. It was more comfortable than his own back at the station, he noted.

'Detective work's all about patience, Doctor. It's a waiting game.'

'We don't have the time, Inspector. People are one jump ahead of us; events are one jump ahead of us. We still haven't come anywhere near catching your Lurker. We still don't know where Wall is, and I still don't know whether Ace is safe.'

'We know she's alive, Doctor. Mr Washington told us that.'

The Doctor looked puzzled for a moment, then he smiled. 'Oh, Mama, you mean? Is that his name? Yes, it would appear that Ace is alive, no thanks to me.'

From his pocket he pulled the dead, buckshot-riddled Cybermat he had taken from Mama. The big American had wanted to put it on the wall when he reopened.

'First time I ever managed to shoot anything dead,' he had said.

The Doctor hefted it in his hand for a moment, staring into its torn casing.

'We're not even managing to keep this thing contained.' He placed it emphatically on the desk. 'What have you got for me, Inspector?'

'The names of the companies you asked for. The ones working in the same field as Peddler. And the address of the blood place. I've already sent some men there. They're fully armed. They know what to expect.'

'Excellent, Inspector.' The Doctor scanned the sheets of paper in front of him.

Advanced electrical and electronic engineering. A highly specialised field, particularly in 1940. Six names, Peddler's among them. Jocelyn & Co., Midlands Electric, Daniel International, Peddler Electronic Engineering, Lemur Engineering, Vital Systems Corporation. Six names. He was assuming a lot. That Wall and his henchmen had brought the Cybermats with them, for instance, but it was just as possible they had made them over the last few days in hiding. That they had previously been based on British soil, yet it was just as possible that they had come from overseas.

He looked down at the dead Cybermat on the desk. No. That at least was unlikely. He had spent the time waiting for Mullen probing about the creature's insides. This one had originally been a squirrel. A red squirrel. These Cybermats were made on Earth. And, very likely, the British Isles. Made in England.

He placed the Cybermat carefully back in his pocket.

'Well, Inspector,' he said leadenly, walking towards the door, thrusting Mullen's pristine leaves of paper roughly into his pocket, 'what are we waiting for?'

He knew what he was waiting for. He cast a backward glance at the telephone. He had made Ace take the number: why didn't she use it?

Ah, well, too much to do, Ace. Another time. Ciao.

The telephone rang. The Doctor pushed back past Mullen and grabbed the receiver.

'Yes…'

He was silent for a long minute.

Then, 'I'm on my way.'

He slammed down the phone and marched past the chief inspector and down the stairs.

'Was it her?' Mullen puffed behind him. He really should be fitter, in his job.

'Yes and no,' the Doctor replied. 'Two things I want you to do, Inspector. First, I want you to find out what's happening with your friend the Lurker, find out what's going on at that blood collection centre. Second, I want you to get Cody McBride out of Lazonby's clutches.'

'Impossible, Doctor,' Mullen replied.

'Inspector…' The Doctor was in no mood to be trifled with. 'We are facing an implacable and, frankly, at the moment inscrutable enemy. We need every scrap of information we can get our hands on. Cody McBride has seen the Cybermen at close quarters. I need to talk to him.'

'What are you going to do, Doctor?'

'I have to see a man. That was him on the phone. He has Ace with him. She's safe. He also says he has some information, which he refuses to discuss with anyone but me. He won't tell me what it is over the telephone.'

He fished his hat from his pocket and clamped it on his head.

'Clever, for a human. I'm going to need to borrow your car.'

They were on the street. Mullen already had the keys in his hand. Before he could react the Doctor had snatched them from his grasp. He dodged past the policeman and into the driver's seat, gunned the engine and lurched forward.

'You can't…! Where are you going?' Mullen was grappling for the door handle.

'Belsize Park,' the Doctor called. 'Clever man, name of George Limb.'

He roared off into the night. Mullen beckoned feebly after him.

'But how am I going to…?'

* * *

A face of blistered, scabrous metal. Wide, weeping holes for eyes. A mouth eaten by corrosion into a loopy, deranged grin.

The huge, grinning head crashed down upon Ace. With a yell she threw herself to the floor as two hydraulic arms crashed in empty air. She rolled around the thing's legs and sprinted for the wall. Anything to put a bit of distance between her and it.

It turned. Slowly. Jerkily.

Its torso was partly tangled up in a huge, filthy, torn length of tarpaulin which flapped and wound about its feet. One of its legs dragged behind it. One arm thrashed erratically. Half of its side was blown away; tubes hung leaking from inside its body. Blood – human blood, congealed, thick – had been roughly smeared over many of its broken joints. Tendrils of human flesh were still attached to its cracked breastplate.

It was dying.

Ace watched, fascinated and repulsed. She had seen Cybermen die before – she'd even killed a few herself – but this was entirely different.

Pathetic. Revolting.

Sad.

The setting merely added to the agonising pathos. The room, bare of furniture, was prinked out in a pink floral wallpaper design, tiny delicate flowers, faded with age. The curtains, drawn across the window, attempted the same drab floral optimism. The carpet was darkly floral. Disease shuffled towards her across a bed of roses.

A part of her wanted to be sick; a part to reach out and touch the thing. It stopped in front of her, swaying slightly. She extended a cautious hand...

With a visceral snarl it lunged, huge arms flailing and closing. Again, Ace tried to dive, but the Cyberman was moving faster now. A metal glove caught her a glancing blow to the head. Dazed, white-blind for a moment, she scuttled across the floor like a Cybermat. The Cyberman swung an arm; she rolled, and felt a metal hand full of her hair ripping at the scalp.

There was nothing in here to fight the monster with. She darted towards the door and grabbed at the handle. The door didn't budge.

It was locked.

Again she had to dive to avoid the lunging Cyberman. Again she rolled around its crippled legs. Even in this state it could easily wear her down. She only had to tire a little.

The Cyberman lurched forward, then stopped. Turning, it had managed to get its good leg tangled in the lengths of tarpaulin. It twisted, trying to free itself. Ace grabbed at a corner of the filthy oilcloth and pulled with all her strength. The already off-balance Cyberman crashed to the floor. Ace leapt over its thrashing body and threw back the curtains. She strained to lift the heavy sash frame. It was stuck. No. Nailed. She ripped the Walkman from her jacket pocket and hammered at the glass.

She stopped. It was hopeless. She could see that, outside in the darkness, the window was barred.

The Cyberman was on its feet, lurching towards her.

There was a loud click. The door to the room swung open. Ace's heart surged. Mr Limb.

She leapt towards the door. There was a figure in front of her. A figure she didn't recognise. Tall, blond, dressed in black.

He was laughing.

She landed at his feet. With a leer he thrust her roughly to the ground in the path of the advancing killer. From behind him he brandished a wooden pole, about five feet in length. Ace recognised it as an old, carved standard lamp, the base and the shade missing. Where the bulb should have been two metal prongs stuck viciously out. An electric flex snaked out through the door.

He jabbed at the Cyberman with it. The Cyberman lurched backward with an electronic howl. He jabbed again. He was driving the Cyberman back into the far corner of the room. Again and again he jabbed, holding the rod to the Cyberman's fractured chest unit. The alien voice box exploded in a scream of circuitry.

And fell silent.

Ace was standing when the man turned to regard her.

'Th-thanks,' she said. 'You saved my –'

'Please,' interrupted the man curtly, 'no clichés.'

Slowly, casually scrutinising her, the man paced around Ace in a leisurely circle, hands clasped behind his back.

'Yes,' he said to himself, 'I see…'

What was his accent? Dutch? German? He was about thirty. Powerfully muscled. Walked like a soldier. A German soldier.

He reached out and touched her bomber jacket, running its material through his fingers.

'Look, who are you?' she asked.

He snapped to attention.

'Captain Hartmann. And you,' he replied, 'are Ace.'

'Where's George?' Ace asked, suddenly frightened. 'What have you done to him?'

He didn't reply. He was staring at the Walkman, still clutched in her hand. With a catlike movement he snatched it from her.

He examined it for a moment and, with a satisfied grunt, began jabbing at the buttons. The little machine began to record.

'What is the function of this machine?' he barked.

'You're the master race,' Ace replied quietly. 'You tell me.'

'I will ask you only once more,' Captain Hartmann whispered.

He meant it.

'First tell me what you did with Mr Limb.'

He told her.

Ace let out a wail. No! That sweet old man.

She lashed out at the Teutonic face grinning down at her. Hartmann deflected her blow with ease. The Walkman fell to the ground and cracked open, its cassette skidding away from the machine.

Ace shot a glance down at the tape. Somebody must be told. The Doctor must be told. With another yell she flung herself at him, kicking the tape into a corner of the room as she did so. He floored her with one punch. The last thing she saw as she tried to clear her head was the man swinging something towards her. The lamp. His home-made cattle prod.

She felt her whole body lurch. She tingled horribly, sickeningly, all over for a brief moment, then London's blackout enfolded her.

Hartmann looked across at the prostrate Cyberman. Let the old man keep his monster. It was practically dead. It was the girl his masters were interested in.

He dragged the unconscious Ace from the room and switched off the light.

CHAPTER 15

The heavy wooden front door of George Limb's house opened slowly.

'Doctor, come in, please, come in.'

The old man seemed shaken.

'Mr Limb, are you all right?' asked the Doctor.

'I have some rather worrying news for you, Doctor. Most perplexing, most perplexing.'

'Ace…' said the Doctor.

George Limb nodded and began shuffling towards a side door.

'I'm afraid since I telephoned you the situation has changed somewhat. I had to go further than I anticipated to make the call. On my way back I had the misfortune to encounter some ruffians. I took evasive action – evidently they were intent on using their fists rather than their brains – and returned to the house. I found the front door ajar, and our young friend gone.'

'Gone?'

'Vanished into the night, Doctor.'

The Doctor slumped against the banister rail.

'Always one step behind. We're still playing catch-up, Mr Limb.'

He drew himself erect; a small, inoffensive man with lightning in his eyes.

'Somebody is playing games with me, Mr Limb. And I don't like it.'

Suddenly he was brisk, businesslike.

'You said you had some other information for me.'

'Yes,' the old man replied. 'I fear I have been irresponsible, Doctor. I fear I might have unwittingly brought misfortune on to young Ace's head. Perhaps on to all our heads.'

He turned at the foot of the stairs.

'After your previous visit it dawned on me that there must be a central collection point for the blood. I have friends in many walks of life, Doctor, and it was relatively easy for me to discover the location of the facility, as it was for me to procure some bags of blood plasma.'

'Mr Limb, you're surely not telling me –'

'I fear so, Doctor. I intercepted the… creature at the centre and used the blood plasma to lure it into the back of a lorry I had hired for the occasion.'

'And you brought it back here?'

'Yes.'

'So where is it, Mr Limb? Where is it?'

George Limb began climbing the grand staircase.

'Well, naturally, I put it in the guest room,' he said.

George Limb stopped outside the room that contained the Cyberman.

'Oh, dear,' he muttered. The door stood slightly open. 'This door was locked, I'm certain. I hope Ace didn't decide to explore up here.'

He pushed the door open and stepped into the shadows.

'You didn't tell her about this?'

'No, Doctor. The young lady seemed to have gone through enough. Besides, how does one speak of the unspeakable?'

Light filled the room.

The Cyberman lay, motionless, against the far wall. The only sound it made was a low, continuous hiss, like the escape of gas.

The Doctor scurried across the room and squatted in front of it.

'Yes, it's as I thought. Its immune system has packed up. Couldn't cope. Hmm… It's a Cyberleader.'

'A Cyber… leader?' George Limb stood over the Doctor.

'Yes…' said the Doctor thoughtfully. 'Different design. Different markings. You can tell from what's left of its head. But what was it doing here?'

'I must say,' said George Limb, 'I feel perfectly dreadful about my hand in all this. I fear of late I have been… a little obsessive about the Lurker. Ever since I had my intuition about what it might be.' He shook his head sadly. 'An old man's tomfoolery. Trying to catch a monster, indeed.'

'A remarkable achievement, Mr Limb. Particularly in someone of your... that is... how old are you?'

'Seventy-eight last month,' George Limb replied. 'And your words are very gracious, Doctor. But nonetheless I feel as if I have meddled in things that man should leave alone. I feel like Dr Jekyll, Doctor. I feel like Dr Frankenstein. I even have my own monster. I feel like a penny-dreadful character in a cheap novel.'

'I don't suppose,' the Doctor smiled, 'you would have a workshop or laboratory in the house, Dr Frankenstein?'

'The cellar!' The Doctor clapped his hands. 'Where else?'

Between the two of them they had just dragged the Cyberleader down three flights of stairs. George Limb leaned against the wall, struggling for breath. The cellar was long and narrow, and poorly lit.

'There isn't much here, Doctor,' Limb apologised. 'I haven't pursued an active scientific life for many a long year.'

'This will do very well,' the Doctor replied. 'We have the main requirement for our little experiment.'

He slapped the long wooden workbench which sat in the middle of the room.

'Our monster has his slab.'

They heaved the Cyberleader on to the bench, the Doctor struggling to keep the torso together, Limb barely able to lift the tree-trunk legs.

'Now,' the Doctor said to the wheezing, groaning man next to him, 'a drip. I take it you have some blood plasma left.'

Still hunched and gasping, George Limb opened an old wooden sideboard that stood in the corner. He fished out a bag of blood.

'We need to set up a drip of some kind,' the Doctor said.

'I...' George Limb croaked. 'I was going to set up a drip for the creature, Doctor, but it was still too active. It smashed up anything within its reach. I still have the equipment.'

'Excellent! Electrical components!'

'Electrical components?'

'Potentiometers. A variable resistor.'

'You're going to build a transformer, Doctor!'

'A transformer. Yes, I am. Components, Mr Limb.'

Suddenly active again, George Limb dragged an old cardboard box from a shelf.

'Lipton's,' said the Doctor, peering at the faded side of the box.

He rummaged around inside. His face lit up.

'Mr Limb, this isn't an old tinned-fruit box. This is Aladdin's cave!'

The old man was struggling to drag a large metal frame across the floor. Like a grown-up rediscovering his childhood toys, the Doctor let his fingers play among the knobs and valves. He stopped. His face became serious.

'Mr Limb, this is perfect. Ace would have loved this.'

With reverential care he lifted from the bottom of the box a grey-painted metal case surmounted by two knobs, a large metal switch, and a single coloured light. Hornby-Dublo was stamped along its side.

'Frankenstein, you see,' said the Doctor, 'had to wait around until there happened to be an electrical storm. Frankenstein wasn't on the mains, Mr Limb. He called upon the power of the Gods, but he couldn't call upon the power of the London Electricity Board.'

He was squatting above a mains socket, set low in the wall. In his hand he held an electrical plug, the lead from which trailed across the floor in the direction of the workbench.

'Whereas we –' he thrust the plug into the socket – 'can!'

At the head of the bench George Limb stood next to the drip and watched the blood-engorged bag leak its contents down a rubber tube into the neck of the inert Cyberleader.

The Doctor scampered to the side of the bench.

'The nine-fifteen for Swansea is now departing from platform ten, calling at Reading, Swindon, Bristol Parkway, Newport, Cardiff, Bridgend, Port Talbot, Neath and... Swansea! Do you like the seaside, Mr Limb?'

'Doctor, really!'

The old model railway transformer lay partly dismantled in front of the Time Lord. With the addition of an alarming array of metal wire and a large, fortuitous block of iron the Doctor had transformed the sturdy, safe-in-the-hands-of-children exemplar of pre-war British engineering into something much more powerful and much more dangerous. Wires billowed from the back of the casing, snaking to different points on the Cyberleader's body.

He tripped the large metal switch. The single coloured light shone.

'I have to get it precisely right,' said the Doctor. 'He needs a very precise current to keep him alive. Too much and I kill him. Too little and he dies anyway.'

'Yes, Doctor...' George Limb sounded perturbed. 'I've been wanting to ask you: in what sense can we consider him – it – alive?'

'Cybernetics, Mr Limb. I shouldn't be telling you, but under the circumstances I think you have a right to know what we're dealing with.'

'Cybernetics?'

'The science of the interface of men and machines. The point at which the organic and inorganic worlds meet and fuse.'

George Limb rubbed his hands with excitement. 'So this thing is half mechanical, half organic. I suspected as much. But why?'

'Efficiency, Mr Limb. Blind, ruthless efficiency. What it really means is the final parasitisation of the living world by the mechanical.'

The old man blinked his strange, slow blink.

'There!'

A regular, slow hum, almost inaudible, came from the Cyberleader's chest.

'Now... notebook and pen, please.'

The Doctor had removed what remained of the face plate from the Cyberleader's head. Two wires connected the Cyber-brain to a slim plastic readout pad on the edge of the bench. With a small screwdriver he began making tiny adjustments inside the open head.

'Difficult... Got to... access the memory circuits. If there's anything left of them.'

He held the screwdriver out to George Limb.

'Mr Limb, when I tell you to do so I would like you to connect these two little elements with the screwdriver.' He licked the nib of the pen. 'Now, please.'

The old man gently inserted the screwdriver into the twisted mass of strange electronics and brain tissue. Numbers burbled across the readout screen. The Doctor scribbled furiously.

'Stop!' he would bark from time to time, and then, 'Again!' – all the time his hands filling the page with lightning-fast, unreadable characters.

A sudden, high-pitched electronic burble from the head made him start. George Limb snatched the screwdriver away in alarm.

'What was that?' the old man asked.

'I'm not sure...' Pensively the Doctor tapped the end of his pen against his lower lip. 'It sounded like some kind of signal. I think we must have accidentally triggered it. A signal... Hmm... But to what?'

He returned his attention to the notepad.

'Ah, well, it's stopped now. I hope.'

'Doctor...' George Limb tugged at the Time Lord's sleeve.

The transformer was starting to glow alarmingly.

The screwdriver was suddenly snatched from the old man's clutch as if by some invisible hand. A burst of digital chittering momentarily squawked from the head.

'What was that?' The Doctor peered into the wrecked brain.

'I think the thing's overloading, Doctor.'

The Doctor grabbed at the lead that trailed from the back of the transformer to the wall, and yanked. The whole setup groaned into lifelessness.

He looked down at the Cyberleader.

'I think that's our lot,' he said.

scanning>
scanning>
signal detected>
activate>
locate signal source> signal source located>
signal source erratic> estimated distance two miles>
scan for hostile life forms> negative>
signal source fading> unable to compute route>
unable to proceed>
shut down> maintain low-level scan>

'But there's so much missing,' the Time Lord sighed. 'Huge amounts of the memory were just erased as he stumbled around the city. He probably didn't even know who he was. An innocent.'

He was sitting in the front room at George Limb's huge oak table, the chess set at his back.

'The killings are all here, in garbled fashion,' the Doctor continued. 'Poor wretches. And before that... It seems that fate has been kind to us after all. He was section leader for a proposed army of sleepers.'

'Sleepers?' George Limb set a tray of tea down on the table.

'Dormant Cybermen, waiting to be revived on a received signal. His job was to prepare for the arrival of the sleepers. To find a secure hiding place for them and to guard that hiding place from intruders. He was killing people even before this Lurker business, Mr Limb. He was just doing it less spectacularly.'

The Doctor idly rotated the saucer of the teacup that had just been placed in front of him.

'The Peddler factory is my guess.'

'What?'

'The proposed location for the sleeper army. Given that I'm sure Peddler knew Wall before their meeting.'

'Doctor –' George Limb was shaking his head slowly – 'where did they come from? Why are they here?'

'A very good question. According to our metal friend they came here from the far future as a result of a time-travel experiment.'

'Doctor… time travel…' The old man's eyes were alight.

'Time travel, yes,' the Doctor snapped, irked at the interruption. 'I thought they had evolved themselves again. It seems that their grasp of time-travel technology in the thirtieth century still isn't up to much. They're stranded here Mr Limb. Earth, 1940.'

'This is really… well… it's all too much, Doctor.'

'Are you saying you don't believe me?'

'No, no,' Limb expostulated. 'Not at all, Doctor. Please, go on.'

'They did what they usually do when their numbers are low. They set up a production plant. They started turning humans into Cybermen on their filthy machines.'

'It's difficult to imagine, Doctor.' Limb sounded aghast.

'It's not so difficult, Mr Limb. Look at what's going on in Europe. And it's barely begun over there, believe me. The real horrors are yet to come.'

'I tend to agree, Doctor. I had ample opportunity to study the rise of Herr Hitler when I was at the Foreign Office. Domination by conquest will never be enough for him, no matter how many victories he wins. He will always have to find another enemy. I honestly believe the man will stop at nothing until he has destroyed the world.'

'And if he gets his hands on Cybertechnology he probably will. You see what we're up against, Mr Limb. Quite apart from the Cybermen themselves.'

'A future technology has arrived in our midst. With all that that promises and threatens,' Limb rhapsodised.

'At the moment there's not much in the way of promise. The threats are overwhelming. A future technology has arrived in our midst in the middle of a war. All sides are desperate for victory…'

'No side will hesitate to inflict the full force of this new technology on its enemy. I know. One of the things you notice in the service of government is how history speeds up during times of conflict. Another is how scruples go out of the window. In truth, that is why I left the civil service, Doctor. That is why I kidnapped the beast. That is why I have told no one else about this, Doctor. Not even Ace.'

'You're a brave man, Mr Limb,' said the Doctor. 'And far-sighted. In one way, though, the war is helpful to us.' George Limb blinked questioningly. 'As I said, fate has been kind. The Luftwaffe very obligingly dropped a bomb on our friend the Cyberleader. That's what turned it into your Lurker. The bomb half killed it, destroyed its memory banks and severed it from communication from the main Cyberforce. Hence the sudden appearance of Mr Wall and associates. The Luftwaffe have unwittingly sabotaged the Cybermen's plans. We have to stop them setting up again. And stop His Majesty's government getting their grubby little paws on them.'

The Doctor closed his writing pad. 'The bomb marks the last piece of coherent data. From there it's all a terrible mess.' He scratched his head. 'But there's still so much missing. We still don't know where he was sent from. We still don't know where the main Cyberforce is based. We still can't explain the colossal explosions.'

'Explosions?'

'There was one earlier tonight. Even over the sound of the bombing, you couldn't miss it. It nearly blew us off the road.'

'And you think that that may be connected to the Cybermen?'

'Well, of course it is, Mr Limb. Nothing produced on Earth could make a bang like that. Not for a very few years yet, anyway And there's something else.'

'I am all ears, Doctor,' said Limb between decorous sips of tea.

'The Cybermen are in disarray at the moment. British Military Intelligence in this age, as in most others, is run by paranoid incompetents; the same is true, only more so, of our enemy across the Channel. And yet I sense an intelligence at work, hovering somewhere in the background. I don't know what it is, but I know it's playing games with me. I can't fathom its nature. At best it is mischievous; at worse, malevolent, reptilian.'

He sprang to his feet.

'Thank you for the tea, Mr Limb.'

The Doctor's cup sat exactly where George Limb had placed it, full and untouched, only colder.

'There is much to be done. The cellar!'

He marched from the room. George Limb finished his third cup of tea and slowly followed him. By the time the old man reached the foot of the stairs the Doctor was engaged in the intricate task of removing the Cyberleader's head from its body.

'Do you have a hammer and chisel, Mr Limb?' he asked.

By the time he left the old man's house the Doctor had the Cyberleader's head in an old tweed bag. He had painstakingly disconnected a jungle of wires, plugs and circuits and chiselled through the more obstinate of the clamps that held the head to the body.

'The Peddler factory,' he had muttered repeatedly under his breath.

Finally, he had hefted the head from the body.

'I'll be back to dispose of the rest of the Cyberleader later, but for now I would suggest you answer the door to no one, and keep out of the cellar. I'm afraid I have to leave you.'

And with that the singular little man had strolled out of the front door, climbed into the driver's seat of a large black police car and driven away.

George Limb had closed the door and stood several moments in thought. This had turned out to be quite a day. What he needed was a nice cup of tea.

CHAPTER 16

The Doctor pushed open the door of McBride's office and peered inside.

'Hello? Inspector?'

The room was dark and empty. 'Hm. Nobody here but us time travellers.'

He snapped on the light and dumped the bag with the Cyberleader's head in it on McBride's desk. The office was still a shambles from his earlier tussle with the Cybermat. The thing that had been the death of Sharkey. He made a mental note: before he left this time period he would have to make sure that he gathered up all the errant pieces of Cybertechnology.

He pulled the Cyberleader's head from the bag and extricated it from the newspaper that George Limb had wrapped it in. The Doctor smiled. George had packaged it as if it was a portion of fish and chips. He stood for a moment holding the silver head in his outstretched hands, looking for all the world as if he was about to deliver the soliloquy from *Hamlet*.

The head glinted in the moonlight. The technology was quite, quite beautiful. The Doctor sighed. So many of the races that he pitted himself against were such brilliant creatures. The Daleks were masters of the most incredible technology, the Sontarans superb geneticists. The science that had been used to create the Cybermen was quite awesome: to be able to take any organ in the humanoid body and repair or replace it, to have the ability to create a fusion of mechanical and organic components, both working in perfect harmony. Here and now, in war-torn Britain, that science could save hundreds of thousands of lives, and he had to make sure that no one ever had the possibility of getting hold of it.

He wondered how the first Cybermen must have felt, waking up to be confronted with a blank metal sheet that had once been a face capable of producing tears and laughter. Did the

155

first Cyber-engineers know that the removal of emotion would result in their total dedication to power and conquest? The Doctor traced a finger around the corroded eye socket, with its teardrop-like indentation. Someone in the distant past of this ancient race must have known what would come from their cybernetic experimentation, someone who had made this painful reminder of the Cybermen's humanoid roots.

The Doctor placed the head on the desk and dropped into a chair, resting his chin on steepled fingers. What had happened to that scientist of conscience? Had he, too, been turned into one of these remorseless silver creatures? Had he been one of the countless Cybermen that the Doctor had destroyed over the centuries? The Doctor tapped the Cyberleader's head with his forefinger. 'Could it even be you?' he murmured.

His ears pricked up at the sound of McBride's creaking staircase. More than one set of footsteps. The unmistakable sound of British army boots. The Doctor hurriedly pushed the Cyberleader's head back into the tweed bag that Limb had given him as the door crashed open.

A dozen soldiers stormed into the office, surrounding the Doctor, their rifles levelled at his head. The Doctor raised his hands, slowly. These men were on a knife-edge, and he'd been in enough similar situations to known that any clowning about on his part at this moment was liable to get him shot.

Lazonby appeared at the door, a smug smile playing under his moustache. Behind him, Mullen lurked on the landing. The Doctor raised a quizzical eyebrow and the chief inspector looked down at his shoes. 'I'm sorry, Doctor.'

Lazonby strode into the office and snatched the bag from the desk. He peered into it and smiled. 'Well, Doctor. How nice of you to provide some hard evidence for us.'

The Doctor kept his hands in the air. 'Evidence of what?'

'Of being a spy! You are accused of passing on government secrets to enemies of the Crown. Take him away!'

The Doctor was seized by two of the soldiers and marched

out of the office. He called back at Lazonby over his shoulder. 'You are dealing with forces that you cannot possibly comprehend, Major!'

Lazonby was oblivious. He pulled the gleaming head of the Cyberleader out of the tweed bag, his eyes wide. He held it aloft like a trophy.

'Perfection. Absolute perfection.'

It was cold and dark at the back of the pumping station, although Wall neither felt the cold nor feared the dark. He was hunting. He moved silently across the black concourse towards his prey. An old man, just standing there, waiting. Easy. Almost too easy.

He could see the man with perfect clarity in the dark. The man could not see him at all. Wall enjoyed the sensation of being so close to the man that their skin was almost touching. Breathing gently on him. Allowing his lips to brush against the old man's hair.

In his hand Wall held a cigarette lighter. He had tweaked and lengthened the wick in order to produce the largest flame possible. Let there be light. He triggered the lighter between the old man's face and his own. Four inches of flame speared upward and danced there.

The man started slightly as the ghostly, pudgy face – eyes twin discs of darkness – smiled in the glow, mere inches from his own face. Quickly, he recovered his composure.

'Who are you?' cooed Wall softly.

'A friend, I hope…' answered George Limb.

The Doctor was bundled without ceremony into the back of an army truck which roared away in a rush of spray. He sat surrounded by half a dozen fresh-faced soldiers. The Doctor sighed. The currency of war. He smiled at the soldier opposite him, but the lad remained stony-faced.

'You do realise that your Major Lazonby is quite deranged?'

157

The young private shuffled uncomfortably in his seat. The Doctor turned his attention to the soldier next to him.

'Is Lazonby a popular man?'

Another embarrassed shuffle. Despite his calm demeanour, the Doctor was becoming increasingly worried. He had to get away from Lazonby, find Ace and get the Cybertechnology out of this time period and, at the moment, he didn't know quite how he was going to do it.

The journey wasn't a long one and the truck soon pulled to a juddering halt. The Doctor was prodded out into the evening air. A drab, faceless building loomed over him. He smiled, grimly. One of the many Military Intelligence buildings that were scattered over London. He had been in enough of them during his time as UNIT's scientific adviser to recognise the type.

A rifle butt prodded him in the small of the back and he was pushed through the double doors. He was shepherded through a maze of corridors to a small, plain room, empty save for a table and a scattering of chairs. 'Oh, dear. This doesn't look very inviting.'

The soldier behind him gestured with the muzzle of his rifle. 'Inside, please, sir.'

The Doctor stepped into the room and drew his finger over the top of the table. It came up thick with dust. 'You could have cleaned up a bit if you knew that you were expecting guests.'

The door slammed and the Doctor's temper finally broke. 'I haven't got time for this! You are all in terrible danger!' He slumped into one of the wooden chairs. 'And I still haven't found Ace.'

The Doctor looked at his pocket watch. It had been exactly twelve hours since he had been locked up. He had paced the cell for a while, then realised that no one was going to bother with him until the morning. He had pulled from his pocket the scrawled list of electronics factories Mullen had given him and looked at it until he feared he would stare a hole through the paper. Jocelyn & Co., Midlands Electric, Daniel International, Peddler Electronic Engineering, Lemur Engineering, Vital Systems Corporation. To amuse himself he had read the list upside down, back to front. He had folded the paper into an aerodynamic shape not yet conceived of by engineers on this planet and tossed it about the cell, casually catching it as, invariably, it returned to him. He had played word games with the names. Constructed elaborate anagrams. Simultaneously translated the names into five hundred languages.

Interesting.

The timing would have been about right. It would make perfect sense…

Perhaps he was getting somewhere after all. If only he could get out of this cell.

Ah, well…

Secreting the list carefully inside his hat, pulling the table into the centre of the room, he had clambered on to it, tucking his legs underneath him in the lotus position, and dropped into a deep sleep, letting his brain sift and assimilate all the events of the previous day.

He had snapped awake at the sound of boots in the hallway. If Lazonby was doing things by the book then…

A key ground into the lock. The Doctor snapped his watch shut, slipped it into his pocket, and hopped from the table, watching the door, expectantly. The door of his cell had opened and an officious little man in a pin-striped suit had entered. The Doctor had caught a glimpse of armed guards outside the door as it swung shut.

The suited man had opened a notebook, had insisted that the Doctor empty his pockets, and mumbled something to the effect that they really should have done this earlier, when he'd been brought in. Grinning broadly, the Doctor had proceeded to remove every apple core and sweet wrapper, every piece of string and useless bit of junk from the capacious pockets of his jacket, simultaneously slipping every bit of anachronistic technology out of sight, his sleight of hand as polished as that of a well-rehearsed magician.

The officious clerk had left the cell an hour later, his notebook stained with apple juice, sweet wrappers stuck to his suit and a half-eaten stick of rhubarb in his hand, none the wiser as to who the Doctor was, or where he came from.

And so the day had gone on: an endless procession of faceless military officials, all asking endless military questions, all jotting down the Doctor's decidedly unmilitary replies, no matter how bizarre. The Doctor had always prided himself on his ability to bamboozle the opposition. He had hoped that by being so uncooperative with this stream of middlemen, the man he really wanted to see – Lazonby – would eventually be forced to deal with him personally.

The Doctor pulled out his pocket watch again. It was late in the afternoon. Outside a hostile alien force was planning to... The Doctor frowned. That was just the point. He didn't know what they were planning to do, and he wasn't going to find out locked up in a cell. He snapped his watch shut, irritably, and paced around the table. He had been the perfect uncooperative guest – surely Lazonby would have to get around to him soon.

With perfect timing a key scraped into the lock again, and Lazonby strode into the room, immaculate as always. The perfect officer. The Doctor watched as he took off his cap, placing it on the table and smoothing back his hair. He pulled down the jacket of his uniform, straightening the creases, and settled into one of the chairs.

'Sit down, Doctor. It is time that you and I had a little chat.'

'Yes.' The Doctor pulled up a chair opposite Lazonby. 'I'd rather like to know what you've done with that head that you took from me.'

The young officer smiled. 'It's being well looked after.'

The Doctor leaned across the desk, his eyes drilling into Lazonby's. 'You really have no idea what you are dealing with.'

'Rubbish! The scientists that we have assembled here are

some of the finest minds in Britain. I'm more concerned with how the Germans have managed to catch up with our research so quickly. No doubt the secrets that you and your accomplices have been passing on to your Nazi paymasters have been of great benefit.'

The Doctor snorted, contemptuously. 'Is that what you think I am? A Nazi spy? Believe me, Major, the paltry scientific research of your war effort is of no interest to me whatsoever. I am concerned with a far greater problem.'

Lazonby regarded the little man slouched on the other side of the table, a shambolic patchwork of paisley and question marks. His clothes were all slightly too large and from a dozen different styles, his hair was unruly and his smile was crooked. An agent of chaos. An enemy of the Crown. Lazonby clenched his fist. He would happily order the execution of this vagrant now, were it not for the head. There was still the question of the head.

Lazonby knew that scientists didn't always cherish the same ideal of order, knew that sometimes, from chaos, leaps of intuition were possible. Lazonby didn't like that harsh fact of life, but he wasn't so regimented that he would ignore it either. He looked at the Doctor again, his eyes narrowing. What scientific knowledge did this man possess? If there was any possibility that this little tramp could help them unlock the secrets of that silver head... He had to know.

'Where did that head come from?'

The Doctor paused, unsure of how much of the truth to tell this strange young army officer. There was a fanatical glint in his eye that worried the Doctor. A glint that he was all too familiar with, but, at the same time, that fanaticism was likely to make him susceptible to ideas, to suggestions.

'Tell me, Major, do you believe in life on other planets?'

Lazonby gave a short, barking laugh. 'Don't be preposterous, Doctor. I am well aware of the hysteria that that young actor, Welles, perpetrated in America the other year, but that sort of nonsense isn't going to happen here. The Americans are well known for their flights of fancy.'

'Really. Whereas stubborn, pig-headed pomposity is the sole prerogative of the British, I suppose. We don't believe it, therefore it must be wrong. What a wonderfully unbalanced way of looking at the world.'

The blow caught the Doctor completely by surprise, and sent him spinning from his chair. He had been aware that his interrogation was likely to get physical, but the ferocity and suddenness of Lazonby's attack was totally unexpected.

The Doctor clambered back into his chair, wiping a trickle of blood from the corner of his mouth. Lazonby had both hands stretched out flat in front of him, frowning at the redness where the knuckles of his right hand had connected with the Time Lord's jaw. As the Doctor watched, Lazonby began to rub the back of his other hand against the edge of the table until it too was as red and sore as its partner. He held both hands back out in front of him and smiled at the uniformity.

'I am not a man prone to belief in the fantastic and the fabulous, like our American cousins, Doctor. The British army could win this war, with precision, and with a positive mental attitude, but the leaders of this country are weak. They don't understand the need for harsh discipline, for a properly regimented fighting force.'

The Doctor frowned. Lazonby was verging on the psychotic. That, and the position he held, made him a very dangerous man. He would have to try another approach. He kept his voice low and calm.

'Major Lazonby, the Nazis, despite all their hatred and aggression, are like amateurs compared to the terror that is facing you. The creature whose head you now possess is one of a race of aggressors to whom the weapons of war of this world look like children's toys. The Cybermen –'

'Are man-made, Doctor. As well you know!' Lazonby sprang to his feet, his face purple with rage. 'The Germans have managed to perfect the battle armour that Peddler was working on! Your treachery had tipped the balance of the war!'

The Doctor's mind was racing. So that was Peddler's secret government work. Battle armour. It would be a tremendous coincidence if it wasn't connected to the presence of Cybermen in this time period.

Lazonby had crossed to the door and called to the guards outside. 'Bring in the other prisoner.'

The door swung open and McBride was pushed roughly into the room. He smiled sheepishly at the Doctor.

'Hey, Doc.'

'McBride!' The Doctor hesitated, waiting for another figure to be pushed through the door. None came. He got up and crossed to McBride, his face grave. 'Where's Ace?'

The American shook his head. 'Doc... I don't know. These big silver guys attacked us. She went after them.'

'What!? And you let her?'

'I couldn't stop her. I'm sorry!'

The Doctor paced animatedly around the table. 'This is serious. She's in terrible danger. Major Lazonby, I want you to tell me everything. Everything that was going on at the Peddler factory.'

Lazonby looked fit to burst. 'I am asking the questions here, Doctor. You and your accomplice are accused of espionage and murder! Now, both of you, sit down!'

The Doctor sat, glowering at the major. 'Have you any conception of what is going on here?'

'I know exactly what is going on here! The Germans have developed their own version of the battle armour using the secrets that you passed to them. Under cover of the bombing they dropped some of it in that silver capsule, then their agents in this country – this man –' he gestured disdainfully at McBride – 'and others, picked up the armour and used it to kill Dr Peddler.'

He leaned in close to the Doctor, his voice calmer. 'You are obviously an intelligent man, Doctor. It's not too late for you to undo the harm you've done. The Germans have already reached the Channel Islands but we could start to drive them back. Think of it. British troops in Cyber-armour; more manoeuvrable than tanks, bulletproof, fast. The war could be over in a matter of months. Peddler's death has given the Germans the advantage that they needed. The suits that attacked the factory were far in advance of our own prototype. But you can help. Forget Berlin. You seem to understand the technology. Replace Peddler. Help us build a British Cyber-army, and we can start to strike back!'

The Doctor stared sadly into the glazed eyes of the fanatical young major. 'Do you really think that the conflict would end if I gave you that technology?' He shook his head. 'I'm sorry. I can't help you.'

Lazonby stood, abruptly. 'No matter. There are others more willing, more patriotic, who will assist us in our hour of greatest need.' He pulled his cap firmly on to his head and crossed to the door. 'You will both be tried, sentenced, and shot as spies and saboteurs.' He turned to McBride. 'If you have any influence with your accomplice then I suggest you start persuading him that cooperation is the only choice for either of you.'

Lazonby swung on his heel and marched out, the door slamming behind him.

McBride pulled his seat closer to the Doctor. He looked with concern at the bruise on the little man's chin. 'They been treating you a bit rough, Doc?'

The Doctor rubbed his jaw, gingerly. 'Our friend Lazonby got a little carried away.'

'Yeah. He's the type who would knock out your teeth, then kick you in the stomach for mumbling.'

'Fortunately, I always carry a spare set.' The Doctor pulled a set of false teeth from his pocket and clacked them like castanets.

McBride smiled weakly. 'So what do we do now? I have to say

I was kind of relying on you to get me out of this mess.'

The Doctor sighed and regarded the false teeth. 'I'm afraid that rescue duties rather lie with our friendly neighbourhood policeman.'

McBride groaned. 'Mullen? Then we are in trouble.'

CHAPTER 17

Colonel T.P. Potter (retired) unscrewed the lid of his thermos flask and poured himself a cup of strong, sweet tea. He raised his cup and looked around the gloomy underground station. All his regulars were there; the alarms hadn't even sounded yet, but his people had already found themselves places on the platform, unfolding their blankets ready for the long night to come. He sipped his tea with satisfaction. His people. Working like a well-oiled machine.

He'd been an army officer for years, fought in the Great War. By the time that Britain had declared war on Germany he'd been considered too old to serve. He snorted into his tea. Too old! Preposterous. Plenty of life left in him. He knew a thing or two about fighting the Hun, and it didn't involve hiding in underground railway stations.

His age hadn't stopped him becoming an ARP warden, though. As soon as war had been declared he had signed up alongside all the others. He wasn't popular in his district, however. Too many of those under his care thought that he was over-officious, pompous, and bossy. He shook his head. Weak people. They needed strong leadership, and his army training made him the perfect choice. Why wait for the alarms to sound? he had asked them. Everyone knew that they were going to sound eventually. Making good use of the time, this was. Far better to get to the shelters early. Avoid the rush and the struggle.

Oh, a few had complained – one woman had even thrown a boot at him when he'd tried to order her into the shelters – but he knew what he was doing. Given time, Potter's army would be the best drilled bunch of civilians in London. He stretched his neck, looking around for the little Scotsman who had kept the tube station entertained the previous night. Potter had been impressed by the performance. Good for morale. He had hoped to see the little man again, persuade him to become a warden as well; a sergeant to his colonel.

He looked up as a metallic clang rang out from the tunnel. Potter frowned. There shouldn't be anyone in the tunnels. He hauled himself to his feet and peered into the Stygian gloom of the tunnel mouth. Another noise, a scuffling. There *were* people in the tunnels. Couldn't be any of his people. All checked and accounted for.

He called over to where a tall, thin-faced man was struggling with a blanket.

'Wilkins! Have you sent anyone into the tunnels?'

Wilkins looked puzzled. 'The tunnels?'

'Yes, man! It's a perfectly straightforward question.'

Wilkins gave him a long suffering look. 'No, Colonel Potter, I have not.' He returned to his blanket. Potter sighed. Wilkins was meant to be his second-in-command, but the man's heart just wasn't in it. He really would have to try to find that little Scotsman, see if he would take over.

Potter put down his tea, pulled on his tin helmet and straightened his jacket. As a uniform it wasn't much but it was all he had, and people always responded better to authority figures if they had a uniform. He pulled a large torch from inside his bag and shone it into the tunnel. It made little impression on the blackness, but he could make out two figures back in the gloom. What the hell were they doing there? They had been told to stick to the platforms and stairwells. He'd heard that people were beginning to sleep in the tunnels over at Aldwych, but he wasn't having any of that nonsense here. He marched down to the end of the platform and called into the darkness.

'You men! What the devil are you doing in the tunnels?'

To his considerable annoyance, the figures didn't reply. He clambered unsteadily on to the rails, pulling his notebook from his jacket pocket. He'd have to take the names of these two troublemakers. He called out again, in his best parade-ground bellow. 'Did you hear me? Come here at once! At the double!'

He grunted in satisfaction as the two figures began to move

down the tunnel towards him. He pulled a pencil out and licked the tip. 'Now, I want to take your names and –'

The words died in his throat as the two figures lumbered into the light of the station. The huge figures filled the tunnel mouth, glittering as the light from his torchbeam reflected off the strange metal of their suits. Behind him he could hear screams and shouts as other people on the platform caught sight of the monsters. He began to back away, stumbling over the tracks as one of the creatures towered over him. 'What the devil are you?

The silver giant reached down and caught hold of Potter's jacket, hoisting him into the air like a rag doll. Potter could see himself, pale and quivering in the polished silver face of the giant. A metal flap dropped away from behind the slitlike mouth and Potter retched as a wave of fetid air, like sour milk, washed over him. A mechanical hum started deep in the chest of the monster and Potter realised it was speaking. The harsh mechanical voice wavered and oscillated. 'WE ARE CYBERMEN>'

'What do you want with us?' Potter whispered. The reply made his blood run cold.

'YOU BELONG TO US>''YOU WILL BE LIKE US>'

McBride sat on one of the chairs watching as the Doctor paced round and round the room. It was making him dizzy.

The sound of a key in the lock again brought McBride scrambling out of his chair. 'So soon? I thought we were meant to get a hearty meal, a last cigarette or something.'

'Whatever his personal feelings towards us, Major Lazonby is liable to do everything by the book – if nothing else, we can rely on that. There will be a full military trial to humiliate us before the firing squad start polishing their rifles. Oh, and I suspect that we'll be shot at dawn, not in the evening.'

McBride went pale.

'No, I rather think that this is our knight in shining big brown overcoat.'

The door opened and Mullen stepped into the room. McBride

let out a sigh of relief. 'Never thought I'd be glad to see you.'

The Doctor beamed. 'Chief Inspector, what a pleasant surprise.'

The big Irishman's face was grave. 'Don't thank me yet. The two of you are up to your necks in it. It's taken a good deal of favour-pulling at a very high level just to get me in here.' He sat down, pulling a pack of cigarettes from inside his coat. He took one and offered the packet to the Doctor, who shook his head impatiently. McBride took one gratefully, and Mullen lit it.

The chief inspector leaned back in his chair, lighting his own cigarette. 'Lazonby is convinced that the two of you are spies, and he's a very influential young man. The only reason that you aren't in a military court right now is that he's too busy with whatever is going on at the Peddler factory, and I wish to hell that I knew what that was.'

The Doctor pulled his seat closer to the policeman, fanning cigarette smoke away with his hands. 'What is going on at the factory right now?'

Mullen shrugged. 'It's locked up tight as a drum. For the moment they're still allowing me access to the murder site, but that won't last for ever. Lazonby keeps quoting obscure wartime Official Secrets Acts.'

'I don't suppose you had any success in getting the Peddler file...' the Doctor asked hopefully. 'No, of course not. Pity. Inspector, you wouldn't happen to know whether or not Dr Peddler had any connection with France, would you?'

Mullen shrugged his shoulders.

McBride leaned forward.

'Doc, on the wall in his office, there was that picture.'

'Picture?'

'Sure, like a map, only painted. One of those little islands off the coast of France. The Channel Islands. Jersey, I think.'

The Doctor clapped his hands with delight.

'Brilliant, Mr McBride. Very well spotted.'

McBride looked directly at Mullen, smiling slyly. 'I'm surprised you didn't notice that, Mullen.'

The chief inspector shuffled, gazed at his feet, and said nothing.

'And now,' said the Doctor, whipping out the crumpled list of factories from his pocket, 'you are going to tell me that Lemur Engineering is based on Jersey, aren't you, Inspector.'

'Let's see... perhaps I should have copied down the addresses. Yes, I believe Lemur was on Jersey.' Mullen replied. 'But you'll not have much joy there. Jersey's occupied by the Jerries.'

'Precisely, Inspector. It all begins to fall into place.'

Mullen was becoming irritated. 'Excuse me, Doctor, but what does?'

'That's where they've come from. Wall and his tall friends. The German invasion must have taken them completely by surprise. They're on the run!'

Mullen and McBride looked dubiously at one another. It was Mullen who spoke. 'Sounds a bit speculative to me, if you'll forgive my saying so, Doctor.'

'Inspector, do you know what a lemur is?'

'It's... an animal. Isn't it? Sort of cross between a monkey and a rat.'

'Strange sort of thing for an English company to name itself after, wouldn't you say?'

'I suppose...'

'Well suppose I told you that you've misread the name, Inspector? That it isn't called Lemur Engineering at all. That it's called Le Mur Engineering.'

'Le... Moo...'

Mullen looked confused. McBride looked no less so. The Doctor cast an exasperated glance at the two of them.

'Le Mur, Inspector. They speak a great deal of French on Jersey. And Le Mur is French for Wall!' The Time Lord slapped the palms of his hands against the door. 'Oh, if only we could get out of here. I'm dreadfully worried about Ace, and about George Limb.'

'Limb – ah, yes,' Mullen suddenly piped up. 'I thought that was the name you said. It sounded familiar so I did a bit of checking up. We've got quite a file on George Limb, Doctor.' The Doctor turned to him in surprise. 'Oh, yes. Quite a file. It seems he was a permanent secretary, first at the Admiralty, then at the Foreign Office. That was on paper, at least. He never seemed to stay put. He seemed to roam from department to department in government, acting as some kind of troubleshooter.'

'Troubleshooter, eh?'

'Or troublemaker, depending on who you ask. It seems he had a reputation as a double-dealer. Stirred up a lot of trouble wherever he went. There's a question mark over his resignation, but it's possible he just tried to be a bit too clever. Stuck his neck out too far; nearly lost his head. Very nearly arrested. He's got friends in high places, though. Very high, if you get my drift. "We will fight them on the beaches…" and all that.'

The Doctor raised an eyebrow, impressed.

'You name it, Doctor. Whenever there was a big international conference, he was there. Versailles in 1919, Munich in 1936. He was even in Russia just before Hitler and Stalin pulled off their deal. God knows why. And that's just the start of the story. When he retires the file really starts to bulge. Everyone in the criminal community in London goes to him. He's suspected of being the brains behind any number of bank jobs, big cons, you name it. We've never managed to pin anything on him, though. What's more he never seems to make a penny out of these jobs. It's like he just does it for the intellectual challenge. The mob bosses go round in Bentleys and George Limb wipes his arse on newspaper. We've checked.'

McBride raised an eyebrow. 'You checked his ass?' he drawled, deadpan.

Mullen glared at him and continued. 'But believe me, Doctor, he's respected right across the London underworld. Respected and feared.'

The Doctor tutted and scratched his head.

'I can go one better,' said McBride. 'You don't get to be a detective without learning to keep your ears open, Doc. I've been listening to what goes on in this building. Limb was here this morning, chatting with our military buddy. He's no fool. He could see who it was useful to get pally with and didn't waste any time introducing himself. Lazonby said that they had another scientist who was willing to help – my bet is he meant Limb.'

The Doctor was speechless.

'I knew there was something funny right from the start,' the detective continued. 'All the streets around his house were deserted. Bomb damage. Rich streets, easy pickings for looters. And yet none of them had been touched.'

'I'm not surprised,' Mullen interjected. 'No criminal in London would pull a stunt like that in George Limb's manor.'

The Doctor was grim-faced.

'I've been used, gentlemen. I think I've just been another – how did you put it, Inspector? – intellectual challenge. I'm a fool. I've been the manipulator for too long, moving the pawns, the chessmaster. I've spent so much time formulating my own schemes that I've missed the fact that there are others better versed in the art of deception and deceit. You have to get us out of here!'

Mullen chewed on his cigarette.

'Wilkins!'

Wilkins started as the voice hissed at him from the darkness.

'Wilkins! Come on, man.'

He looked around, peering into the gloom, trying to find the source of the whispered voice. 'Down here, man.' Potter was on the floor, crawling in the trench between the tracks. Wilkins looked around in panic, trying to see if the two silver giants had seen them.

'What the hell are you doing, Potter? They'll kill you!'

Potter shook his head. 'We've got to get out of here. If we're quick we can get away now. Come back with reinforcements. Jump to it man!'

Wilkins shook his head. 'You're mad, Potter. You saw what those things did to Frank.'

Potter was silent for a moment. Frank had been a good man. One of the younger men in his small army of followers, excused active service because of asthma. When the Cybermen had emerged from the tunnel he had been at the far end of the platform, closest to the stairs. When the screams had started, Frank had made a vain attempt to get people out of the way, ushering them towards the emergency exit. Potter, hanging helpless in the grasp of one of the monsters, had only been able to watch as its partner had unclipped a stubby silver tube from the mass of instruments on its chest and levelled it along the platform.

Potter closed his eyes, recalling the rattlesnake noise of the gun, the smell of charring flesh and the screams that had echoed around the tube station. no one had dared disobey the silver giants after that. Not that anyone was in a fit state to. A motley collection of old couples, middle-aged women and a young woman with a baby. They had all clustered protectively around the young woman as the Cybermen had herded the twenty or so frightened Londoners off the platform and into the tunnels, pushing them ever deeper into the maze that wound its way under the streets of London.

Now they had stopped. The Cybermen were pulling bricks from the wall, widening a hole that led even deeper, probably into the sewers. Potter had realised that once they were in the sewers, they were lost. Someone had to go for help, and as the senior officer it was his duty to try.

Moving as quietly as his old frame would allow him, he had crawled through the mass of huddled, frightened people to get to Wilkins. Back down the tunnels there would be more people starting to shelter for the night: policemen, soldiers even. He had hoped for an ally in Wilkins to get back to the relative safety of the tube stations, but, as he looked at the pale and shivering librarian, Potter realised that he was on his own.

The harsh, mechanical voice of a Cyberman made them both start. Potter pressed himself into the shadows between the tracks. This was it. His chance for freedom. His chance for glory.

The waiting Cybermen were forcing the others through the ragged hole in the tunnel wall. Wilkins hurried over, waiting for Potter to be discovered, waiting for the crackle of that terrible gun. His heart pounded as the terrible blank gaze of the Cyberman swept down the tunnel, then he was pushed into the deep blackness of the sewers, the giant figure squeezing itself through the hole after him.

Potter breathed a sigh of relief. It had worked. He hadn't been spotted. He waited a while longer, lying quietly in the gloom, waiting for any sign that the Cybermen had missed him. Once he was sure that he was safe, he clambered to his feet and made his way to the hole that had been torn into the brickwork. He peered inside, the smell of the sewers almost making him retch. He could hear distant footsteps, distant sobs.

He turned back to the tube tunnels with grim determination. If only he hadn't dropped his torch. Still, no matter. His eyes would soon become accustomed to the dark. It may not be the Hun that he was fighting, but Colonel T.P. Potter (retired) was going to show what he was made of. Hands outstretched, feeling his way along the grime-encrusted wall, he began to make his way down the tunnel.

'This is going to work! Goddamn it, this is actually going to work.'

'Shut up, McBride,' Mullen hissed into his ear. 'Prisoners aren't meant to talk to their escorts.'

'Be quiet, both of you, we've got company.' The Doctor nodded at a group of pinstriped officials who had just appeared at the far end of the corridor.

Mullen prodded McBride in the back with the snout of his

Webley, and the trio of chief inspector, private detective and Time Lord made their way towards the main doors. They were given a curious glance by the men approaching them, and McBride could feel sweat prickling on his scalp, but as soon as they saw the gun in the hand of the chief inspector they scurried off, not wishing to get involved with what were, quite obviously, dangerous criminals.

McBride had been expecting the alarm to sound at any time in the last few minutes, ever since they had stepped from outside their cell, in fact. Mullen had considered the Doctor's plea for freedom, pulled his gun from his holster, then called for the guard outside the cell door.

The young corporal had been very unsure about releasing his prisoners into Mullen's custody, but the big Irishman had launched into a terrible temper, towering over the soldier, demanding to know what right he had to obstruct the course of justice. He had pointed out, quite reasonably, McBride thought, that if the prisoners were in all likelihood to be executed, it was vital that the police obtain a full statement about the particulars of the Peddler murder.

There was a moment when McBride was certain that the corporal was going to refuse, but in a stroke of genius Mullen had threatened to go to Lazonby. The soldier had gone white, and had practically offered to escort the prisoners to Mullen's car himself. Now they were nearly at the big double doors. Only a few more seconds.

McBride closed his eyes in despair as two armed guards stepped in front of them, blocking their way. Mullen tried to brazen it out, hauling his ID from inside his coat.

'Chief Inspector Mullen, Special Branch. I'm taking these two men back to the station for interrogation.'

One of the soldiers, almost as big as Mullen himself, stared at the three of them.

'Are you, indeed? Well no one has informed me of any prisoner transfer.' He gestured to an office doorway with his gun. 'If you would wait inside for a moment, sir, I'll just get authorisation for you to leave.'

McBride stared at Mullen in panic. The chief inspector was obviously racking his brains for some reason why they had to leave immediately. They could see the big, black police car outside the door for God's sake!

'Excuse me.'The Doctor had slipped in between the two men, pushing the soldier's gun out of the way. He stared up at the hulking guard, his eyes twinkling. 'I really don't think that you need to get any authorisation.'The Doctor's voice was soothing, musical. 'The chief inspector has all the authority he needs: he's an officer of the Crown.' The soldier's eyes were beginning to glaze over. McBride could feel his own eyes going. He shook his head violently, trying to concentrate. He glanced over at the other guard. He, too, was being drawn in by the Doctor's calming tones.

'Surely the two of you are going to be far busier with getting everyone into the shelters… There is an air raid on, after all.'

McBride frowned. No there wasn't. He was just about to open his mouth when the drone of the first siren cut through the foyer of the building.

Suddenly, there was pandemonium. People rushed all around them, and the two guards raced off, trying to keep everybody in some form of order. The Doctor smiled at his two companions. McBride grinned back.

Mullen shook his head. 'You've the luck of the Devil himself. How the hell did you know that there was going to be a raid just then?'

The Doctor tapped the side of his nose. 'Come on, Inspector, your chariot awaits.'

The three of them pushed out through the double doors and raced across the car park to the big Rover. McBride winced at the freezing rain. He'd been cooped up inside for too long. He pulled his trench coat tight around him and bundled himself into the back of the car. The Doctor hopped into the driver's side, looking far too small in the worn, leather seat. Mullen tossed him the keys and they roared off into the night.

The Doctor had been on the main road less than a few seconds, when he turned into a small side road, hurling the car around the corner. Mullen looked apprehensively at the speedometer, but said nothing. He clung on to his seat as the Doctor threw the car into a series of tight turns.

'Well then, Doctor, now that I've sprung you from the clutches of Major Lazonby, where exactly are we going?'

The Doctor was peering through the rain-splattered windscreen, his face a mask of concentration, struggling to see over the dashboard of the police car as it raced through the East End. He sped around another corner.

'You, Inspector, are going to go with Mr McBride, round up whatever forces you can muster, and raid the Peddler factory.'

'What?'

'Without doubt the Cybermen will be setting up another processing station. Their forces are weak. They'll be looking to strengthen them. If George Limb is working with Major Lazonby he'll undoubtedly have engineered a truce with Wall. Which means the Cybermen now have access to the resources of the Peddler factory.'

'And how the Devil do you expect us to get in? Walk up and knock on the front door?'

'You're a policeman conducting a murder inquiry. Get a warrant!'

'That's going to be damn near impossible, Doctor. I'm going to –'

'I don't care what you have to do! The atrocities that are taking place in the Peddler factory have to be stopped now!' There was a deathly silence in the speeding vehicle as the two men stared at each other. McBride drew in a sharp breath as a building loomed out of the night. The Doctor snatched his eyes back to the road and the tyres on the Rover squealed on the wet tarmac as he wrenched the wheel round and brought the car skidding to a halt.

They were outside Mullen's police station.

'I'll meet you both outside the Peddler factory in half an hour.'

McBride let out his breath. 'Where are you going, Doc?'

The Doctor was grim-faced. 'To George Limb's house.'

CHAPTER 18

The big Rover pulled up outside the terraced house in Belsize Park and the Doctor clambered out of the driver's seat. The street was silent and empty, the distant sounds of the sirens almost melodic. The Doctor stared up at Limb's house. It was dark and silent, like its neighbours.

The Doctor peered through the window. No one. No light, no fire in the grate, no sign that anyone was home at all. He pulled on the front door. Locked. Rummaging in his pocket, the Doctor brought out a safety pin. A few minutes fumbling with the lock, and the door was open.

He stepped into the gloom of the hall and listened. Still nothing. He was about to reach for the light switch, when he realised that there was an air raid on. The last thing that he wanted at the moment was to have to deal with two hundred pounds of German bomb.

He delved into the pockets of his jacket again, pulling out a box of his everlasting matches. He struck one, and the hallway was lit by a soft white light. Slowly, the Doctor began to pad through the house.

The cellar was empty, as he had expected, all traces of the Cyberleader's body removed. That at least was some small consolation. He moved through into the lounge.

Everything was as you would expect of a elderly man living alone in Belsize Park. Magazines stacked in a rack, books arranged neatly and alphabetically on shelves. The Doctor crossed to the small bureau tucked against the wall. He leafed through a stack of papers. Nothing. Nothing but old newspapers, gas bills that had been paid, and library tickets. A backward-folded map of London lay on top of the pile. A series of ink-blue crosses traced a broad arc across its streets. The trail of the Lurker. Despondently, the Doctor stuffed the map into his pocket.

Where had the man kept all the important documentation?

The sound of ack-ack fire made the Doctor look up. Of course. The spare room. If the Cyberleader had been kept up there then perhaps Limb had used it to store things of equal importance.

He scurried round to the foot of the stairs and began to make his way up. There had been no sign of life in the house, but it didn't pay to get too confident. He peered up on to the landing. The upper floors of the house were as empty as the rest.

He crossed to the flower-patterned spare room. The light from his match made the shadows dance and flicker. The room seemed empty but he had to be sure. He pulled the blackout curtains across and switched on the light. It was just as he had seen it before. Empty. No indication of anything unusual.

The distant crump of falling bombs made the Doctor start. He was wasting his time here. Limb had covered his tracks too well. He snapped the light off angrily and tried to slam the door.

He couldn't.

The door was jammed on something. The Doctor reached for the light switch again. There. Under the door. Something small and plastic.

The Doctor rose to his feet clutching the audio cassette. No doubt about where that came from.

'Ace.'

Potter stumbled for what felt like the millionth time. His hands were slick with grease and dirt, and his shins were bleeding from his repeated clashes with the rails of the pitch-black tunnel. He had no idea of how far he had gone. It could have been a mile or a hundred miles; in this blackness there was no way to tell.

He slipped again and crashed to the floor, his glasses tumbling from his nose.

'Damn and blast it.' He scraped around on the floor, desperate to find them. His fingers raked through the accumulated grime of years of commuters. He was beginning to despair. He had hoped that his eyes would become accustomed to the dark, but the total blackness had refused to give way, the sign of light that he had expected at the end of the tunnel had refused to come.

His hand brushed against something that whipped away from under his touch. Rats? He could hear things scuttling in the darkness. He scrabbled desperately for his glasses.

There.

Thank God. He slipped them on to his nose, peering into the velvet dark. 'Is anybody there?' he hissed.

More scuttling.

Potter strained his eyes. He realised that he could see something – a glow. Faint. Red. Two glowing embers, almost like eyes. Exactly like eyes.

Potter stared about him with growing panic. There were more of the eyes now, the blackness around him growing steadily brighter with a deep-red glow as the things began to converge on him from out of the blackness. He could feel small shapes scurrying over his feet; hear the chattering of dozens of sets of metallic teeth.

He scrambled desperately against the wall, kicking out at his attackers. The floor of the tunnel was alive. Potter turned and ran.

Behind him he could hear a rush of movement, a gnashing of teeth, the splash of water as the tide of creatures pursued him though the dark of the underground.

He stumbled, catching his foot and crashing to the floor again, floundering in the shallow water of the tunnel. The blackness around him lit up with the eyes of the creatures, and he closed his eyes, waiting for the end. The end of Colonel Potter. The end of his one chance of glory.

The blackness was suddenly pierced by a brilliant white glare. Potter peered up. Towering over him was one of the Cybermen, light from a cowling on the top of its head turning the gloom of the tunnel into daylight. For the first time Potter caught a glimpse of the small metal piranhas that surrounded him and he screamed.

The Cyberman grasped him in a huge metal gauntlet and hauled him out of the water. It raised its other hand and held it level with

Potter's head. There was the flare of a brilliant blue spark, and Colonel Potter knew no more.

In the shadow of St Paul's Cathedral, a borrowed police car stood in a side road, ticking quietly as its engine cooled in the rain of the November night. The Doctor stood outside the police-box shell of the TARDIS, his hood pulled over his head to ward off the rain, as he tried to extricate the key from around his neck.

He slid the delicate metal shape into the lock and, with a subtle series of clicks, the door swung inward. The Doctor vanished inside, slamming the door behind him.

The interior lights of the TARDIS rose in intensity as the Doctor strode into the console room, the heavy circular indentations on the walls glowing softly. The background hum of machinery changed in pitch too, settling into a steady purr, like a contented cat.

The Doctor crossed to the central console, a vast array of complex controls and twinkling lights that rose from the floor of the room like a huge mushroom. He patted the console affectionately. 'Hello, old girl. Yes, I've missed you, too.'

He shrugged out of his duffel coat, and pulled the cassette from a pocket, tossing the coat into a pile on the floor of the console room. The far side of the control area looked like a young boy's bedroom. Clothes and shoes were scattered everywhere, jumbled up with books on nuclear physics and juggling, a Scalextric set and a box of Newberry Fruits.

The Doctor paced round the console, jabbing at buttons. The technology before him could decode the most complex alien computer programs, could link itself with his own brain, was even capable of independent thought; but as for playing a cassette tape from twentieth-century Earth...

'Why they didn't fit TARDISes with in-flight entertainment, I'll never know.'

He poked at a few more switches, then crossed the room and pushed open the door that led into the bowels of the ship.

The corridors that ran through the TARDIS were practically limitless, though the Doctor knew his way around all of them. Well, most of them. His companions, however, tended to like their quarters close to the console room, and Ace had been no exception.

She had claimed that if there was going to be some emergency, she would rather not spend the bulk of her time trying to find her way around a maze of corridors that, to her mind, looked all the same. This way she could keep an eye on the Doctor. He hadn't complained, at least it meant that he had been able to keep an eye on her.

Until now, at any rate. What would Limb have done with her? A theory was struggling to formulate itself in his mind, and it wasn't pleasant. Thank heavens the man was confined to one small planet in one narrow time period. The Doctor shuddered to think what he might do with time and space to roam around in.

Why had Ace brought an audio cassette with her to 1940, in spite of all his warnings? Why had she left it at Limb's house? She was a bright girl: he fervently hoped she had left the tape as a clue.

He stopped outside the door to Ace's room. There was a 'Do Not Disturb' sign on the door handle – stolen from a hotel in Coventry. The Doctor pushed the door open.

The room was a shambles, more so than the console room. Clothes of every description were scattered everywhere. The bed was unmade – a huge, cuddly dinosaur perched on the pillow – and empty coffee mugs lurked in every corner. The desk in one corner was piled high with souvenirs from Ace's time with him, the pinboard above it covered with photographs. He picked up a bar towel from the back of the chair. 'Welcome to Iceworld'. So long ago. So long since he had picked up this rebellious teenager.

He dropped the towel and peered around the room.

'It's got to be in here somewhere.'

He spotted a set of headphones on the floor alongside the bed 'Aha!'

He grasped the headphones and followed the curly lead until it vanished under a mountain of T-shirts. He pushed them to one side, revealing the ghetto blaster that he had built for her.

He hauled it from the floor and dumped it on to the bed, dislodging the dinosaur, which rolled inelegantly into the corner. The tape deck was a jumble of different styles and scientific eras. The advanced electronics of the Time Lords mingled with Alpha Centaurian acoustic equipment and the valve technology of Earth. A slot for a cassette tape nestled under the front of an ancient Bakelite radio. The Doctor pressed the eject button and a battered cassette slid into his hand.

' "Rage Against the Machine". How appropriate.'

He slipped Ace's tape into the deck and listened to her encounter with a young-sounding man. German. The sounds stopped abruptly, and the room was filled with screeching guitars.

The Doctor rewound the tape and listened again. Master race? Nazis. George Limb was in league with the Nazis. He closed his eyes.

Ace.

This had to stop. He had to stop it, now.

Hoisting the ghetto blaster on to his shoulder, the Doctor marched back out to the console room.

The drone of the air-raid sirens was joined by something new and unearthly as the TARDIS began to fade from the shadows beneath St Paul's. The wet pavement was lit up with an electric blue glow as the battered police box melted into transparency and leaves swirled into the space that it had occupied. The square patch of dry tarmac where the TARDIS had once stood slowly darkened as the rain soaked into it, and soon there was no indication that anything had ever been there at all.

Moments later a small patch of scrubland behind Southwark Power Station echoed with the same alien trumpeting, and the rain began to bounce off something large and invisible. Then, with a final groan and a loud thump, the TARDIS materialised.

The Doctor struggled through the door, manhandling Ace's ghetto blaster by its shoulder straps. He pulled the door shut and locked it, then slung the music box over his shoulder. He peered into the night, squinting as the rain ran off his forehead and into his eyes. He could see the Peddler factory ahead of him, and a cluster of people outside the main doors.

Mullen, if things were going to plan.

He scurried over to the road, the sodden grass squelching under his feet. The strap of the ghetto blaster bit into his shoulder. Ace was right. It *was* too heavy. When all this was over he would build her a new one. A lightweight one.

Mullen looked up in alarm as he heard footsteps pattering over the road. He spun round to see the Doctor emerge from the gloom.

'About time. We'd just about given up on you.' He looked at the jumble of technology hanging from the Doctor's shoulder.

'What in the name of God is that contraption?'

The Doctor ignored him. 'Is McBride here?'

The private detective appeared at Mullen's shoulder. He looked at the Doctor's grim face with concern. 'Did you find Ace?'

The Doctor shook his head. 'No. But I know who has taken her.' He peered at the half-dozen or so policemen trying to huddle in the doorway of the Peddler factory.

'Is this all?'

Mullen looked hurt. 'It's the best I could do, Doctor. There is a war on, you know. Besides, all were dealing with are a few of Lazonby's soldiers and Peddler's scientific chappies. They shouldn't put up too much of a fight.'

'Oh, you're up against considerably more than that, Inspector. Our friend Mr Limb is best of friends with the Nazis as well as the Cybermen.'

Mullen's face tightened. 'Nazis? The bastard. And you think that they might be inside the factory?'

187

The Doctor's steely eyes flickered over the darkened building. 'I don't know. But I think we should exercise a little caution, nonetheless. We have no way of knowing how many Cybermen have been created by now.' He wiped rain from his eyes. 'Have you tried to get in?'

Mullen nodded. 'I've sent a couple of men all round the place. There's no sign of any soldiers, but there are some damn funny noises coming from the lab. All the doors are locked. We'll probably have to break them down.'

'Oh, I don't think there'll be any need for that.' The Doctor pulled a hairpin from his pocket and trotted over to the door.

A ripple of mirth went though the policemen, quickly stopping as the huge double doors swung inward. The Doctor turned to them and gestured inside the building. 'I think we'd all feel better if we got in out of the rain, don't you?'

The policemen swarmed past the Doctor, spreading out through the darkened foyer. Mullen, McBride, and the Doctor followed them in, cautiously peering around the deserted building. Mullen pulled out his gun.

'I don't like this one little bit, Doctor. Where is everyone?'

The Doctor heaved the ghetto blaster on to the reception desk, and beckoned to McBride. 'You have some local knowledge of the factory, Mr McBride. Where would they all be?'

McBride pointed down one of the darkened corridors. 'The lab is down there. There are some offices and workshops too. My guess is that they'll all be hard at work.'

Mullen nodded. 'Right then. Come on, you lot!' He strode off down the corridor, his men in tow. McBride was about to follow, but the Doctor held him back. McBride looked down at him. The little man's eyes twinkled out of the dark. 'Just before we go rushing into the lions' den, Mr McBride, I want to discuss a little idea with you.'

Lazonby marched back and forth in his small, military office, constantly checking his watch. Wall sat at the desk, his face unreadable behind his glasses. Every time Lazonby looked over at him, all he could see was his own face, reflected back at him from those little black lenses. Wall hadn't moved for over an hour. Lazonby was beginning to lose patience.

'When am I going to be able to see some progress? You promised me that you would be able to set the lab up in no time at all. You've taken all my men, as well as all of Peddler's. How much longer is this going to take?'

Wall smiled at him. 'Patience is a virtue Major Lazonby,' he trilled. 'What we are putting into practice here is the stuff of dreams. Surely you don't wish to rush the greatest technological breakthrough that the world has seen in the last fifty years? You really must try to cultivate a sense of occasion.'

There was the dull crump of an explosion from somewhere in the distance. Lazonby looked pointedly at him.

'There is no point in cultivating a sense of occasion if we are all to be blown to kingdom come whilst we wait. I need results now!'

There was another distant thump. Lazonby looked up, puzzled. 'That wasn't a bomb. That came from inside the factory!' The thump came again. A look of pure rage crossed the major's face. 'Someone has got in!' He snatched his gun belt from the desk. 'Come with me.'

Wall didn't move.

Lazonby leaned close. 'I said come with me.'

Wall leaned back in his chair. 'You will find that I am a man who doesn't take kindly to being threatened, Major Lazonby. I understood from our mutual friend Mr Limb that we were to be partners – that we were meant to be working together. If these circumstances change, it would be most… unfortunate.'

'I don't respond well to threats either, Mr Wall, particularly from civilians. Now, we are going to find out exactly what's going on down at the lab.'

'I really don't think it requires both of us, Major.'

Lazonby pulled the gun from his holster. 'I think it does, Mr

Wall. After all, we are meant to be partners.' The smile faded from Wall's face as he looked at the gun. He stood, brushing down his black coat, and crossed to the door.

Outside the laboratory doors, several of the policemen were using a heavy wooden bench as a battering ram. Huge metal shutters sealed the lab off from the rest of the factory. The policemen were making a lot of noise, but very little impression on the big shutters. Mullen waved at them to stop. Where the hell had the Doctor got to? No doubt he could get them open in seconds. He looked around for him, just in time to see the Doctor appear from the end of the corridor, that peculiar collection of technology still hung over one shoulder.

'You don't seem to be having much luck, Inspector.'

Mullen grunted. 'Perhaps if you were to lend a hand, Doctor.'

The Doctor frowned.

'Where's McBride got to?' Mullen asked.

'He's gone to find something for me.'

The Doctor put the ghetto blaster on the floor and crossed to the shutter doors. 'Hmm. This is going to take more than a hairpin for us to get in.' He rummaged in the pockets of his jacket. 'Now, somewhere around here I should have –'

A shot rang out in the corridor. Plaster exploded from the ceiling, and policemen scattered for cover. Mullen reached for his Webley.

'I really wouldn't do that, Inspector.'

Mullen raised his hands slowly. 'Lazonby.'

The young major came slowly down the stairs. Another man scuffled in the shadows behind him. Mullen stared at the little figure. It could only be Wall. He fitted perfectly the description that Peddler's secretary had given.

Lazonby kept his back against the wall, covering the group. His eyes darted back and forth between Mullen and the Doctor.

'Well, now, Chief Inspector, breaking and entering, and conspiring with a known spy. I didn't realise that the police force had become quite so corrupt.'

'Or the military,' Mullen snarled. He pointed at Wall. 'This man is wanted for murder.'

Lazonby smiled. 'Mr Wall is helping us with the war effort.'

Wall looked over at the dents in the shutter door. He seemed panicked. 'They've been trying to get into the lab. Shoot them, Lazonby. Shoot them all.'

'What a fabulous solution.'

The lights suddenly snapped on, momentarily blinding everyone. The Doctor stepped in front of the shutters blocking the lab, like an actor stepping on to the stage.

'Why don't you shoot us all, Major. A bullet right between the eyes. Very neat. Very ordered. A very military solution to the problem.'

All eyes were on him.

Lazonby's gun wavered between the little Time Lord and Mullen.

The Doctor fixed him with a piercing stare. 'Earlier today, I asked you if you had any comprehension of the evil you were dealing with. Now I'm going to show you.'

He reached into his pocket.

Mullen held his breath as Lazonby's gun swung round to centre firmly on the Doctor. He could see the major's knuckles going white as his finger tightened on the trigger.

With unnatural calm, the Doctor pulled Ace's cassette tape from inside his jacket. He bent down and slipped it into the slot in the front of the ghetto blaster. Lazonby's gun followed every movement.

The Doctor pressed 'play' and straightened, clutching his lapels.

The voices of the German and Ace boomed out in the silence.

'What is the function of this machine?'

'You're the master race. You tell me.'

'I will ask you only once more.'

'First tell me what you did with Mr Limb.'

There was a sharp, coughing laugh; tinny over the speakers. The Doctor crossed his fingers. If anything was going to tip the balance, then the next few seconds were vital. The German's voice filled the corridor again.

'Mr Limb? My dear young girl, your friend Limb is a traitor. He has been working for us for six years or more. He has been a vital source of information to the Reich.'

There was the sound of screaming and breaking furniture, a brutal electrical crack, then silence.

The Doctor leaned down and snapped off the cassette player. Lazonby stared at him in silence. His finger slackened on the trigger.

Wall gripped him by the shoulder. 'It's a trick. A trick, do you hear me. This man is cunning, ruthless. He's a traitor. Don't listen to him, Lazonby!'

The Doctor took a step towards the pale and quivering army major.

'Have you ever seen the results of partial Cyberisation on a human subject, Major?'

Lazonby raised the gun again, in trembling hands.

Mullen drew in another breath as the Doctor took a step closer.

'Has Mr Wall shown you what the Cybermen do to their human subjects?'

The Doctor transferred his gaze to Wall. The little man cowered behind Lazonby, peering at the Doctor through his blackened glasses.

'Don't listen to him, Lazonby. We're partners. A British Cyber-army, remember.'

The Doctor kept his voice low and calm. 'Have you ever wondered why Mr Wall never takes off his glasses?'

Lazonby swung his gaze towards the cowering Wall. Those damned reflective little glasses. Sweat began to run down his brow. He was an officer of the British army. He had to do what was right for his country. If Limb was in league with the Nazis...

With the enemy...

The Doctor took another step closer. His eyes switched to the barrel of the revolver, now only inches from his face.

'Ask Mr Wall to take off his glasses.'

'Shoot him!' screamed Wall.

'Ask if you can see his eyes.'

'Kill him!'

'Now, McBride! Now!'

The Doctor ducked.

The gun went off.

A wall of the corridor exploded inwards as an engine of hissing pistons and cold metal crashed through it. Peddler's prototype Cyber-armour creaked and groaned as McBride tried to control it. A gangly collection of metal beams and crude electrics, lashed to the American with leather straps.

A metal-clad arm flailed out and bricks scattered across the corridor. The Doctor and Mullen threw themselves to one side as the ceiling collapsed.

'Concentrate, McBride!' yelled the Doctor.

'That's easy for you to say, Doc!'

A metal arm punched through an office door.

'This thing seems to have a life of its own!'

The Doctor dodged as McBride stamped towards the shutter doors. The Cyber-armour was crude and unsophisticated, but very powerful. McBride struggled with the joystick, desperate to bring the machine under some sort of control.

Bullets ricocheted off the metal framework as Lazonby fired shot after shot at him. He could hear the Doctor shouting at him, urging him to open the doors to the lab.

McBride raised both arms of the clumsy metal suit, and brought them slamming down on the metal shutters.

There was a screech of rending metal, and McBride felt himself toppling forward as the doors gave way. The suit collapsed into the lab with a resounding crash. McBride struggled out of the wreckage. He hauled himself to his feet, and found himself face to face with a scene from hell.

The smell hit McBride first. A dark, rich stench of decay, laced with the coppery tang of blood. The smell of a charnel house. The smell of death. He staggered to his feet, pulling a handkerchief from his pocket and covering his nose. There was another odour – an earthy, human scent. There was a huge rent in the floor. Concrete lay all around, shattered like toffee. McBride could see wet brickwork glistening through the hole. The sewers.

Around the walls of the lab were tall, curved bays interlinked with tubes and cables. With a start, McBride realised that it was the sphere, split apart like an orange. Each segment held a body, but there was no way that McBride could describe any of the occupants as human.

Pipes and wires wound around exposed bones; raw, wet, torn flesh glistened between chrome plates. Blood pooled on the floor and thick hydraulic fluid pumped through transparent tubes into chest cavities that had once held hearts and lungs. A corner of the lab was piled high with discarded organs. A butcher's window of human offal.

Cybermats squirmed over the bodies like metallic leeches, their teeth snipping at flesh with the precision of a surgeon's scalpel. McBride could hear them chittering to each other – a tinny noise, like laughter. He could hear people entering the lab behind him. A whispered prayer from Mullen. The sound of one of the policemen being sick.

Lazonby pushed past him, his gun hanging limply at his side, staring at the tableau before him. He wandered, dazed, into the centre of the laboratory, transfixed by the figures clamped into the Cybermen's machines. Old men. Women. Being taken apart, piece by bloody piece. The cold, hard technology of the Cybermen replacing flesh and blood.

Lazonby could hear the Doctor's voice, clipped, without emotion, echoing throughout the lab.

'Do you see now, Major Lazonby? The truth? What the

Cybermen really are? What it is that they really do? There is no perfection, no ideal, no brave new world. You know what the Nazis are doing across the Channel; how can you possibly condemn them and condone this? This is everything that you are fighting against.'

Lazonby said nothing, his jaw hanging slack. Where were his perfect, glittering soldiers? Where was his symmetry, his order? The disembodied head of the Cyberleader sat on a silver pedestal, wires and cables snaking off into the workings of the sphere. Lazonby moved closer to one of the elegantly curved segments. He stared. The figure inside had once been a man. Boxlike machinery sprang directly from his chest, wheezing and clicking. The arms and legs were shining metal and plastic, but the head...The face was peeled back, metal plates were bolted directly to the skull. Thin grey hair wisped from under the steel skull cap. Through those terrible blank eye sockets Lazonby could see human eyes.

The eyes suddenly snapped open.

Lazonby choked back sobs as the figure staggered out of its alcove, arms outstretched. He could see what had once been an elderly man through the terrible tangle of machinery. The monstrosity pulled itself clear of the sphere segment, trailing wires and weeping cables.

The creature that had once been Colonel T.P. Potter (retired) lurched towards Lazonby and somehow, falteringly, forced its larynx to work.

'Help... me... Help... us...'

He suddenly straightened, his arms swinging back down to his side. His eyes glazed over, and a deep hum started in the controls strapped to his chest. As Lazonby watched, Colonel Potter died, and a new Cyberman grated its first words.

'INTRUDERS>'

Lazonby raised his service revolver and shot Potter clean through the head. The half-Cyberman collapsed backward in a spray of hydraulic fluids.

Suddenly, the machinery all around the lab changed in pitch, the Cybermats hissed, agitatedly. The Doctor caught Lazonby by the arm. 'I think we'd better get out of here, Major.'

Lazonby shook him free and turned towards Wall. The little man cowered as Lazonby strode towards him.

Suddenly, there was a high, metallic screech from the centre of the lab. Something exploded from the hole in the floor. Not Cyberman, not Cybermat. Powerful arms pulled it across the floor, a metal tail thrashing at the air. Lazonby spun and emptied the remaining chambers of his revolver into the thing. It spun across the lab, crashing into a corner. It mewed pitifully as sparks flew from its casing – a tragic, wailing sound, somehow familiar. All colour drained from Lazonby's face, and the heavy revolver clattered to the floor, as he realised the nature of the Cybercreature. A baby. Full-sized Cyber arms grafted directly on to its tiny torso; the tail of a Cybermat where the legs should have been.

He rounded on Wall, clamping his hands on either side of the little man's face and hauling him off the floor. Wall squealed and wriggled, but Lazonby held him firm.

'What have you done? What have you turned *me* into?' His voice was a strangled whisper.

With a sudden jerk, Lazonby snatched the glasses from Wall's face, letting him fall to the floor. Wall gave out a high-pitched gurgling scream, and Lazonby staggered back in horror.

Twin camera lenses stared out from the pallid, puglike face – chrome and glass nestling into the clean white bone of the eye sockets. Wall writhed on the floor, flailing blindly. 'Light! Too much light!'

The Doctor crossed the lab to the Cyberleader's head, and began to wrench it from the pedestal. A Cybermat hissed at him, teeth snapping; the Doctor batted it away with his hat. With a crunch the head came free.

There was a sudden cry from McBride.

'Doc, look out!'

A metal arm rose from the huge rent in the laboratory floor as a Cyberman hauled itself out of the sewers. The Cybermen in the sphere segments were beginning to stir. McBride looked around for any kind of weapon. In a corner was a pile of army uniforms, torn and bloodied – all that was left of Lazonby's troops. Nestling among the cloth was the glint of gunmetal. McBride bent down and snatched a rifle from the pile. Bullets twanged around the laboratory as McBride loosed off shot after shot against the emerging Cyberman.

Lazonby joined him, rummaging in the pile of uniforms and staggering to his feet clutching a heavy machine-gun.

He snapped off the safety catch and unleashed a stream of bullets into the lab. The Cyberman reeled under the impact and vanished from view, crashing back into the sewers. Lazonby smiled grimly at McBride.

Suddenly, the floor of the lab shattered as Cybermen punched their way up from underground. McBride couldn't see how many pairs of arms flailed through the smashed concrete. Four, no six. One by one the Cybermen hauled themselves through the floor. McBride raised his rifle and fired shot after shot. He could see the two that he and Ace had come up against – the charred one and the one with the bent handle – towering a good foot above their newly converted colleagues – Lazonby's former troops. They swatted his bullets away as if they were flies. Mullen and his policemen scattered as energy bolts danced through the lab, sending brickwork flying.

Lazonby unleashed another barrage of shots against the advancing giants. They staggered under the impact, but kept coming. Equipment shattered around them, smoke and flame belching from the conversion machinery. The Doctor was suddenly at his side, the Cyber head under his arm.

'It's no good, Major. We have to get out of here, now!' He had to shout over the roar of the Bren gun.

Lazonby didn't look at him. He kept firing, tears streaming from his face.

'My fault, Doctor. All my fault. Get out of here. Find some way to finish this.'

He shoved the Doctor away from him and stumbled further into the lab, staggering from the recoil of the machine-gun. He fired again and again. At the Cybermen. At their machinery. At the things that had once been people. Firing as if that alone would erase the terrible mistake that he had made.

The Doctor staggered to his feet. McBride caught him by the arm, and hauled him towards the shutter doors, coughing from the acrid smoke that now filled the lab. 'C'mon Doc, there's nothing you can do for him.'

McBride hauled himself over the shattered remains of the prototype Cyber-armour. The Doctor turned and peered back into the blazing laboratory. He caught one last glimpse of Lazonby, wreathed in smoke, surrounded by Cybermen, his Bren gun still blazing.

Then a silver arm came chopping down, and the gunfire stopped.

The Doctor scrambled over the wreckage and out into the corridor, scooping up the ghetto blaster as he went. Mullen and McBride were waiting for him, the policemen already heading for the front door.

McBride began to hare off down the corridor. The Doctor meandered after him, prodding at the head. Mullen exhaled noisily. 'Come on, Doctor, let's get out of here.'

The Doctor shook his head. 'I don't think we're in any danger out here. The Cybermen are going to be far more concerned with repairing their equipment than pursuing a handful of people like us.'

McBride stopped and pointed at the head dangling from the Doctor's hand. 'What about that?'

'Oh, I doubt that they consider it that important.'

There was a rending crash from behind them. They all spun.

Silhouetted against the inferno of the lab were the Cybermen, weapons drawn, gnashing Cybermats writhing around their feet. In front of them stood Wall, the light glinting horribly from the cameras embedded in his skull. He pointed at the trio of chief inspector, detective, and Time Lord.

'Kill them.'

'On the other hand…' said the Doctor.

PART FOUR

CHAPTER 19

'Unlucky in love, lucky at cards. Isn't that the saying? Well, you'd have thought that with all the bad luck I'd had with the fair sex over the last few years, my gambling would be pretty good. Not a chance. If there's a situation where some poor sap is going to come off the worse for wear then it's a pretty safe bet that the sap in question is going to be me, and at the moment the situation is about as bad as it gets. I'm trapped in a factory, during an air raid, with a horde of murderous metal monsters from outer space. They've got ray guns, we've got a little man with a home-made jukebox. My hand ain't looking too strong. Only once in my life I've had an Ace up my sleeve, but I lost her, and now I'm not sure if I'll ever see her again.'

Ace's midriff still felt sore from the electric shock it had received. She had no idea where she was. She had recovered consciousness to find herself bound and gagged on the floor of a tiny, propeller-driven aircraft, flying through darkness. The aeroplane had bucked and lurched alarmingly, buffeted by winds. In front of her, at the controls, Captain Hartmann had turned briefly and smiled at her. Such a friendly smile. It had made Ace's blood run cold. She had been relieved when he returned his attention to the matter of piloting the little craft through this hurricane.

They had landed – God alone knew where – and two uniformed German soldiers had hauled her unceremoniously, like an old sack, from the plane, and dumped her on cold, wet tarmac. Powerful searchlights cut through the drizzle and darkness. All she could make out behind the walls of light were low concrete bunkers, all around. It was through a metal door in one of these bunkers that Ace had been hauled, struggling and shouting – as much as she could shout behind her gag.

Low corridors. Harsh electric lighting. And now this.

* * *

The room didn't seem to fit with the outside of this place. The bed was big and soft and hung with drapes, like something out of a fairy-tale palace. The carpet was thick and scattered with rugs. A real tiger skin. Ace had never seen one before. Dried flowers stood around in vases. There was even a large, elegant fireplace.

It was blocked off, of course, with a metal plate. The door to the room was made of heavy wood, and locked. The window was tiny, receding into a wall several feet thick.

As the sky slowly lightened through the tiny window, all Ace could see was long grass and a few trees in the distance. She was near the sea – of that she was sure. Something in the air. A tang. Occasionally, she even imagined she could hear it.

God, it was quiet here.

Footsteps would occasionally approach the door, and then recede again. She had been brought breakfast: the door had been opened and a tray laden with cold meats and cheeses, bread, butter and hard-boiled eggs, a carafe of water and a jug of coffee, had been deposited on the floor by a wordless German soldier.

She had eaten the meal eagerly. It was the first food to have passed her lips since the curry she had eaten at George Limb's house. She had gulped down the coffee. Must keep alert: she didn't know what was in store for her here.

She had been allowed out twice to go to the lavatory.

This luxurious captivity was getting on her nerves.

Finally, the door swung open to reveal Captain Hartmann, still smiling, hands clasped behind his back. He had changed his clothes for a uniform: gleaming black boots, black jodhpurs, black jacket done up to the neck. A silver death's head on one side of his collar, two lightning flashes on the other.

SS.

Ace felt herself shuddering. For the first time, the truth hit her. This wasn't simply the uniform of some stock baddie in a third-rate war film. These people were real. What they did was real. The films hadn't exaggerated – far from it: for the sake of the censor they had underplayed what these people did.

She couldn't stop herself from shaking.

'I trust you have recovered from the rigours of the journey.'

He was a model of polite hospitality.

'Like you care. Where am I?'

'You are our guest. While you are with us you will be extended every courtesy. There is a guard outside your door at all times. Please inform him if there is anything we can provide for your comfort.'

Ace shook her head. 'I can't believe this! You electrocuted me! You rammed a cattle prod into my guts!'

Hartmann shrugged. 'Regrettable but necessary.'

'But then you Nazis are good at treating people like cattle, aren't you?'

He smiled. 'Propaganda and lies. You must bear in mind, young woman, that there is a war on. Each side always tries to paint the other in the worst possible light.'

'Oh, no, mate. I know all about you lot. Everybody does. Believe me, when this war ends, it won't be pretty. You're going to lose, and then you'll get it in the neck. They'll be stringing you up like dogs.'

'Lose?' He slapped his thigh. He seemed to find the prospect hilarious. 'Already we control most of Europe. We have even planted our victory standard on British soil. We cannot lose!'

British soil? Ace was beginning to panic. That was impossible. It never happened.

What if the Doctor was right? What if the thing he so feared had come to pass? The Cybermen were here, for God's sake. Everything was screwed up. Maybe history had gone wrong.

Hartmann took his hands from behind his back. He was holding Ace's Walkman.

'I am very curious to know what this is,' he said blandly.

'What does it look like, Herman? It's a Sony Walkman.'

'What is its function?'

'Get stuffed.'

'Your language is very strange. I am not familiar with many of the expressions you use; but this last one – this… get stuffed. That, I think, I understand.'

'Do it, then. Go on, bog off.'

Suddenly, Hartmann's tone was flinty. He wasn't smiling. 'This, as I said earlier, is a guest suite. There are other rooms in this complex which are considerably less comfortable.'

He turned on his heel and marched out of the room. The door swung shut behind him.

The day dragged on. With nothing else to do, Ace tried to make herself comfortable on the absurdly luxurious bed. Tried to sleep.

Where was she? Where was the Doctor? Was there any way he could find her here?

It was no good; she couldn't sleep. Somewhere, deep down, far off, she could hear the faintest of noises. Screams. Rhythmic screams, one after another. For nearly an hour they continued. Ace blocked her ears but she could still hear them. If anything they seemed to get louder.

Then they stopped.

Silence.

The silence was louder than the screams. It seemed to go on for ever. Day through the tiny window became night.

And then footsteps again. Hartmann. She sprang to her feet. The door opened and the SS captain stood before her. His face was unreadable now. A mask. Again he was holding her Walkman.

'What is the function of this device?'

'Why don't you just –'

He brought the back of his hand hard across her face. She staggered and fell beneath the weight of the blow.

'I do not wish to hear any more of your degenerate filth!'

He turned again and walked from the room. The guard moved in to take his place – easily sixteen stone of muscle and mindless obedience. He grabbed Ace hard by the wrist and hauled her to her feet. Not waiting for her to regain her balance he dragged her from the room and down a long, grey-tiled corridor.

At the end of the corridor was a metal door, painted the sort of drab, depressing green which, even in Ace's day, denoted some official, functional, and unpleasant purpose. Hartmann held the door open as the guard pulled the kicking, struggling Ace through it.

Beyond was a wide, low-roofed area, plain concrete supported by stocky concrete pillars. The floor was black with burn marks; the space was devoid of furniture, save for a single workbench. The guard threw Ace to the floor at the foot of this bench. It was about eight feet in length, and very heavy. On its surface, at each corner, was a leather strap and buckle. Another leather strap, along the side of the bench, held a series of vicious-looking wooden canes in a row. The top and sides of the bench were flecked with crusty, reddish-brown stains.

The room smelled of raw meat.

'When this complex was in civilian hands it was a scientific and industrial research facility,' said Hartmann. 'This area was used to test the resilience of materials and chemical compounds. I understand they used to conduct some quite extreme experiments here. We use it to test the resilience of human flesh. Our experiments are no less extreme.'

Ace felt her breathing quicken. She was shaking. Her mouth was dry, her mind empty.

'Suddenly you have nothing to say,' Hartmann smirked. He ran his forefinger lightly across Ace's cheek. She flinched. 'That will change.'

He nodded in the direction of the far wall. The guard dragged Ace towards three doors in a row, all metal, all green. She didn't struggle. She was numb with fear. The anonymity of the concrete expanse, of the official-looking doors, somehow exacerbated her fear. The central door was pushed open and she was thrown through it.

* * *

The room Ace found herself in was small, empty, and dim. She huddled herself into an uncomfortable corner, knees drawn up to her chin, rocking slightly, struggling to fight back tears.

Where was the Doctor?

She thought of all they had been through together. She thought of the Cybermen. Daleks. Dangerous enemies: dangerous times. Somehow it had all been a game compared with this. Hitler. Real Nazis this time.

They mustn't win. The Earth would become a hell. She would tell them nothing. She would give them no clue to the future. Why hadn't she listened to the Doctor? Why had she brought her Walkman with her, in spite of his many lectures?

They would take her out, strap her to the bench and beat her until she told them everything she knew.

She would tell them nothing.

They would flay her back with their birches. They would probably kill her.

Her thoughts bounced and echoed around the tiny room. She had to stop this. She would drive herself mad this way. This was what they wanted. This was why Hartmann had placed her here to wait.

Her eyes were becoming accustomed to the weak light filtering through the glass in the door. She began looking around her, minutely scrutinising the walls, anything to take her mind off the area outside the door. The bench.

There was some writing on the wall, low down, close to her head. Indelible pencil. 'This used to be my office,' it said. 'Now it is my cell. Tomorrow they will come for me. Jacques Millais. Engineer. Remember me. Pray for me.'

There were other messages. Different hands. Different tones of voice: some defiant, some pitiful, some merely names, written, it seemed, with the last reserves of their owners' strength. All desperate not to be forgotten. A memorial wall. It reminded Ace of the memorials that would go up after this most hideous of wars was over. Walls commemorating the millions who would die in battle, the millions who would be murdered in the death factories.

She was going to be one of them. One of the millions to die in a holocaust that happened thirty-odd years before she was born.

And she wouldn't be forgotten either. She scrabbled around in the pockets of her jacket for a pen, a pencil, anything. If only she had managed to hang on to her rucksack.

No pen. She fished out a bunch of keys. The keys to her mother's flat in Perivale. She laughed bitterly to herself. The flat hadn't even been built yet.

They would have to do. The surface of the wall was only plaster. She would scratch her last words into it. What to write? Somehow 'Ace woz 'ere' didn't seem appropriate. What was it the Doctor used to say to her? She struggled to recompose the words in her head. 'There is always evil to be fought. Evil thrives on neglect. It thrives on ignorance, on apathy, on hypocrisy. It thrives wherever we allow these things to grow unchallenged. It thrives wherever we turn our face away from need. Wherever we close our eyes, evil thrives.'

Yes.

She began scratching into the plaster, gouging out her final message to a world that would never read it, would never understand its meaning. A world gone mad.

Ace stopped. There was a noise coming through the wall. A tapping. She scratched with her key. The tapping came again. Scratch. Tap.

At last, 'Hello...'

A man's voice, very weak.

'H-hello...' Ace replied, nervously.

'You're new,' the man said. A northern accent. Yorkshire?

'Yes. I was only brought here last night. Can you tell me where I am?'

'Aye. This used to be the materials-testing area. Now it's –'

'No, I mean, I don't even know what country I'm in.'

'You're still in Britain, believe it or not. However many of us the bastards torture and kill, this is still Britain. This is Jersey.' The man laughed lightly. 'Dear old Jersey. We used to come here for holidays when I were a lad. All the way from Huddersfield. It were lovely. I jumped at the chance to move here…'

Jersey. Ace strained to remember her history. That's right. The Channel Islands. The only British soil occupied by the Nazis.

'What is this place?'

'This used to be the Le Mur compound. A research facility. Highly specialised stuff. Electronics. Before the Krauts moved in… I used to work here. We all did. Now they're killing us, one by one. I think I'm the last. You're the first outsider they've brought here as far as I know.'

'But why?'

'Every day they take me out and beat me. I don't feel it no more. The pain… I don't see the uniforms, or hear the questions. All I see is the smiling faces of me dead mates. It feels just like the old days again.'

The man's voice seemed somehow light, far away.

'Oh, this were a good company to work for. At first. It brought a lot of jobs to the island. Engineers, scientists. We were a happy bunch. Up until Dr Peddler left.'

'Peddler? Did you say Peddler?'

'Dr Peddler. Good old boy, Peddler…'

'Dr Peddler was here?'

'Oh, aye. Of course. Dr Peddler set this place up, along with that Wall.'

'Wall?'

'He always used to buy us a present at Christmas, Dr Peddler. Every one of us, a different present for each of us. Very thoughtful. Aye…'

'Tell me about Wall!' Ace was struggling to stop herself shouting.

'Oh, Wall. I didn't take to Wall much. None of us did. Wall were the businessman. Dr Peddler, he were the scientist. In the end they had some kind of falling out and Dr Peddler left. It were never so much fun after that. Things started to go downhill. That were a year or two back. He used to cycle here every day, Dr Peddler…'

'Please, this might be important. Tell me what happened here. When Dr Peddler left.'

'Well… they'd always been very secretive about what they were doing here, but it got worse after Dr Peddler left. Wall sacked loads of us. I lasted longer than most, but in the end I went too, along with the rest of them. Wall put practically everybody out of work. Personally I were glad to see the back of the place. There were something funny going on here. Dr Peddler were very unhappy at the end, I knew. Then the Jerries came. They had to bomb their way into the place. It took planes, tanks, dynamite, you name it.'

'And then what happened?' No reply. 'Please… it might be important. What happened next?'

'Nothing at first. Then they started rounding up everyone who'd worked here. They dragged us all back in and started asking questions about the work. Trouble was, nobody really knew what were going on, except Wall, and he vanished. They keep talking about battle armour, but I don't know anything. I keep telling them I don't know anything at all. So they beat me, and –'

The man's voice faltered.

Ace could here footsteps approaching. She sensed the man tense. There was something horrific about the approach of footsteps in a place like this.

The man started to laugh quietly to himself.

'I don't know anything… I don't know anything I don't…'

The footsteps stopped outside the cell of her invisible companion.

'Quickly,' Ace shouted. 'Tell me your name.'

For some reason she had to know.

'What…'

'Your name!'

They were opening his door. They were inside the room.

'Napley. Sid Napley.'

211

'I'm Ace,' she yelled, tears streaming down her cheeks. 'I'm Ace!'

'Ace…' the dreamy voice came again. 'I like that. Goodbye…'

She heard the door slam. She heard dragging sounds from outside. The chink of metal buckles, the slap of leather straps.

She tried to curl herself into a ball, eyes shut tight, teeth clenched, covering her ears, choking on sobs.

CHAPTER 20

The Doctor, Mullen, and McBride huddled at the top of the stairwell, listening for sounds of Cybermen on the floor below. Mullen was pale and sweating and McBride was still catching his breath. Only the Doctor seemed calm. He was kneeling on the floor tweaking at controls on the ghetto blaster, the head of the Cyberleader lying beside him.

When the Cybermen had appeared McBride had thought that it was all over, but the Doctor had wrenched a control on his box of tricks and a deafening, electronic screech had filled the corridor. The Cybermen had staggered, disorientated and, in that moment, the three of them had managed to vanish into the gloom of the factory.

Now they were playing a dangerous game of hide and seek in the darkened corridors, the Cybermen tearing the building apart trying to find them, spurred on by the raging Wall. They were beginning to run out of hiding places; McBride was beginning to run out of patience.

'Are we just going to sit here until they catch us? If the Cybermen don't get us then those... metal rats will.'

The Doctor shook his head. 'I've set up a jamming field that disguises our biorhythms. We can't be detected by their scanners. We just have to avoid being seen.'

A Cyberman appeared at the foot of the stairs, the light from its head sweeping the corridor. The trio ducked back into the shadows. The Cyberman moved off and Mullen let out a sigh of relief.

'What we need is a bomb to finish the blessed things off,' said Mullen. The Doctor stared at him. Mullen shuffled uncomfortably. 'What did I say?'

'Chief Inspector, you're a genius.'

'What are you on about, Doc?' McBride hissed. 'Where the hell are we going to get a bomb?'

The Doctor raised a finger and pointed upward. McBride looked up, puzzled, then, as the distant sound of ack-ack fire and explosions reached him, he suddenly realised what the Doctor had in mind.

'Oh, no...'

The Doctor was a frenzy of activity. He pulled his hat out of his pocket and jammed it on to his head. He tapped maniacally at controls on the ghetto blaster. 'Now, listen to me, both of you. I'm going to set this to give out another disruptive burst. As soon as it goes off, run. Head for the ground floor and start switching on the lights and pulling all the blackout curtains down. As soon as the Germans see this place lit up, it'll make an irresistible target. If any of you see any Cybermen, smash whatever window you're at and get out, head for the police box by Southwark Power Station.'

Mullen scratched his head. 'But there isn't a police box by –'

The Doctor shushed him. 'Trust me, Inspector.' He looked at them both, steely-eyed. 'Now, when I say run, run.'

He pressed the button on the ghetto blaster.

'Run!'

McBride had never run so fast in his life. As the electronic screech filled the factory he had bounded down the stairs, taking them two at a time. Huge figures filled the corridor, reeling drunkenly. McBride dodged past them. Typical – he got the corridor with the Cybermen in it.

He sprinted around a corner into a corridor lined with windows, all of them draped with thick, black curtains. He found the light switch, snapped it on and began tearing at the heavy cloth. Outside, in the night sky, he could see searchlights and hear the drone of bombers.

Russian roulette with Hitler.

'I hope you know what you're doing, Doc.'

It took him several minutes to clear all of the windows. He got to the far end of the corridor and looked around. No Cybermen.

214

He darted through a door marked 'Conference Room' and found himself in an expansive room with more external windows. He closed the door, put on the lights and started pulling the blackout curtains open. He was half-way along the wall when he heard the door open behind him.

McBride spun to see Wall in the doorway. A Cyberman loomed behind him. Wall slithered into the room, his camera eyes firmly centred on McBride.

'No escape for you.'

He launched himself at the American and the two of them crashed to the floor. McBride struggled to keep Wall's hands from his throat. He was fighting like a man possessed. Those cold, unblinking lenses stared down at McBride.

'All my work, all my plans, ruined because of you and that spiteful little Doctor.'

McBride tried to ward off the blows raining down on him. He twisted and fought. He got his foot under Wall's stomach and pushed.

The little man flew across the room, crashing against the door. The Cyberman levelled its gun. McBride ducked behind the conference table as the weapon crackled. The window behind him exploded into a million pieces and cold air and rain billowed into the room.

McBride braced his back against the heavy table and heaved. It toppled over and crashed to the floor. Using it as cover, McBride launched himself towards the shattered window, but something caught hold of his leg. Wall again, slithering over the floor like a huge reptile.

'No escape,' he hissed. 'You will be like us.'

McBride could see the Cyberman taking aim. He reached down and hauled Wall to his feet. There was the harsh discharge of the energy weapon, and Wall convulsed in his hands. Smoke curled out from his collar and the cameras embedded in his eye sockets spat flame. Wall gave out a long, warbling scream.

McBride let the smoking body drop from his grasp and hurled

himself through the broken window. Behind him he could hear the rattle of the Cybergun, and splintering wood.

He hit the ground hard, the breath punched from his body. He scrambled to his feet and began to run, eyes closed, waiting for the noise of the gun again.

There was a colossal explosion behind him and he was hurled to the ground. He looked around. The Peddler factory was ablaze, not only with the electric lights but with fire. In the darkened city it shone out like a beacon. The German bombers had already started to use it as a target and, as he watched, another fireball tore through the building sending bricks and shrapnel high into the night air.

McBride suddenly realised that he was in a very dangerous place. He hauled himself off the wet road and began to run again, towards the looming shape of the power station. Where the hell was this police box? And what good would it do him to find it?

There was another explosion, louder this time. It made McBride's ears ring. He thought that he could hear his name being shouted. He shook his head to try to clear it .

'McBride!'

He *could* hear someone calling him. He looked up, wiping the rain from his eyes. There was a figure standing outside a police box, waving at him frantically. The Doctor. He sprinted forwards, collapsing inside. The Doctor slammed the door shut.

McBride lay on the floor, panting, desperately trying to recover his breath and clear his head of the noise.

The noise.

There was no noise. There were no explosions, just a quiet, contented hum. He looked up. The Doctor was beaming down at him. 'Hello, Mr McBride. Glad to see you're still with us.'

McBride groaned. 'Mullen?'

'Over here, McBride.' The familiar Irish lilt floated across the room.

McBride staggered to his feet, helped up by the Doctor. As his eyes cleared he got his first look at the inside of the police box. His jaw dropped.

The Doctor looked at him quizzically. 'Aren't you going to tell me that it's bigger on the inside than the out?'

McBride shook his head and crossed to where Mullen was watching the destruction of the Peddler factory on a huge (colour!) television screen. 'I always knew that you weren't from Perivale.'

CHAPTER 21

Ace cried until no more tears would come.

The muffled sounds from outside her door were mercifully short. The footsteps receded into silence, accompanied by the same dragging sound as before.

Ace sat with her back to the wall. She was numb. She was beyond caring about memorials, about her own life or death. Her fear had gone. She felt calm, she felt cold. Above all, she felt anger. Cool, rational, implacable anger.

She had no weapon, but she could improvise. The keys that were to have carved her memorial would serve another purpose. A bunch of keys clenched in the fist, prongs outward, made a particularly vicious knuckle-duster. She would fight; she wouldn't let the Doctor down. She would fight the only way she knew how – the way she had always fought. The next Nazi who came through the door, she would carve her memorial on his face.

Footsteps. She crouched to spring.

The door opened slowly. She was on her feet and surging across the cell.

She stopped.

'You…'

'I hope they didn't hurt you, my dear.'

George Limb shuffled into the cell.

'Get away from me. Hartmann told me all about you.'

'And what exactly did the good captain tell you?'

'That you're working for them. That you've been working for them for years.'

'Not strictly true, Ace. Let us just say that they have been of far more use to me than I to them.'

'Do you know what they are? Do you know what they do to people?'

'Indeed I do, Ace. A ghastly rabble, I agree. But I am a realist, my dear. A small man trying, like everybody else, to stay afloat upon the riptides of history. Herr Hitler and his gang are here. Indeed, they are everywhere. They are a fact, and facts, however unpalatable, have to be addressed with unflinching realism. I am sure you have heard the expression "the road to hell is paved with good intentions"… Come.'

He beckoned her from the cell.

'I first became aware of the National Socialists in 1923. Hitler attempted an armed uprising. It was a fiasco, and he ended up in prison, but it was clear from his conduct in court that this man had… potential. From then on I have taken a close interest in the party's fortunes. I tried, largely through dear Winston, to get the British government to take this man seriously, but with little success. After the Germans invaded Czechoslovakia there was an international conference held in Munich to try to secure the peace in Europe. The prime minister of the time, Mr Chamberlain, attended, and so did I. Immediately, I saw it for the farce it was. The very fact that the conference took place was an absolute indication of the Allies' lack of resolve. Chancellor Hitler walked all over them.'

'"I have in my hand a piece of paper…"'

'Precisely.'

No. She wouldn't listen to this. She fixed her eyes across the concrete expanse on to the lethal wooden bench with the straps. 'You're a user, Limb. You've manipulated and lied to me ever since I first visited you with Cody. You sent us into that factory, didn't you? You knew how dangerous it was going to be.'

'I have never lied to you, Ace. Believe it or not, I have a high regard for your courage and resourcefulness. And if you recall I advised you not to break into the Peddler factory.'

'You knew we were going to go in.' Her voice was low and resentful. 'You knew.'

'If you must blame me for that, accuse me only of bowing to the inevitable, and perhaps of being a little opportunistic. I was… curious. You and Mr McBride had come to me with the beginnings of an interesting story. I wished to – as it were – stir things up a bit. See what floated to the surface.'

'You could just have asked me what was going on. Like a fool, I'd have told you…'

'Openness and trust are not the hallmarks of the fool, Ace. They are virtues, to be highly prized – though I am aware of my own shortcomings in those areas. Sadly, however, the information one can receive from the mouths of others is invariably of limited use: however loyal, diligent or indeed intelligent they are, they inevitably colour the facts with their own prejudices. They see in part what they want to see. Moreover, they see only that which is obvious and ignore only that which is important.'

Ace was barely listening.

'Hartmann said you were going to give the Nazis Cybertechnology, you creep. He said you set me up to be brought here.'

'You were never in any danger from Captain Hartmann, my dear. Of that I can assure you. I'm afraid it was necessary to make these people… an offering…'

'An offering?'

'As I said, you would not have been harmed. You are under my protection. I have assured Captain Hartmann's superiors that you are one of very few people on this planet at this time who can shed light upon the technology of the Cybermen.'

In spite of herself, Ace laughed.

'Don't look at me, mate. I'm as in the dark about what makes the tinheads tick as you are.'

George Limb smiled. He blinked his strange, slow blink. Suddenly, Ace knew what that blink reminded her of. A lizard.

'Such colourful language. You know, when I was in Whitehall my language was considered too colourful. I think it embarrassed people. Civil service reports and memoranda are terribly dry things. Come, walk with me.'

'You're not listening to me, are you? I don't want anything to do with this, and I don't want anything to do with you.'

'Ace, I hope you will in time forgive me for all the injustices which have been inflicted upon you recently. All I can say is that they were necessary. I am playing a very delicate tune on the fragile strings of time.'

'I trusted you. The things you said. The light in your window.'

'Lights attract many things, Ace. The lost traveller, the doomed moth, the overcurious intruder. Lights lure ships on to the rocks.'

'Is that what it was, then? A wrecker's light?'

'I hope not, Ace. I hope not.'

Slowly, he began to walk towards a corridor Ace hadn't noticed before, hidden in shadow behind a concrete pillar, another blank, grey-tiled, underground thoroughfare. Warily, Ace followed.

'I have something for you,' said Limb. 'In here.'

He stopped outside yet another of the anonymous green doors.

'One moment,' he said, and disappeared through it. When he re-emerged he was holding Ace's rucksack.

'You left your bag at my house,' he said, handing it to her.

'I didn't exactly have time to pack. That bastard Hartmann electrocuted me.'

'Oh, believe me, Ace, I no more approve of their methods than you do. We live in times of great violence, times when the rights of the individual seem to count for little. This will not change, even after this war. Of that I am sure. But then I suspect you would know more about that than I.'

He walked on up the corridor. It ended in a pair of grey metal double doors.

The guard on the doors snapped instantly to attention.

'Oh, ah, Heil Hitler, and so forth,' said Limb, vaguely waving a hand in the air as the guard opened the doors for them.

Beyond lay a huge, brightly lit expanse of white plaster and metalwork, gigantic machines, pipes and valves, towering thirty feet into the air. And along one massive wall, rank upon rank, row upon row, scores of Cybermen stood in a honeycomb of cavities, inert but upright, as though to attention, lifeless, embryonic, waiting to live.

Grey-uniformed guards and white-coated technicians moved like insects across this technological cliff face.

'My God…' Even Ace was astonished. She had never seen so many Cybermen.

'Impressive, isn't it?' said Limb. 'Unfortunately, there is a problem. It seems that the finest scientific minds in the Third Reich are no nearer to understanding Cybertechnology here at its heart than I was in my bedroom in Belsize Park. All we can do now is wait.'

'What for?'

'The Doctor, of course. To come and rescue you. I am afraid you will have to play the hostage a little longer, Ace.' He gestured absently to a nearby soldier. 'Uh, guard…'

The soldier approached.

'Return the young lady to the guest suite. And be pleased to inform Captain Hartmann that she is to be extended every courtesy whilst she is here. Any further attempts to frighten her and to undermine my plans and I shall not waste my time speaking to the captain's superiors. I shall be reporting directly to my friends in Berlin.'

The guard seized Ace by the arm.

'Gently, please,' Limb counselled.

'Suppose the Doctor doesn't come?' Ace snarled.

'I understand the Doctor well, my dear, though not half as well as I should like. In many ways he reminds me of myself, although I am sure I flatter myself by the comparison. I have no doubt that so resourceful a gentleman will have no difficulty in deducing your whereabouts and attempting to effect a rescue. My, how exciting…'

With a flick of his hand he dismissed the guard and turned away.

CHAPTER 22

Dawn was breaking over London. From the fourth-floor window of his office Cody McBride, Private Detective, and Chief Inspector Patrick Mullen, Special Branch, watched the now-peaceful sky slowly lighten. Below them people were waking, emerging from shelters, re-engaging with their daily lives. The city had lived through another night. And what a night.

McBride was ransacking the pockets of his various identical trench coats.

'Out of smokes… out of whisky. Man, I've got to get my life together.'

'You're surely not wanting a drink at this time, man,' Mullen exclaimed.

'A cigarette would do,' McBride replied.

'Here –' Mullen fished a battered packet of Rothmans from inside his overcoat – 'have one of mine. And while we're on the subject…'

From the back pocket of his trousers he plucked a slim metal hip-flask and unscrewed the top.

'Take a nip of that,' the policeman said, smiling. 'I intend to.'

McBride gratefully took a slug from the flask. 'Sorry, I got no glasses,' he said. 'They kinda got smashed.'

'Very wise,' said Mullen. 'We should do the same. *Sláinte.*'

'Say what?'

'Pardon?'

'What?'

The policeman grinned.

'I may have misjudged you, McBride,' he said. 'You're not like most of the Irish Americans I've met. Most of them are red-hot Republicans. Give half their money to the IRA.'

'Me,' said McBride, 'I'm a Democrat, and I give half my money to Mama. Nah, I'm too busy trying to earn a buck to get political. Say, where's the Doc?'

'The Doc,' said the Doctor, bustling through the door, 'is here. I'm sorry to have kept you waiting, gentlemen. I've been working on the head.' In his hands he held the corroded, dead head of the Cyberleader.

'You got plans for that, Doc?' McBride asked. 'Cause it'd make a helluva plant pot.'

'Sorry, Mr McBride,' the Doctor replied. 'I need this. There's still a great deal to do.'

From his pocket he pulled the now-crumpled map he had removed from George Limb's house. He spread it across McBride's desk.

'Inspector,' he said, 'do these crosses mean anything to you?'

With his finger he traced the crescent of ink marks made by Limb.

'Well…'

'They mark the trail of the Lurker,' announced the Doctor. 'Now…' He fished a pen from his pocket. 'These explosions…'

'Explosions?'

'Yes, yes. The ones nobody's supposed to know about. The ones that the newspapers put down to a new type of German bomb… You remember?'

'Yes.'

The Doctor handed the pen to Mullen.

'Give me a rough idea where they occurred.'

The chief inspector scored the map with a number of broad, heavy gashes.

'That's about the best I can –' He stopped. 'Well I'll be!'

The Doctor smiled.

The trail of the detonations followed that of the Lurker almost identically.

'Doc,' McBride cut in, 'are you saying it was the Lurker?'

'No. I'm saying the Lurker was being followed. Stalked.'

'By whom?'

'Or what,' said the Doctor darkly. 'I'm about to find out.' Suddenly he was brisk. 'I must leave you. It's time to take the fight to the enemy. And I still haven't recovered Ace,' he added grimly. 'I've been very neglectful.'

McBride cast his eyes to the floor. In the excitement he had all but forgotten his tough lady ally.

'Before you go, Doctor,' said Mullen, 'I've telephoned the station. Sent some men to Belsize Park to arrest George Limb. He won't escape this time.'

'He already has,' the Time Lord replied. 'He's a very slippery customer.'

'What's his game, Doc?' asked McBride.

'Chess,' said the Doctor curtly. 'You know, half of London saw the Cybermen's escape pod flying over. Only two people understood what it meant. One of those was Peddler, who, I believe, had seen it all before. The other was George Limb, and just how he knew I have yet to find out: although it wouldn't surprise me if that devious old man hadn't simply deduced it from first principles.'

Mullen looked troubled.

'So how will we ever catch someone like that?'

'Oh, don't worry about Limb,' said the Doctor. 'I've an appointment with him on Jersey.'

'Jersey?' McBride butted in. 'How in the hell d'you know he's on Jersey?'

'That's the trick with chess players,' said the Doctor. 'Once you work out their game you can generally predict their moves. That's all there is to top-level chess. No one ever makes a move without knowing how their opponent will respond. Jersey is where Wall and his Cybermen came from. It is where the main Cyberforce is based. George Limb knows this. I know George Limb is on Jersey, and he knows I know. He is waiting for me there.'

Mullen shook his head slowly, a smile of incredulity and admiration playing about his lips.

'We could use you on the force, Doctor. The criminals wouldn't stand a chance.'

'Yeah,' said McBride, 'and I'd be out of a job. Get outa here, Doc.'

'Yes.' The Doctor smiled. 'It is time I was leaving. Goodbye, gentlemen.'

'Doctor,' Mullen cut in as the Time Lord was disappearing through the door, 'is there anything else we should do here? Any loose ends we should tidy up?'

'Just keep your eyes open and your mouths closed,' the Doctor replied. 'This whole episode must remain our secret. It shouldn't be too difficult. Heaven knows, there's enough else happening. Oh, and take care of yourselves, gentlemen. Don't forget, there's a war on.'

He turned and began descending the stairs.

'Ah,' said McBride, 'relax. The war's as good as won. The United States'll be in soon enough.'

He reclined on his chair and put his feet on the desk.

'Ain't that right, Doc?' he called after the vanished Time Lord.

'Oh,' the Doctor's voice floated up the stairs, 'I really couldn't say…'

scanning>
signal detected>
activate>
locate signal source> signal source located>
scan for hostile life forms> negative>
proceed>

For three hours the Doctor had waited in the grey drizzle of the Southwark morning. He had begun the day by picking his way around the ruined shell of the Peddler factory, satisfying himself that no trace of Cybertechnology remained in the ruins. The TARDIS still sat in the shelter of the power station: the Doctor stood in its shadow, holding the head of the Cyberleader. From the severed neck two wires now protruded, joining what was left of the inner workings of the head to what looked for all the world like a battery-tester – a small needle gauge and a pair of frequency dials set into a yellow plastic box.

It was worryingly crude, but in the time available...

The Doctor only hoped it would work.

Beyond the limit of the Doctor's hearing the head was transmitting a high-frequency signal. Every so often it would squawk electronically, the needle would dance wildly, and the Doctor would make swift, minute adjustments to the dials.

Gently...

```
scan signal source area>
alien life form detected>
analyse> humanoid> non-terrestrial>
search data files>
subject identified> planet of origin Gallifrey>
presume hostile>
arm>
prepare to detonate>
prepare>
prepare to det>
prepare to>
prepprep>
preprrpreprprrr>>>
```

Time Lord and time bomb stood facing each other across the expanse of waste ground. Very slowly the rhythmic bleeping from the Cyberleader's head was dropping in pitch. It was clearly, painfully audible now. The Doctor began to walk slowly towards his quarry, still making delicate adjustments to his lash-up.

Carefully... The Doctor knew that a slip of the wrist now would obliterate him, the power station and much of Southwark. Only the TARDIS and the source of the explosion itself would be left standing.

By the time he stood over the machine the whistle from the Cyberleader's head had become a low hum. He looked at the thing in front of him. It stood about waist high: a flat, circular surface with a rounded underside on a pair of short, flexible legs on broad feet. Its top sported an array of coloured lights, readouts, and inset controls.

'So you're the thing that's been blowing up half of London,' the Time Lord murmured.

Lights flickered menacingly across the surface console of the squat machine.

Gingerly, the Doctor reached towards it. 'Here goes…'

He keyed a sequence of buttons. The surface lights flickered once more and then died.

The machine toppled on to its side into the mud.

Suspended outside space and time, the TARDIS hung immobile and hummed to itself.

If the Cybermen's little toy was to trigger any more explosions it could do so in the TARDIS, where no one except the Doctor would feel the effect.

The Time Lord was on his knees in a corner of the console room. The device lay next to him, upside down, legs in the air. He had removed a panel from its exposed underside and was rummaging around inside.

'Yes… I see…' he muttered to himself. 'You generate a force field around yourself and then trigger a plasma explosion just outside the force field. Now… we shall remove the force-field chip, for a start… Temporal anomalies are bad enough. Indestructible ones are quite out of the question.'

He placed a tiny piece of microcircuitry in his pocket.

'But why?' he muttered. 'No Cyberman was ever so well armed. You must be very important to them… Ah!'

He peered deeply into the machine's interior.

'You're some sort of command-relay unit! In effect a portable battle computer, capable of constantly receiving and processing new data and updating and relaying orders. Very clever! And presumably you were sent here with your big friend as a sort of advanced reconnaissance mission.'

The machine emitted a low beep, almost as if agreeing.

The Doctor continued. 'Spy out the land, formulate a battle plan and then send in the cavalry. Then he got hit by a bomb, his homing signal was damaged, and ever since you've been running about London like a lost dog trying to find him.' He tickled the metal underbelly of the console. 'You know, you remind me of an old friend of mine...'

The Doctor groped blindly about the floor where he knelt. His fingers closed on one of his jeweller's screwdrivers. He gingerly inserted it into the guts of the command unit.

'Let's see,' he murmured, 'if I can't make you dance to a different tune.'

In a remote storage bay, deep underground, deserted and empty, the stillness was ripped in two by the asthmatic shriek of the Doctor's old TARDIS taking material form. The door to the blue box opened and the little Time Lord emerged. Grimly, he planted his battered hat upon his head.

Jersey.

He pursed his lips and let out a low, enticing whistle. Responding with an electronic burble, the squat form of the Cyber-command unit waddled after him.

'Stay,' said the Doctor. 'I'll call you when I need you.'

The walking time bomb slipped into the shadows.

'Now... the front door, I think.'

Having pushed open the unlocked doors of the storage bay, the Doctor sauntered down the corridor beyond, whistling tunelessly to himself, umbrella slung jauntily over his shoulder.

It was a matter of yards before he was challenged by an SS private.

'Halt!' the young soldier barked. 'What are you doing here?'

'Oh, nothing much,' replied the Doctor. 'Just out for an afternoon stroll. Is it the afternoon? It's so difficult to tell when one has just materialised, particularly when one is underground. I don't suppose you could...' He paused, struck by a sudden thought. 'You know, I'm not sure I've ever said this to a human before...

Would you be so kind as to… take me to your leader?'

The soldier had unslung his rifle and was pointing it at the Doctor's head.

'March!' he barked.

'Certainly,' the Doctor replied.' "Colonel Bogey"?'

And, shouldering his umbrella military-style, he set off down the corridor at a brisk pace, half singing, half humming the irreverent old tune. 'Hitler… ta ta ta tum tum tummm…'

The late Major Lazonby would have felt quite at home in Captain Hartmann's office. Save for the massive portrait of Hitler dominating the back wall, the two rooms looked almost identical. Everything was neat and in order and, in so far as was possible, green.

Hartmann was not a happy officer at present. He had just concluded what he quite rightly regarded as a highly hazardous – and probably pointless – mission; flying a tiny aeroplane into the heart of enemy territory, kidnapping a teenage girl and flying out again in the middle of a storm and a major night-time bombing raid. What could a foul-mouthed girl possibly tell them about the technology they were trying to unravel here?

He had been told virtually nothing about what was going on: Colonel Schott, his commanding officer, was playing his cards close to his chest and telephoning Berlin a lot. All he had been told was to place himself at the disposal of the feeble old Englishman who had given them the tip-off about the girl, and who had arrived a few hours previously by private plane. The Englishman reminded Hartmann of Colonel Schott. They both seemed to rely on friends in high places rather than the dynamism and dedication demanded by the New European Order. They should both have been put out to pasture years ago.

He was in no mood to be lenient when the guard came to the door and reported an intruder in the compound.

CHAPTER 23

'Name?'

The Doctor had merely carried on playing with the end of his umbrella.

'I told you.'

Hartmann slammed his hand down on his desk.

'Doctor is not a name! It is a professional designation. What is your name?'

'You have my identity card.'

'I have an identity card for an organisation which doesn't exist, stamped with the year 1980 and containing somebody else's photograph. I am not a patient man, and I will not be trifled with!'

'I doubt you'd be able to pronounce the name I was originally given. I've come for my friend Ace.'

'Ah, now we are getting somewhere.'

'Is George Limb here yet?'

'You are a friend of Limb's?'

'No, I'm afraid we won't ever be friends. Too much of a difference in outlook. Now, I should like first to see my friend Ace, and then to have a little word with Mr Limb.'

Hartmann sat down, not knowing whether to be amused or infuriated at this little man's attitude. He was used to the fear spread by his uniform, by the death's head, by the twin lightning flashes. The SS were feared right across Europe. This man was not afraid of him, and Hartmann didn't know what to do. He couldn't inflict pain on him – not until he had established whether or not this man was under George Limb's, and hence Berlin's, protection.

'And if there's any going, I'd love some tea. It's been a strenuous few days.'

'Guard,' Hartmann called. 'Fetch the Englishman.'

'Ah, Doctor. Good of you to join us.' George Limb grabbed the Doctor's hand and shook it with genuine enthusiasm. 'There is so much to discuss. Come, please.'

He clapped the Doctor on the shoulder and ushered him from Captain Hartmann's office.

'Thank you, Captain,' Limb said, dismissively, over his shoulder.

They walked up the corridor together, Limb leaning slightly on the Doctor's arm.

'Quite a place, eh, Doctor?' he said. 'Carved out of solid rock, for the most part. What could have done that, eh?'

'I've seen more impressive factories,' the Doctor replied.

'Oh, I don't doubt it,' chuckled Limb. 'Although I'll venture we managed to surprise your young friend Ace.'

'Yes, where is Ace?' asked the Doctor testily. 'I should like to see her without further delay.'

'Please, Doctor. Accept my assurances. Ace is quite comfortable. Indulge an old man for a few moments. Observe...'

He pushed open the heavy set of double doors and, casting off the support of the Doctor's shoulder, threw his arms wide.

'Look, Doctor.'

The ranked, inert Cybermen gazed sightlessly down on the pair.

'Mmm,' said the Doctor flatly. 'So here they are.'

'I have to admit, Doctor, I was most impressed. I arrived here for the first time last night, and I really didn't know what to expect. But this...'

'Tell me, Mr Limb, when did you first find out about the Cybermen?'

'When you told me about them, Doctor. You and the young lady, in your different ways. I saw the sphere coming down over London, as did everybody else, of course. It was clear to me that this was not a product of any technology I had seen before. Allied to my suspicions about the non-human nature of the Lurker, the truth began to dawn.'

'Yes, a very impressive piece of deduction,' said the Doctor.

'Sherlock Holmes again, Doctor. Once you have eliminated all impossible solutions what remains, however improbable it seems, must be the right answer. The finer details, such as the location of this place, I discovered from its former director, Mr Wall. He was surprisingly forthcoming.'

'I'm sure the promise of Major Lazonby's cooperation made him only too willing to talk to you. I should inform you, by the way, that both Wall and Major Lazonby are dead. Peddler's factory is rubble.'

'Oh dear.' Limb cast his eyes downward. 'What a senseless waste of life.'

'Why have you lured me here? I assume it is because in spite of your guile you are as out of your depth as the rest of your species with Cybertechnology.'

'I fear so, Doctor. I did try to fathom its depths myself – that is why I captured our friend the Lurker – but the shortfall in my scientific knowledge was just too great.'

'You must know,' said the Doctor in a low voice, 'that I will not help you revive the Cybermen.'

'I trust you will change your mind soon enough, Doctor.'

'Your trust is sadly misplaced.'

George Limb sighed. 'My… associates are apt to be a little heavy-handed. One would hate to have to allow them to focus their attentions on our young friend Ace.'

'I'm disappointed in you, Mr Limb. I would have expected something more sophisticated from that Machiavellian mind of yours.'

The old man looked wistfully about the vast room.

'It's the times we live in, Doctor. They bring out the very worst in men. In London I had little need to resort to such crudities. The criminal world accorded me a reputation far more formidable than anything I felt I had actually earned. The major players treated me with a wholly undeserved respect, whilst the likes of our friend Sharkey were absolutely petrified of me. It is quite remarkable, the power of suggestion.'

'Indeed. But not here.'

'Sadly, no. These people are in thrall to a master. Whatever else his failings, and they are many, Chancellor Hitler has made such an impression on the minds of these people that a mere penpusher such as myself stands no chance of competing. No, here – ashamed though I am to have to resort to such methods – I'm afraid I have no alternative but to threaten violence.'

'I see…'

'But come, Doctor, let us not be uncivilised. Please, come with me.'

The old man began ascending a metal staircase set into the wall opposite the dormant Cyber ranks. The Doctor followed. Close to the lofty ceiling a walkway ran the length of the wall, and behind it a long window looked out across the white-and-chrome abyss. Next to the window was a door, which George Limb now opened.

'They have given me Dr Peddler's old office,' he said, 'which is rather nice of them. Come in… Come in.'

He picked his way into the large room, obviously once elegant and comfortable, now a mess. On one wall, thick with dust and grime, a framed photograph of a young Dr Peddler, arm in arm with a woman carrying a child, hung next to a calendar showing photographs of pastoral tranquillity. Jersey before the occupation. The calendar was two years out of date. Office furniture and the day-to-day paraphernalia of business management vied with large and obscure pieces of heavy machinery. The room seemed to have been used largely for the storage of junk. In a far corner, partly obscured by the desk, sat a squat, black machine, looking for all the world like a giant inverted child's spinning top. Grubby glass portholes ringed its neck and pipes as thick as a tree trunks bulged from a dirty metal skirt, covered in grease and burn marks, before disappearing into the underside of the thing.

The filing cabinets which still lined the walls, and the drawers of the large mahogany desk, had been ransacked. Files and papers lay scattered across the desk and floor; pens, paperclips, and blotters lay in piles where they had been upended.

The overall effect of discarded machinery and trashed paperwork conjured in the Doctor visions of some futuristic, post-apocalyptic bureaucracy gone haywire.

George Limb moved a pile of papers with his foot.

'I think our German friends must have been looking for answers among Peddler's notes. I don't think this office has been used since he left. Except as a junkroom.'

'Cybermen don't need offices.'

'From what I understand, Dr Peddler succumbed to certain… ethical qualms about the Cyber process, and resigned rather swiftly.'

'You have never seen the way they make Cybermen, Mr Limb. It's horrible. In London Dr Peddler was working on a method of harnessing Cybertechnology without the terrible human cost. Worthy but doomed. Cybertechnology can never provide any answers for the human race, Limb. Surely a man of your undoubted genius must see that.'

'You flatter me, Doctor, but, as you surely realise, genius ultimately is not a function of the intellect but of the imagination. And my imagination is on fire at the moment.'

'The whole world is on fire at the moment.'

'In London you called me Frankenstein, Doctor. Mary Shelley called Dr Frankenstein the Modern Prometheus. Prometheus, bringer of fire. Yet I alone am the bringer of fire! It is I who am poised to give birth to the modern world. And, like Frankenstein, I am peopling that world with monsters!'

The Doctor tutted. 'I expected more of you,' he said. 'Just another mad scientist.'

Limb reached down among the pile of papers and extracted a small wooden box. He slid back the lid to reveal a set of chessmen.

'Apparently Dr Peddler was a player,' he said. He pulled a board from a drawer in the desk and laid it out, almost lovingly. 'I should deem it an honour if you would grant me a game, Doctor.'

Colonel Schott poured himself a stiff brandy. Not for the first time he wished he had retired before the war started. Before Hitler.

Hartmann and all his sort gave Schott a headache. Brave, certainly, but dedicated to the point of fanaticism. In Schott's day military service had been a noble career; the officer class had been a class above. An élite. Not any more.

Schott had served with distinction in the Great War. He had been at Tannenberg with General Hindenberg. He had been wounded on the Somme. The Iron Cross, First Class, now sat upon his chest. He was too old for this National Socialist nonsense. Everything was turned on its head. That a captain – a mere captain – should be able to get away with such insolence. But Hartmann was SS, while Schott was Wehrmacht. Regular army. Rank didn't come into it; everybody here – Schott included – was frightened of the SS.

This had seemed like an easy ride at first. Second-in-command on some sleepy little island off the coast of France. Then they had discovered this place. Those silver giants. The news had shot up through the chain of command, apparently to Reichsführer Himmler himself. Himmler was sending someone. He loved this sort of thing. In the meantime he, Schott, was in charge, with instructions to liaise with the highest-ranking SS officer on the scene: Captain Hartmann.

Hartmann had spent the previous twenty minutes haranguing Schott about discipline and security. The entire complex was awash with enemy aliens, he had ranted. When Himmler's representative arrived he would put Schott on a charge.

To address a senior officer in such a way… It would have been unheard of in Schott's day. He downed the brandy. There was nothing he could do, and he knew it.

The situation was getting more complicated by the day. Schott recognised what was happening – it happened all the time nowadays. There was the usual power struggle going on in Berlin over who was going to control this new discovery. Everybody jockeying for position under the Führer. Goering vying with Himmler vying with Hess vying with God knew who. Which meant that, as ever, it was uncertain exactly whom he was supposed to be taking his orders from. At the moment he was leaning towards Admiral Canaris at the Abwehr – the Wehrmacht intelligence bureau. Canaris was a man Schott respected. Distinguished naval career. One of his own kind; one of the officer class. It was Canaris who had put him in touch with the old Englishman, with instructions that he was to be given full cooperation. It was a strange situation, and one that Hartmann, he knew, found intolerable. Schott had sent Hartmann himself to collect the girl: partly because he could fly an aeroplane, and partly just to get him out of the way for a short while.

Now the Englishman had turned up, unannounced. And then another little man had turned up. Hartmann was right: on paper their security looked farcical.

Moreover, the situation in Berlin could change at any moment, leaving Schott exposed and vulnerable. Sooner or later someone would come and take charge. Schott just hoped that he could keep things running smoothly until that time.

The brandy bottle was low. He poured what was left into his glass and peered lovingly into it, watching the crazy reflection of the overhead light bulb playing on its golden surface.

Two men – one old, one ancient – sat hunched over a chessboard. One, white-haired and frail, sat on his handkerchief, spread in a genteel manner across an enormous metal pipe that jutted from an obscure, filthy and, above all, dead machine. The other, short and grizzled, his colossal age betrayed only by the depth of blue-grey in his eyes, sat on the edge of a swivel chair much too large for him, his foot resting on an old piece of engine. Around them old paperwork lay in piles, boxes of valves and knobs teetered against one another or lay, their sides split, contents spilling out across the floor.

Outside the window, across the chamber, the blank-faced Cybermen stood in rows, impassive as ever. Remorseless foot soldiers, devoid of hope, devoid of fear, never surrendering, never retreating.

Beneath their unseeing gaze the Doctor advanced his king's pawn.

'What do you hope to gain from Cybertechnology, Mr Limb?'

George Limb mirrored the move.

'A very astute question, Doctor. You should know that I have no desire whatever for personal gain. Wealth and power mean nothing to me. I suppose the answer must be knowledge, Doctor. Knowledge for its own sake.'

'Knowledge carries with it responsibility. You can never escape that fact.'

King's knight to king's bishop three.

'All my life I have been a collector of knowledge, Doctor. Take my little... consultancy back in London. Frankly, the whole business is far more beneficial to me than it is to my clients. I hire out my services for one reason and one reason alone: doing so enables me to chart the varying currents flowing through the criminal underworld. I have to keep my information network fed from as many sources as possible. Invariably I learn more from my clients than they learn from me. Naturally, I have to charge a certain amount of money. Criminals immediately become suspicious if one is not seeking to line one's pockets. To a man, they have a depressingly narrow outlook on life. It's the same with the Nazis.' He sounded almost wistful. 'It will be the same with the Cybermen, I have no doubt.'

King's knight to king's bishop three.

'I can assure you, it will not be the same with the Cybermen.'

George Limb chuckled. 'You know, Doctor, there is a popular rumour in the criminal underworld of London that I am omniscient. All-seeing. My word –'

'Then surely you can see that you are out of your depth, man.'

Knight takes pawn.

'I have been playing these games for most of my life, Doctor. You forget I was with the Foreign Office for decades.'

'Why did you retire? With Churchill as your patron –'

'Churchill was my true friend, and my undoing. He had assured me many times that he had no intention of taking the highest office. Unwisely, I allowed my emotions to cloud my intellect. I believed him. As Prime Minister his hands are tied, and so are mine. I no longer have access to him. I stalemated myself, Doctor. So I did what I had to do. I destroyed my power base. I sacrificed my queen, if you will… And now here I stand. Cybertechnology, and the ability truly to shape the future, in my grasp. I am aware that if dear Winston could see me now – if any of my unimaginative countrymen could see me now – they would have me shot as a traitor. A Nazi. But I have put myself above the petty interests of nation states in the service of a more far-sighted approach. I am merely interested in the balance of power. Certain outcomes to current hostilities ought to prove more… interesting than others, in terms of the long-term destiny of mankind. No, it has never been a question of what the Nazis could learn from me. It was a question of what I could learn from them. Information. It is my passion. It is my nourishment.'

'Information and manipulation.'

'I do find the future a fascinating place, Doctor. I like to feel I'm… a citizen of it.'

'Rubbish!' The Doctor sounded angry. 'You can't possibly know how mankind's destiny will unfold. Let alone consciously control it. No one can know all of the ebbs and flows of future history, even within this one set of variables. And every point in space-time has an infinity of alternatives.'

'If the truth is as I suspect it is, I envy you your somewhat advantageous perspective, Doctor.'

'It is. And you shouldn't. The responsibility which comes with such knowledge is a heavy one.'

'And yet you are here. An anomaly. Creating havoc with, as it were, the time-lines.' He smiled apologetically.

The Doctor's face was grave. 'Sometimes I'm appalled by my own recklessness.'

'Captain Hartmann… yes, yes I remember you.'

The voice, tinny down the phone, was nonetheless measured, cultured and intelligent. Hartmann believed the Deputy Reichsführer's words. Reinhard Heydrich, the man with day-to-day responsibility for running both the SS and the Gestapo, had a reputation as a formidable thinker with a staggering eye for detail. It was said by some that he had a file on everybody of note in the Reich. It was said by others that he didn't: that he carried the information in his head.

'And how is Jersey?'

The Blond Beast, they called him in some quarters. Degenerates and scum.

'Herr Deputy Reichsführer, I have to report that things are not as they should be. I believe that Colonel Schott, by his lack of positive action and by the fact that he has fallen unduly under the influence of enemies of the Reich, has jeopardised the security of this highly secret operation.'

'Which has already got all Berlin buzzing with rumour and gossip, Hartmann. Your silver giants are the talk of the Chancellery.'

'Sir, Colonel Schott seems to be taking all of his instructions from an elderly English civil servant named George Limb.'

'Limb… yes, I've heard of him.' The Deputy Reichsführer was legendary for his calm manner. It was said he always talked as if he was seducing a woman. *'What exactly is Limb doing to unravel your little mystery, Hartmann?'*

'At present, sir, he seems to be playing chess with another enemy alien.'

'I see… And old Schott is just sitting on his hands, eh? Probably half cut on brandy. Very well… let's see… Schott… He's Canaris's man, isn't he? It might be appropriate to give the admiral a shot across the bows… Yes. You must act as you think fit, Captain. On my authority, of course. Don't let me down, Captain. Good day.'

'Heil Hi –'

Hartmann stopped. The phone was already dead.

* * *

'A poisoned pawn. Precisely what I should have expected from you, Mr Limb.'

George Limb rubbed his hands with glee. He was enjoying himself immensely.

'This is a most interesting game, Doctor. Even I am finding it difficult to predict the outcome. What would you say to a small wager?'

'What had you in mind?'

'My one regret is that I don't live in an age of better communications. It is the curse of my singular profession that I need information at my fingertips all the time. Economics and technology at present are too slow to require or provide such a facility. We lack what I might perhaps call... information technology, if you will forgive my rather vulgar coercion of the noun.'

The Doctor nodded, smiling slightly.

'And you believe that Cybertechnology will deliver the future you so long for. By giving it to both sides you are trying to trigger a technology race. An arms race.'

'Precisely, Doctor.'

'Hideously irresponsible!' The Doctor turned away angrily.

'Oh, come now. I was only trying to speed up the inevitable. It doesn't take a genius to see that the future is going to be poised in a... a balance of terror, if you will. Unfortunately, by destroying the Peddler factory you have upset that balance. Thanks to you, Doctor, the Nazis will inherit the Earth.'

'If you think that any combination of threat and persuasion will induce me to give those people the secret of Cybertechnology –'

'I am an old man,' Limb interrupted. 'I am impatient. The future is my one and only motivation. That is what I live for. I will sacrifice anything to speed up history. To put the future within my grasp. But there are other ways. If the mountain will not come to Mohammed...'

'What do you mean?' queried the Doctor suspiciously.

'Time travel, Doctor.' The Doctor was silent. 'Back at my house in

Belsize Park you said that the Cybermen had travelled backward in time to get here. I find that fascinating. Moreover, I believe that you know far more about the subject than you care to reveal.

The Doctor said nothing. When Limb spoke again it was a low, urgent, rasping voice.

'Give me the secret of time travel.'

'Impossible,' the Doctor said curtly. 'I have certain responsibilities above and beyond this planet.'

'Hear me out, Doctor, please. A wager. If I win the game you will tell me what I most wish to know and I will make sure that Berlin closes this place down permanently. If you win I will still have this place closed, and face the consequences. You and Ace will be free to go, your secrets intact.'

'An interesting proposition,' the Doctor mumbled, chewing on a rook. 'It would certainly save a lot of bloodshed and misery. Check.'

CHAPTER 24

Captain Hartmann strode towards the room where Ace languished, a renewed sense of purpose driving him forward. Heydrich had spoken: no one could stand in his way now.

The guard on the door snapped to attention.

'Open it!' barked Hartmann.

The door swung open to reveal Ace, slumped on the bed, staring at the ceiling. She didn't bother to glance at him as he entered the room.

'Stand!' he shouted.

She ignored him.

'On –' in two strides he had crossed to the bed – 'your –' his hand reached out; he seized her ponytail in his fist – 'feet!' He yanked. Ace let out a gasp. She felt her hair tearing away at the roots. In spite of herself she pivoted upward until she was standing in front of her captor.

'Until now you have enjoyed an undeserved status here. Let me inform you of how your situation has changed. You are now simply a hostage. You will be used to force the Englishman and his insolent little friend to revive the Cybermen.'

'The Doctor's here...' For the first time since she arrived on this island Ace felt a real surge of hope. 'He'll never help you.'

'If they refuse I will shoot one of your fingers off. If they still refuse I will shoot another finger off. All of your fingers, all of your toes. Then your nose. Then I shall remove your tongue. Then I will blind you. I will continue this process until you are nothing but a bloody, limbless torso. Then I will shoot you. Then I will shoot them.'

'Then you'll shoot yourself, I hope.'

Hartmann smiled. There was nothing appealing in his smile now.

'You have spirit, girl. You would have made a good German wife. Come.'

He turned, dragging Ace by the hair, and marched from the room.

Like vultures, three black-clad soldiers, soul-dead, absolutely obedient to orders, clustered around one defenceless victim, waiting for the kill.

'Checkmate,' said George Limb. 'A delightful game, Doctor. You sacrificed your queen too easily.'

'Hmm…' said the Doctor. 'You know, I once played chess with a being from another dimension for the survival of the universe. Happily for the universe, on that occasion I won.'

'Was it a close game?' Limb seemed ready to accept anything, his eyes burning brightly.

'Not really. I cheated. What was at stake seemed to justify it.'

'I trust you are going to honour our arrangement?'

'Certainly, if you are.'

George Limb nodded.

'I will see to it that this place is closed down, Doctor. And you will provide me with a time machine…'

'Oh, yes,' the Doctor replied. 'That's easily done. You're sitting on one.'

With surprising speed the old man sprang to his feet.

'This thing…'

'… is the Cybermen's space-time capsule, yes. That, believe it or not, is what they arrived in. From… oh… centuries in the future and almost certainly the other side of the galaxy. Unfortunate, to end up on Jersey on the eve of the Second World War. Oh, well…'

With a resigned air the Doctor raised himself from his seat and squatted in front of the ugly bulk of the inert machine. He pulled a handkerchief from his pocket and began rubbing it hard against the dirt-black side of the machine, smearing away swathes of grease to reveal a row of dingy buttons and readouts. Slowly he began pressing buttons. The machine began to emit a low hum – a throb which resonated through the floor of the derelict office.

'Yes, I see their problem. This looks like an experimental model.

It would probably only have held two or three of them. The calibrators they used to navigate this thing are on the blink. That's why they ended up here. That's why they were stuck here. Cybermen never had much of a command of time travel.'

George Limb hovered anxiously over the Doctor.

'Oh, don't worry, Mr Limb. After I've tinkered with it it will serve your purposes perfectly well. Where – or perhaps I should say when – would you like to go?'

'Forward, Doctor. I don't care about the year, as long as it's significantly forward. Some time in the next century should do the trick. The future!'

The door crashed open. Hartmann stood there, pistol in one hand, Ace's hair in the other.

'You have no future, old man. Neither of you. Out.'

Limb stood as if rooted to the spot. The Doctor, still crouched by the alien machine, gazed levelly at the SS officer and said nothing.

'Don't listen to him, Doctor,' Ace muttered grimly.

Hartmann pointed the pistol directly at her head and smiled viciously. 'Who won?' he asked.

'Er, he did,' acknowledged the Doctor a little sheepishly.

'Wrong,' said Hartmann, jamming his pistol into Ace's temple. 'You both lost. Now move!'

George Limb looked archly at the Doctor.

'Prepared to sacrifice the queen again, Doctor?' he asked.

'No,' said the Doctor flatly, and began walking towards the door.

'Let's see you talk your way out of this one.'

Ace now stood next to Limb, their backs to a pillar, the barrel of Hartmann's pistol hovering between them.

'Alas…' George Limb began.

'Silence!' barked Hartmann. 'Hurry up, Doctor.'

Across the room the Time Lord was scampering from Cyberman to Cyberman, checking fluid links, taking readings, wiping away the odd fleck of dust from their casings with the sleeve of his jacket.

'Yes, yes,' he said petulantly. 'Excuse me…' He manoeuvred one of the lab-coated scientists to one side. The flower of Germany's scientific genius stood around, muttering among themselves, watching as the little man flitted in and out of the alcoves and conduits that snaked around the dormant Cyber-army, tutting and flapping and humming to himself.

He stopped at the end of one of the rows and patted an inert Cyberleader on the silver dome of its head-casing.

'Yes, of course,' he said to the motionless giant. 'You'll be first.'

'Is everything in order, Doctor?' asked Hartmann tensely.

'It seems to be,' the Time Lord replied. He strode back to where the SS captain held his captives at gunpoint.

'There's just one more thing to be done.'

He fished into his pocket and began rummaging around.

'Slowly, Doctor,' warned Hartmann.

'Don't panic, Captain,' the Doctor replied, withdrawing his hand. Between his thumb and forefinger he was holding what appeared to be a whistle. He raised it to his mouth and blew. No sound emerged.

'A dog whistle,' he said. 'Inaudible to the human ear. Although in your case, Captain Hartmann, being one of the master race and so on…'

'Do not try to make a fool of me, Doctor. Carry on with your work.'

'I've done all I can,' said the Doctor. 'You see, these are sleeper Cybermen. They are on shutdown. In order to revive them you need one of –'

The double doors at the far end of the room crashed suddenly open. In waddled the little Cyber-command unit.

'– those,' finished the Doctor. 'Here, boy! Good boy!'

And, like an obedient dog, the lethal console trotted across the room and stood attentively at the feet of its new master.

'Stage One revival,' said the Doctor. 'Initiate.'

The console chittered and burbled electronically for a few moments. Lights on its flat surface winked in sequence.

The whole, huge room, scientists and guards, and prisoners, felt the thrill of energy which rippled across the walls, through the tubes and wires that linked the Cybermen together. The blaze of light, the throb of power.

'Well, Dr Frankenstein,' the Doctor quipped to Limb, 'impressed?'

George Limb smiled and nodded gently in assent.

There was a crackling, tearing sound from the Cyberleader's alcove. Its giant arms twitched and jerked for a few moments. It slowly moved its head from side to side, taking in its surroundings. Steam billowed around it as the newborn colossus stepped forward into life.

'Morning...' chirped the Doctor. 'Sleep well?'

The Cyberleader scanned the little figure standing in front of it.

'WHERE IS WALL>' the Cyberleader grated.

'Wall is dead,' the Doctor replied matter-of-factly.

'WHO REVIVED ME>'

'I did,' said the Doctor.

Hartmann stepped forward.

'Welcome, my friend. I am Captain Hartmann of the Third Reich. It was I who ordered your revival.'

With a low electronic hum the Cyberleader scanned the cluster of people in front of him. Hartmann, Limb, Ace.

'HUMANS> YOU WILL BE CONVERTED> YOU WILL BE LIKE US>'

'We of the Third Reich are more than human,' said Hartmann. 'Together, your race and my race, we have a mighty destiny.'

The Cyberleader scanned the Aryan officer again.

'YOU ARE HUMAN>' it droned. 'YOU WILL BE CONVERTED> YOU WILL BE LIKE US>'

It stepped towards the Cyber-command unit. Hartmann laid a hand on its huge arm. With a hydraulic hiss the arm swung backward, throwing the astonished captain across the room.

'A useful lesson in eugenics,' murmured the Doctor. 'Now, on with the show.'

The Cyberleader stood before the squat console-on-legs, and extended a hand. There was a crackle of power from the little unit and the Cyberleader staggered backward. It attempted to approach the unit again. Another crackle.

'I'm afraid I've taught it to bite,' said the Doctor. 'Command override program, authorisation Theta Sigma.'

There was a whirring from inside the head of the Cyberleader. For a moment it seemed off balance, disorientated, flailing and struggling to remain on its feet. Then its arms fell to its sides.

'Good,' said the Doctor. 'Raise your right arm.'

There was an electronic burble from the Cyber-command unit. The Cyberleader raised its right arm.

'Down,' said the Doctor.

The arm fell to its side.

Around the room the cocoon-like alcoves were glowing with life. Everywhere the sleepers were waking up. Cybermen stepped from the walls into the room, on to gantries, down ladders, down into the centre of the room.

It took Captain Hartmann a moment to register that his great plan had gone badly wrong. Recovering himself he scrambled to his feet and ran for the door.

'Guards!' he yelled. 'Kill them!'

Of the few guards who had been milling about the room, some raised their rifles and fired upon the silver giants. The Cybermen ignored the gunshots. Other guards followed the lead of their captain, who was tearing down a nearby corridor.

'Checkmate,' said the Doctor.

Hartmann reached the guardroom in moments. Half a dozen soldiers sat around in shirtsleeves, reading or playing cards.

'Get up!' the captain screamed. 'We're under attack! The Cybermen!'

He lunged at the intercom on the wall.

'This is Captain Hartmann! This is Captain Hartmann, acting on behalf of Colonel Schott...'

* * *

In his quarters Schott was half asleep on his bunk. Strauss waltzed scratchily around his new gramophone. He leapt from the bed as Hartmann's voice ripped through his tranquillity.

'…We are under attack! I repeat, we are under attack from the Cybermen! Break out heavy machine-guns! All units to the Cyber-chamber! The Cybermen are to be annihilated! I repeat: the Cybermen are to be annihilated!'

What on earth…? Hartmann had exceeded his authority this time. Donning his jacket, holstering his pistol, the old colonel marched out into the corridor, determined upon a showdown.

Outside, in the corridor, men were charging about in a frenzy of activity. The pride of the Reich armies, infantry and SS, were not to be put to flight by a bunch of machines on legs. Four men dragged a heavy, floor-mounted machine-gun towards a nearby intersection. Others were passing out Schmeiser machine-guns and grenades. Hartmann appeared from a doorway and began shouting instructions.

'Captain Hartmann!' bellowed Schott. 'What exactly is going on?'

Hartmann didn't reply but kept issuing bursts of instructions to the continuing stream of men pouring into the corridor from all sides of the complex. A young Wehrmacht private appeared around a corner, ran past Schott and up to the SS captain, breathless.

'Sir, I have to report that the assault squads are assembling at the east and west entrances to the Cyber-chamber.'

'Good,' said Hartmann. 'I shall lead the assault myself.'

'Hartmann!' Colonel Schott placed himself directly in the path of the captain. 'What is happening?'

'The Cybermen are coming to life,' said Hartmann curtly. 'The man who calls himself the Doctor is reviving them. They are hostile.'

'On whose orders did he begin the revivification process?' Old Schott's face was like thunder.

'Mine,' said Hartmann. 'I suggest that you return to your

quarters until we have contained the threat. Once we have shown them how we fight, the Cybermen will be prepared to listen to what we have to say. Unless of course you would like to lead the assault yourself.'

Schott looked the SS officer up and down. He looked down at his own hands, venous, liver-spotted, trembling slightly. He hadn't seen action since 1918.

'No,' he said, quietly. 'No... You carry on, Captain.'

Slowly, he turned and retreated to his brandy and Strauss, and the comfort of his bunk.

Captain Hartmann stood motionless, staring at the metal double doors that separated the Cyber-area from the rest of the underground compound. Behind him was a frenzy of chaotic activity. Troops were marshalling; grenades were being passed out; a big Spandau machine-gun was being dragged noisily along the tiled floor by four grunting, sweating infantrymen.

Somehow, Hartmann felt – and appeared – far from the noise, the chaos. He was drinking in that peculiar sense of absolute calm, of deep tranquillity, which always surrounded him like a suit of enchanted armour before a battle. The imminence of danger, of bloody conflict, worked on Hartmann like a soothing balm.

He believed, as his Führer believed, that the cause for which he fought was divinely inspired. The Cybermen were testament to this: a gift to the German nation from the gods. What other explanation could there be? Hartmann had been in Vienna when Hitler had claimed the Spear of Longinus from among the Habsburg crown jewels. The Spear of Destiny. The spear which had pierced the side of Christ – carried into battle by Charlemagne, carried into battle by Frederick Barbarossa, the unearthly power on which the Holy Roman Empire had been built. A direct channel to Heaven. The Spear was the symbol of the great Destiny of the German people: the Cybermen would be the instruments of that Destiny.

The battle to come was a test. It fell to him, Captain Hartmann, to prove the German people worthy of the gift.

Closing his eyes, he breathed deeply and slowly. In the darkness behind his eyelids he could see the Spear, lit up as bright as day.

'I think that should do the trick,' said the Doctor. 'Terminate revival process.'

There was an electric burp from the Cyber-command unit and the chamber was filled with the sound of machinery winding down. About three dozen of the silver giants stood in a circle around the Doctor and the little, humming console. Their computer brains throbbed with strange new instructions – pirate machine codes, program overrides which each new mind accepted like sweets from a stranger. Newborns, innocent and unknowing, they gazed upon the little man who was their sworn enemy and waited for a loving word to drop from his lips.

'Destroy,' said the Doctor. 'Destroy everything.'

An SS lieutenant ran up to Hartmann and saluted smartly.

'The assault groups are ready, Captain,' he announced. 'Shall we commence the attack?'

'No,' replied the SS captain, his eyes still closed, a gentle smile playing across his lips, his voice little more than a whisper. 'I shall lead the attack myself.'

Even for Ace, it was getting loud in there. Weapons drawn, the Cybermen were firing on the machinery that lined the room, firing on the cocoons in which they had lain and those in which their still-dormant brothers even now slept by the hundred. The Cyber-wall was erupting with repeated mini-volcanoes of steam and sparks. Foamy, glutinous Cyber-fluids oozed from pipes and dripped and slid between panels and crevices, or exploded in waves of grease and mineral salts into the huge room. The whole, vast hibernation unit was starting to glow a deep red.

'I think it's going to blow!' she shouted to the Doctor over the constant hissing and exploding. 'We should get out of here!'

'I agree,' the Doctor replied. 'I'm planning something of a grand finale, and I really wouldn't want to get caught up in it. Where's –'

He didn't finish the sentence. At that moment there was a loud, dull explosion and the metal double doors that separated the Cyber-chamber from the rest of the compound flew inward off their hinges.

Ace coughed, choking on smoke. Further explosions followed. Through the haze and confusion she could see Cybermen staggering under the impact of the staccato blasts, reeling, struggling to orientate themselves.

The doors at the other side of the expanse burst open. More smoke. More explosions.

The Cybermen whirled in confusion.

A German stick-grenade rattled across the floor and stopped at Ace's feet.

It didn't explode.

In an endless split second she had stooped, picked it up by its wooden handle and hurled it back into the smoke. The metal head of the deadly device burst before it hit the ground.

Ace felt a tugging at her shoulder. The Doctor was pulling her behind a heavy concrete pillar. He dropped on to his haunches, one hand clamping his hat to his head, the other tugging Ace down with him, as a hail of machine-gun fire raked the air above them.

'I didn't expect them to respond with such force,' he yelled.

The room was full of grey- and black-uniformed soldiers, firing on the Cybermen at point-blank range. The Cybermen seemed confused, stumbling and dancing under the hail of bullets, firing randomly, still hitting more of their own equipment than anything else.

A Cyberman collapsed, sprawling and writhing, sickly white sputum gushing from a chest unit ripped apart by a grenade and a ballet of heavy bullets.

'Don't just stand there,' the Doctor bellowed into the confusion. 'Defend yourselves!'

He leaned towards Ace.

'They're disorientated,' he said. 'My fault, I'm afraid.'

Machine-gun in hand, Captain Hartmann paused in a pipe-lined alcove and surveyed the chaos. The Cybermen were difficult to kill – that much he could see – but a few had gone down under the combined effects of explosives and close-range machine-gun fire. He smiled. His forces were slowly gaining the upper hand. He was proving his point. Soon the Cybermen would see it. Their raw power was perfectly complemented by the dynamism and courage of the Reich soldiery.

A Cyberman spun round in front of him. Its blank eyes held his gaze. It raised its gun until it was level with his head, and fired.

Hartmann hurled himself to one side. He felt a burning on the left side of his face. He couldn't see out of his left eye. A superb commando, he let his instincts and training take over. He dropped to the ground, rolled around the Cyberman's legs, and scrambled for the shelter of the metal staircase.

His left eye was useless. He struggled to focus with his right. Something had changed. The Cybermen seemed more alert now; more aware of what was happening to them. In an instant they had formed themselves into two ranks, back to back, firing their weapons in a continuous rhythm of energy pulses at the suddenly disorganised German troops. Suddenly their mêlée tactics – get in close, hit the giants with everything they had, then get clear – didn't seem to be working. Now it was his troops who were taking a pounding – a chorus line of broken German bodies were dancing like rag dolls under a hail of enemy fire.

'Fall back!' Hartmann screamed.

CHAPTER 25

The dignified, graceful, mellifluous tones of German civilisation could no longer drown out the screams and roars of German barbarism.

Colonel Schott lifted the needle on Strauss and ended his dream of better days.

Outside his room they were dragging bodies back from the Cyber-chamber.

He opened the door and emerged on to a scene that took his mind flying back to 1917. How many times had he stood in his trench on the Western Front and watched the ragged lines of dead and dying soldiers returning to shelter – or the burial pit – in the aftermath of battle? Only the mud and the blood were missing from this retreating army: in their place burns, lesions, suppurating sores – the inevitable kiss of Cyber-fire. Massive internal damage too, had Schott but known it. He remembered, twenty-odd years ago, standing by a French roadside watching a cohort of German infantry limping back from the front line after a mustard-gas attack by the British at Ypres. The same burns, blistering, horrible, yellow-brown mutilations. They had been like tormented beasts, blind and wailing and begging to die.

That was what this reminded him of. The burns – and the pleas – were the same.

Only now it was his men. Good men.

Boys.

Captain Hartmann staggered along the corridor, one hand clasped over his face.

'Hartmann.' Schott could barely stop his voice from trembling. 'What happened?'

'They're strong,' the captain spat. He lurched past the colonel, clutching the wall for support. His hand fell away from his face.

'My God…' Schott felt sick.

Hartmann had no hair on the left side of his head. His skin from the top of his head to his neck was blistering as he stood there, seething with hundreds of tiny, swelling and popping bubbles. His left ear had melted from his head. His left eye was closed, the lid sunk deep into the socket.

Schott struggled to compose himself.

'How many men have we lost?' he asked.

'Probably thirty,' Hartmann replied. 'Dead or dying.'

A young medical orderly ran past. Hartmann grabbed him by the shoulder.

'Give me a shot of morphine,' he ordered.

The orderly froze, staring at the captain's head. His mouth trembled; the colour drained from his face.

'Give me a shot of morphine!' Hartmann demanded.

The orderly fumbled in his medical bag. Clumsily, he prepared a syringe as Hartmann rolled up his sleeve. He closed his one remaining eye and drew in a deep, shuddering breath as the drug entered his bloodstream.

He could still see the Spear.

After a moment he shook himself, then lurched off down the corridor.

'Bring that gun forward!' he barked. 'We'll finish this once and for all.'

Schott watched as Hartmann's twisted figure turned the corner.

No. This was absurd. Thirty men. There couldn't be more than half a dozen soldiers – army or SS – left in the compound. It wouldn't do. Most of these were Schott's men and Schott would not stand by and see the few that remained butchered on some death-or-glory whim of Hartmann's.

Along the corridor he could see the heavy Spandau gun being dragged forward.

He retreated into his room, shut the door, and picked up the telephone.

Hartmann was right about one thing – this had to be finished. Schott would make sure that it was done properly.

* * *

258

In the Jersey *feldkommandentur* Kommandandtur, formerly Government House in St Helier, General Schumacher was entertaining. It wasn't often that he had a guest as distinguished as SS Brigadier General Kraus. More to the point, Kraus was here in a very special capacity: as personal representative of Reichsführer Himmler.

'Welcome, Brigadeführer,' Schumacher fawned. 'I trust you had a pleasant journey.'

He stood at the bottom of the main staircase, resplendent in his best dress uniform. Smells of cooking hung about the halls.

'The journey passed,' Kraus said flatly. 'I should like to inspect these – what do you call them?'

'The notes of the scientist who was for some years in charge of the Le Mur compound – a Dr Peddler, I believe – refer to them as Cybermen.'

'Cybermen, yes. I should like to see these... Cybermen as soon as possible.'

'Well, of course, of course.' Schumacher laughed nervously. 'But first I hope you will sample some of our hospitality. You must be hungry and tired after your journey.'

'No,' Kraus replied. 'Reichsführer Himmler wants my report as soon as possible.'

'A little food, Brigadier. A little wine, perhaps, and then we can go –'

'I know all about you, Schumacher.' Kraus had a voice that could cut glass. 'You and that old fool Schott. Soft living. Squandering the wealth of the Reich, wasting time, drunk half the time, stuffing your bellies. Is this what you think the Führer means by total war, Schumacher?'

'Well, I –'

'I have seen what total war means, Schumacher. I have been in Poland. One month, it took us, to kick the life out of that filthy swamp. One month, and even now we are relentless. And so it will go on until all subversive elements are crushed underfoot. The communists, the Jews...'

So it was true, the rumours of Kraus's activities in Poland.

Schumacher shuddered involuntarily.

All SS officers were difficult, but Kraus was among the worst. Arrogant, sadistic, fanatical. As a general, Schumacher outranked him, of course, but as an SS officer, and one acting on the specific instructions of Himmler... Besides, Schumacher was terrified of him.

The general was playing for time. He had been worried by what Schott had told him – about Hartmann, about the Englishman Limb, and about the other little man who seemed to have turned up from nowhere and to know more about what was going on than anybody else. He wanted to check that all was well underground before taking Kraus down there.

In his office the telephone rang.

The smoke was starting to clear. The Doctor coughed and beat the dust from himself with his hat. From a pile of rubble he fished his umbrella.

'Are you all right?' he asked Ace.

'I think so,' the girl replied, looking around the shattered chamber.

Lacking orders, lacking an enemy to kill, the Cybermen now stood motionless amid the devastation. A few of their number had died. The Cyberleader himself, first-born of this new army, lay twisted and still amid the debris, his head-casing shattered. The survivors paid their fallen comrades no regard.

'What was that, anyway?'

'Round One, I suspect. Where's... Ah!' He trotted across to the Cyber-command unit, standing like a giant upside-down toadstool in the middle of the battlefield. 'Not damaged,' the Doctor muttered. 'Good.' He began punching buttons on its flat surface.

'Doctor,' Ace asked, 'how are we going to get out of here?'

'The Cybermen will carve a path for us. That's the main reason I revived them. I hoped by a show of strength – a lot of flash and thunder in here – I could persuade our hosts to leave. I've programmed our little friend here to blow itself to pieces. A plasma explosion. It will reduce this place to atoms and I had rather hoped there would be no one in it. Unfortunately, I hadn't bargained for our mad captain. I think we should probably get out of here before they try to drive a tank in, or something equally insane.'

He patted the little Cyber-console.

'You know what to do, don't you?'

The command unit burbled back at him.

'Doctor...' Ace was struck by a sudden thought. 'Where's George?'

'I'm here.'

The voice seemed to come from the mouth of a dead Cyberman, lying on its back against a wall with half of its hydraulic guts missing.

'Help me up, would you, my dear.'

Now Ace could see an arm flapping behind the fallen silver giant. Faded tweed, brown-leather elbow patch. Definitely not SS.

Straining, Ace rolled the Cyberman's body over and into the room.

George Limb emerged, coughing.

'Thank you,' he said. 'I though it prudent to – as it were – play dead until the shooting stopped. Unfortunately, having crawled behind our friend there he seemed to... settle.'

'Are you hurt?'

Ace was shocked at the note of concern in her voice. The old man seemed hunched, cradling his left side.

'It's... nothing,' he said. 'I'm glad to see that you two are unscathed.'

He shuffled over to the Cyber-command unit.

'So... am I correct in my assumption that this is the device which was causing those rather alarming explosions in the East End of London?'

'Don't touch it!' the Doctor snapped. 'In fact, don't touch anything. In fact, stand over there. We shall be leaving shortly.'

The Doctor rapped hard on the head of the nearest Cyberman.

'Come on,' he said testily. 'Wake up.'

The Cyberman twitched into life. So did its fellows.

'I take it you have a prearranged means of escape from the island,' said the old man.

'Something like that,' the Doctor replied. 'We shall take you with us as far as the mainland, whereupon we shall hand you over to the authorities.'

'Ah,' said George Limb. 'I take it, then, that you do not intend to honour our little wager.'

'All bets are off. It's far too late for that. Besides, I doubt you could honour your side of the bargain now. You might have powerful friends in all manner of governments, but we are dealing with a mad SS officer with a death wish. Your friends are in Berlin, and he is just down the hall.'

'I don't suppose I could persuade you just to let me go. I could disappear somewhere, live out the rest of my days quietly, perhaps grow cabbages. That's what the Roman Emperor Diocletian did, you know...'

'Mr Limb,' said the Doctor coldly, 'you are lucky that I am prepared to hand you over to the British authorities. Now, stay behind me. Ace, watch him.'

The Doctor prodded a Cyberman in the back with his umbrella.

'After you,' he said to it.

Ace didn't like this at all. Was the fact that she was flanked between twenty towering Cybermen supposed to make her feel safe? She didn't like the rather sinister tone of dark familiarity the Doctor had adopted when talking to them. She didn't like the slightly twitchy way they moved in response to his barely worded commands. How did they know what he meant? Why were they acting like puppets to his dark puppetmaster? And what if his control over them wasn't as complete as he thought? She felt as if she was at the circus, putting her head into the mouth of trained lions.

They entered the corridor.

'Fire!'

Facing them, perhaps twenty yards away, was the huge, floor-mounted Spandau machine-gun.

Bullets exploded from the end of it. The Cybermen in front of them reeled beneath the impact. Heads and chest units exploded in sparks and fluids.

'Get down!'

For the second time the Doctor pulled her to the floor.

'Back,' he whispered. 'Crawl.'

The three of them, Time Lord, teenager, and septuagenarian, wriggled among falling Cybermen, back the way they had come.

Like the doomed millions of an earlier conflict, the silver colossi kept on walking, dead-eyed, into the spitting mouth of the huge machine-gun.

Colonel Schott, veteran of that futile, bloody conflict, stood in the darkness and the rain outside one of the huge entrances to the compound, engaged in a three-way debate with General Schumacher and Brigadier Kraus. The only light came from General Schumacher's purring staff car. Behind them a squad of heavily armed infantrymen waited tensely. Away in the darkness a giant Panzer growled.

Schumacher was being evasive, as usual.

'I'm sure Colonel Schott is exaggerating this small incident, Brigadier,' he simpered.

'I can assure you, I am not!' Schott was in no mood to play the usual game of placate the SS. 'My men have been wiped out in there. SS men, too.'

'This is madness, Schott,' Schumacher snapped. 'We'll never get a tank in there.'

'We must, General. Those monsters are invincible.' He lifted his Luger from its holster. 'Whatever happens, I'm going back in there.'

'You surprise me, Schott,' said Kraus, smirking. 'I didn't think you had so much mettle. I shall ride with you. The Reichsführer is anxious to know how the giants perform in battle.'

He turned to the huge tank and mounted its front end.

'Return to your supper, General Schumacher,' he mocked. 'I shall report your gallantry to the Reichsführer in the morning.'

The Doctor was on his feet as soon as the three had regained the cover of the Cyber-chamber, frantically jabbing buttons on the little control console.

'I've set this thing on a timer,' he said to Ace. 'I'd better make a few adjustments. It doesn't look as if we're going to get out of here as quickly as I thought.'

A noise from the far end of the room made him stop.

A pistol being cocked.

Hartmann, standing in the far doorway.

'Get away from that thing, Doctor.' He limped forward.

'Hartmann…'

The man didn't seem to hear him. His one functioning eye seemed unfocused.

Why didn't they stop coming?

Only two men were left manning the Spandau gun. Four others lay dead at its base, destroyed by Cyber-fire. The young medical orderly was feeding the massive belt of bullets into the belly of the gun, and an even younger private was keeping a relentless pressure on the trigger.

The Cyber ranks were being decimated.

It didn't seem to make any difference. They just walked forward, unflinching, being blown apart, returning fire with those death rays of theirs.

'It's useless!' the private shouted. 'They're nearly on top of us!'

'We're dead anyway!' the medical orderly returned. 'Keep firing!'

The first Cyberman now stood level with the gun. Almost casually it reached up with one hydraulic hand and closed its fist over the end of the barrel. The precision-bored steel tube was crushed like tin in its grip. The gun, still trying to spew its bullets, exploded in the faces of its two-man crew, ripping itself apart.

Where was he? Why was everything so bright?

Images swam in a morphine haze before Captain Hartmann. He could hear music, distant, deep.

Crashing, majestic music. He recognised it.

What was this place that rose, cathedral-like, around him?

The Grail Castle.

That was it! The mission! The destiny of the German people! It was him! It was him, after all!

Europe was a wasteland of decadence and decay. That's what they were fighting for, wasn't it? He had ridden out with his fellow Knights. Out across the world he had faced death, he had faced danger, he had faced Giants! And he had come to this place.

And there it was before him. The Grail.

'Hartmann…'

It was full. Full of a golden liquid. Colours played off its golden surface, reds, greens, winking and flashing at him.

And only he… Only he was pure enough.

'Hartmann…'

The voice sounded so far away.

He struggled to focus on the little man hunched over the sacred vessel.

'Amfortas…'

The King. The Wounded King. Guardian of the Grail.

No.

The Wagnerian chorus in his head reached a machine-gun crescendo and died.

He wasn't. He wasn't the King.

Something was wrong.

He knew this man…

'Hartmann! Listen to me!'

This man had done something to him. Visited some terrible retribution on him.

This man and this… thing.

The Grail.

No. It wasn't... It...

Something was wrong.

His face burned.

The two men stood, facing each other, across the cauldron, dancing with light.

Hartmann raised the pistol in his right hand, took aim along the barrel, pulled the trigger.

Elsewhere in the complex a colossus was rumbling through the earth. A Tiger tank: forty tons of steel, all but impenetrable – the largest and most formidable weapon in the German Panzer fleet.

Next to the driver, in the seat where normally the wireless operator would have sat, Colonel Schott was hunched, grim and silent, his pistol in his hand. Behind, in the gunner's turret, Brigadier Kraus was perched, already looking for all the world like the conquering hero, head and shoulders jutting through the gunner's hatch, watching, waiting.

Kraus was not the man Schott would have chosen to die alongside, the old colonel reflected with melancholy. Still, how many people in this or any other conflict had the luxury of choice in such matters? He raised the hatch above his head and peered out.

Behind the tank marched the squad of infantrymen. The sense of unease among them was tangible. Battles weren't meant to be fought underground.

'Herr Colonel,' the driver ventured to Schott, 'these corridors were not built to take a tank. Some of these corners –'

'Silence,' barked Kraus. 'Look at this place. It couldn't have been built without heavy earth-moving equipment. These corridors have seen worse than this.'

'But Herr Brigadeführer –'

'Keep your cowardice for the Wehrmacht mess room. Drive.'

* * *

266

'Hartmann!'

Shot after shot the captain pumped into the Cyber-command unit.

The bullets ripped through its surface console. It let out an electric howl. Its legs sagged.

The Doctor closed his eyes in despair. If only he had left the force-field chip in a little longer. Short cuts. Dangerous.

Hartmann's pistol arm sagged. He looked breathless and confused.

Ace, seizing the moment, launched herself into the wounded officer. He cannoned into the foot of the metal staircase and lay there panting, mumbling to himself, his one eye hypnotised by something in the middle distance.

The Doctor was leaning over the Cyber-console, scratching his head in anxiety.

Oh dear…' he said. It looked up. 'I wonder what this is going to do to the Cybermen…'

Outside, among the Cyber-ranks, confusion reigned. Of the thirty-odd Cybermen who had emerged from hibernation, over half were still on their feet, their function – until a split second ago – unimpaired. Now their computer brains were crashing.

Shutdown procedures took over. The elaborate information network that linked them tried frantically to reinitialise itself, bypassing the crippled battle computer. Anti-viral programs cut in.

The confusion didn't last.

Finally:

DAMAGE ASSESSMENT>
MASSIVE DAMAGE TO SLEEPER FORCE>
RETURN TO THE HIBERNATION CHAMBER>
DESTROY ALL HUMANS THE VICINITY>
DEFEND>
REBUILD>

* * *

267

With a roar, the tank swung around the corner.

Brigadier Kraus stared in awe and horror at the silver giants.

The Cybermen reacted to this new threat with one mind. In perfect synchronisation they turned; within a split second they had analysed the vehicle, broken it down bolt-by-bolt, data files had matched the design with known weapon types, infrared sensors had revealed the exact positions of the occupants.

They began pumping energy bolts into the front of the tank's fuselage, and into the gun turret.

With a whimper Kraus dropped back into the gunner's chair. He was shaking uncontrollably. He felt a dampness in the seat of his SS uniform.

The front of the tank was beginning to glow. The driver snatched his hands from the controls.

'Kraus!' yelled Schott. 'Don't just sit there, fire the damned gun!'

The SS Brigadeführer was slowly shaking his head. His mouth hung open.

'Impossible…' he said. 'Those things… Impossible…'

The driver was scrabbling at the lock on his escape hatch. It was too hot to touch, but he touched it anyway. Panic numbed the pain.

'Don't be a fool,' shouted Schott.

The driver wasn't listening. He was hauling himself through the red-hot metal opening. Within seconds he was standing on the body of the tank. He could see the infantry soldiers around him being cut to pieces by Cyber-fire. It was the last thing he saw before he, too, was hit by a score of energy bolts. The body fell back through the hatch and lay, slumped over its controls.

His aged heart pounding, Schott crawled from his seat into the centre of the tank. There was only one hope.

'Kraus, get out of the damned way!' he barked.

Kraus merely whimpered at him. Was this the Butcher of Cracow?

Schott struck the senior officer hard across the face. It seemed to bring him to his senses.

'Kraus, we have to fire the gun! If you won't do it, I must –'

'No. We have to get out of here!'

Kraus began scrambling up the turret.

'You saw what happened to the driver.'

He was half-way out when the energy bolts hit. Still inside the tank, his legs twitched and kicked, catching Schott in the face.

SS Brigadeführer Kraus hung there, his legs dangling inside the fuselage, his body limp across the gun turret, like a broken soldier-doll.

The tank trundled on, driverless.

'It's no good,' the Doctor said quietly. 'The console is ruined. I can't disarm it. I can't stop the countdown.'

'Doctor…' Still cradling his left side, George Limb stepped forward. 'Are you trying to tell us –'

'In less than two minutes there is going to be a massive explosion. I can't stop it. We will all be killed.'

'The TARDIS…' Ace chimed in hopefully.

'We would never get there in time,' said the Doctor. Ace had never heard such a note of finality in his voice. He seemed utterly resigned to their fate. 'I'm sorry, Ace.'

There was a flurry of movement. With a speed that belied his age, George Limb was bounding over to the metal staircase which ran up the wall of the chamber.

At the foot of the stairs Captain Hartmann still lay, drooling and mumbling to himself.

Seeing Limb's approach he seemed to stir from his morphine dream.

This man…

The Englishman…

Hartmann's fist closed on the pistol which now lay at his side. He raised it and pointed it directly at Limb's head. His finger pulled the trigger all the way back.

There was a click.

'A Walther P38, Captain,' said Limb. 'Seven bullets. You fired seven bullets into that machine.'

Limb straightened up. From under his jacket he produced a stubby, silver tube. A Cybergun.

'Heil Hitler,' the old man said evenly, and discharged the gun's lethal burden. Hartmann's already-prostrate body arched under the impact and then fell back on to the metal stairs, dead.

'Limb!' the Doctor shouted. 'What are you doing?'

'Don't try to stop me, Doctor,' the old man replied. 'I bear you no malice, but I will shoot you if I have to.'

'I know what you're planning, Limb. Don't do it! The machine is dangerous! You risk damaging the fabric of space-time!'

'I am sorry, Doctor. I would wish you both well, but in the circumstances it seems pointless.'

The old man was already hauling himself up the stairs towards Peddler's office.

'Doctor, what's he on about?' asked Ace.

'The Cybermen's time machine. I left it powered up. He's going to try to escape in it. Escape to the future.'

Limb made the gantry at the top of the stairs and disappeared into Peddler's office. The Doctor bounded for the staircase.

'I've got to stop him!' he yelled. It was no longer just a case of the destruction of this compound. A tear in space-time could mean the end of everything.

George Limb scrabbled at the clasps that held shut the glass hatchway to the podlike device. For all its future technology the device was mechanically crude. He hefted open the hatch and climbed inside, closing and locking it behind him.

The machine was already humming with power. The controls – two levers, one button – looked childishly simple. He pressed the button.

Outside the Cyber-chamber the tank ran on. Schott struggled to aim the massive 88mm gun. He let fly with its deadly payload, directly into the massed ranks of Cybermen. The effect was impressive. A dozen Cybermen, at least, were caught in the blast and obliterated. A wall came down.

The tank lurched over fallen masonry and Cyber bodies, crushing them like eggs.

Schott clutched his chest. It was tight. He could barely breathe. He would never manage to reload that huge gun and get another round off, he knew. Somehow, Schott had to stabilise the tank. Crawling back to the front of the vehicle, he realised it was hopeless. It was like climbing into an oven. Outside he could still hear the crackle of Cyberguns. He had struck a blow, but he had failed. He slumped on the floor of the tank and reflected back on his days. He had never been much of a warrior, really. He certainly hadn't expected to die in battle.

Colonel Schott smiled to himself and waited for the end.

As he entered the office the Doctor's ears were hit by a deafening squeal, like nails on a blackboard but amplified tenfold, all the time rising in pitch. It was coming from the machine in the corner.

He could see Limb inside. He hammered on the glass.

The old man looked up, and smiled.

The Doctor began hammering the buttons that ringed the outer body of the capsule in a frantic, improvised attempt to power it down.

Hopeless.

The machine was fully powered. Only Limb, from inside, could stop it.

Ace looked with venom at the disabled Cyber-command unit. She was going to be blown to pieces in less than a minute, and all because of that stupid-looking thing. She aimed a kick at its side.

Her foot never connected. The wall to her side suddenly exploded inward. Masonry toppled around her. She lost her footing and fell to the floor.

Her jaw dropped in disbelief.

Bearing down on her was the biggest tank she had ever seen in her life.

She was lying right in the path of its caterpillar tracks.

She felt the first oh-so-gentle pressure of those crushing wheels on her foot.

She closed her eyes.

'Ace!'

The Doctor was standing on the gantry outside Peddler's office. He had run out when he heard the wall collapse. Now, he could only look on as his young friend met with an end too horrific to contemplate.

In less than thirty seconds she would be granted a death that was at least instant. Total, painless oblivion.

It shouldn't be like this.

Oh, Ace…

O-o-o-h-h… A-a-a-c-e…

There was a wailing in his ears. A tempestuous wind.

Everything was still.

Frozen in time.

The time capsule…

It was difficult to think. Moving was like wading through treacle. The Doctor gripped the handrail and, oh, so slowly, began to haul himself back down the stairs.

This was the hardest thing he had ever done. He was moving against time.

Below him the world moved by millimetres.

But there was hope.

He reached the bottom of the stairs, swimming across the frozen waters of time. If he could just reach Ace.

Time was slipping fractionally forward.

He grasped the sleeve of his motionless companion's jacket and hauled her from the path of the tank.

So hard to think…

The TARDIS.

Pick her up... Carry her, somehow...

Out through the great gash in the wall...

Bodies...

Where was he?

Hard to remember...

The TARDIS...

He could feel its presence. It was here somewhere. He could feel its call.

It was about all he could feel.

Concentrate...

Corridors...

All look the same...

Concentrate...

See it... Picture it...

Stairs... Stumbling... Falling through syrup...

Concentrate...

Through the porthole of the Cybermen's time capsule George Limb watched the world blur and fade. He didn't care. It had always been a place of unreality to him – a tangled forest of meaning and inference, connections and discontinuities. People were puppets in a dumb show where the strings were hopelessly and endlessly twisted together. Jerk one and the whole world went into a grotesque and mindless dance.

He drew in a breath. He felt new sensations invade his body... his consciousness.

He felt new – as new as a just-cooled world, hanging in space.

He felt as old as the old, black cosmos, and as huge, and as thinly spread.

His mind was alight with images. His own life – gone in a flash. The lives of others. Countless others, breathlessly fast. The lives and thoughts and physical sensations of beings whose existence he had never even imagined. The thoughts of atoms.

The thoughts of all creation.

He felt himself being stretched. Stretched over all space, all time.

The pain...

He screamed – a voiceless, soundless scream of primal creation...

The Doctor lurched forward, dropping Ace.

'What...? Where...?'

'Come on!' he barked, grabbing her by the hand and hauling her to her feet.

The Cyber-control unit... They had seconds before it went up.

The TARDIS sat in front of them. He already had the key in his hand and aimed at the lock.

He hurled himself through the door, dragging Ace behind him.

CHAPTER 26

The Doctor leaned on the TARDIS console, trying to recover his breath. Trying to clear his head.

Next to him, Ace stood, looking around, confused.'

'What happened?' she asked. 'One minute I was under the wheels of a German tank... and now I'm here...'

'George Limb happened,' the Doctor replied. 'That wretched time machine. I warned him... a dreadful, leaky contraption. The time distortion when he started it up brought everything to a virtual standstill. Including the Cyber-console. Including the tank.'

'But... not you.'

'No.' He smiled. 'Not me. Not quite.'

'I don't think I've understood anything that's happened today,' said Ace. 'I thought the past was supposed to be less complicated than the present. What was all that business with the Cybermen?'

'It's quite simple,' said the Doctor. 'No, actually it's not. You're right – it's very complicated. I just made it look simple. The Cybermen's brains are part organic and part computer. Naturally they form part of an integrated network, with the Cyber-command unit at its centre.' He paused briefly, satisfied himself that Ace was taking it all in. 'The command unit is simply a task-dedicated Cyberman with colossal processing power and the sole function of relaying instructions to the sleepers. And, of course, the thing about computers is they can always be reprogrammed. Even computers as complex as that little fellow. Provided you're clever enough to do it, of course.'

'Which you are, I suppose.'

'It worked, didn't it?'

Suddenly Ace grinned.

'George beat you at chess,' she said.

'Oh, it might have looked that way...' said the Doctor airily. 'Really it was all part of a larger game strategy. I hoped to be able to avoid a bloodbath out there. He seemed to offer the prospect of that. I needed to keep him on our side. He's a very slippery man.'

Ace looked sceptical.

'And anyway,' admitted the Doctor, 'my chess is a little rusty.'

He began flicking switches on the TARDIS console.

'I'm afraid I was less than honest with him. I'd never have been able to get the Cybermen's time capsule working properly. It really was a horrendous lash-up. Still, in a way George Limb got what he always wanted. He was obsessed with knowledge, contact, communication. When he stepped into that time capsule his being would have been shredded through time and space. For a moment he would have touched every single point in space-time.'

Ace winced. 'That's horrible. I liked him at the beginning.'

'I think we both did,' said the Doctor. 'He wasn't an evil man. Not really.'

Ace was suddenly downcast.

'There was a man back there. He was locked in the cell next to me. His name was Sid Napley. He was so brave. So... calm. He'd worked there before the Germans came. They thought he knew about the Cybermen. They took him out and beat him to death. They beat him to death for information he didn't even have.'

She was close to tears. The Doctor put his arms around her, and pressed her face to his hearts.

'Men aren't evil for the most part, Ace. Think of the good that can come out of the worst of situations. Think of Sid Napley. Think of Cody.'

Ace sniffed. 'Cody wasn't fooled by George Limb. Not for a moment.'

'He's a young man of very sound judgement, our Mr McBride,' said the Doctor, turning back to the console of his ship. 'And resourceful. Provided he can learn to get on better with the official law-enforcement agencies, I think he's got quite a future ahead of him.'

His hands flickered over an array of buttons and levers.

'Come on,' he said to his young companion. 'Let's get out of here.'

And, pressing a final switch, he threw the TARDIS spinning into the vortex.

EPILOGUE

'*London, England, November 1940. Staring out of my window at a city bustling with life. Another night of bombing over. Another day to ignore it and get on with the business of living. Another day to realise that the Germans are the least of our worries.*

'*The Doctor never came back. I hope that he found Ace. No, I know that he found Ace. He would have been back if he hadn't. Mullen told me that there was a lot of military activity on Jersey. Explosions at a secret factory. No prizes for guessing who was responsible for them.*

'*Mullen and I... well, I think this is the beginning of a beautiful friendship. Two days after the Doctor had left, I got a call at my office. It was Mullen. He was over at a pumping station in east London. Good policeman that he is, he had followed up the number on Wall's card. He sounded strained, and I knew that something was wrong when he told me that he had sent one of his flatfoots over by car to collect me. Ten minutes later I was in a car driven by Constable Quick, sirens blaring.*

'*Mullen met me at the door of the pumping station as the stretcher-bearers took a body out. The caretaker, apparently. The poor devil had broken his neck. Mullen led me by flashlight into the depths of the building. Everywhere you looked the pipes were scratched and scraped. Cybermats. It made my skin crawl.*

'*The noise was incredible. The pumps were going flat out.*

'*He led me over to a ladder and handed me the torch. I looked down. Sewers were not high on my list of places that I wanted to see at the moment. Mullen said nothing, but I could tell by the look on his face that something was wrong. Very wrong.*

'*I took the torch from him and clambered into the pipe, cursing as my trench coat got smeared in what I can only hope was oil. The brick passageway was huge and dank. Impressive*

Victorian building. I edged my way into the gloom, my shoes slipping on the curved floor. I flashed the beam of the torch around the walls, and my heart stopped.

'Against the wall were tall plastic cocoons. I crossed over to one, peering through the transparent shroud. Staring back out at me was the blank, inhuman face of a Cyberman. I shone the flashlight down the tunnel. As far as I could see there were cocoons, hundreds of them. Each of them holding a Cyberman. So that's why Wall and his goons had kept the pumps going. They were trying to keep the tunnels dry. They were trying to get at this army.

'Hundreds of cocoons.

'Hundreds of Cybermen.

'Waiting.

'The Germans are the least of our worries.'

They talk of the triumph of the machine,
but the machine will never triumph.
- D H Lawrence

THE MURDER GAME

by Steve Lyons
(Featuring the Second Doctor, Ben and Polly)

Landing in a decrepit hotel in space, the time travellers are soon
embroiled in a deadly game of murder and intrigue.

ISBN 0 563 40565 1

BUSINESS UNUSUAL

by Gary Russell
(Featuring the Second Doctor, Ben and Polly)

The Doctor must battle against the evil multinational SenéNet – but
what terrible secret is the company hiding?

ISBN 0 563 40575 9

Doctor Who adventures out on BBC Video:

THE WAR MACHINES

An exciting adventure featuring the First Doctor pitting his wits against
super-computer WOTAN – with newly restored footage …
BBCV 6183

THE AWAKENING/FRONTIOS

A double bill of Fifth Doctor stories… a rural village hides a terrible
secret from the Civil War in _The Awakening_, while the distant world of
Frontios sees a fledgeling colony of humans under attack from the
gravity-controlling Tractators…
BBCV 5803

THE HAPPINESS PATROL

The Seventh Doctor battles for the freedom of an oppressed colony
where misery is a sin …